Underneath the Fireflies

A THRILLER

MARIANNE SCOTT

crowecreations.ca
Ottawa Canada

Underneath the Fireflies © 2023 by Marianne Scott

First Crowe Creations print edition January 2023

Designed by Crowe Creations
Text set in Times New Roman; headings set in Arial

Cover photo needpix.com
Cover design © 2023 by Crowe Creations

Crowe Creations
ISBN: 978-1-998831-03-6

For my grandsons, who think that
having a grandmother who writes mystery novels
is the most wonderful thing in the world.
Kind of like having your own personal superhero.

"She ran away."
"She was promiscuous."
"Serves her right."
"That's the way Indians are."
—Town gossips.

Scout

I N THE SALAL BUSHES FORMING a line at the shore, Scout crouched down, his four legs settling upon the warm earth as he watched the waves heave, heard their whisper and swish over the sands of the night beach. The beach at Lewis Landing on Galliano Island, one of British Columbia's Discovery Islands, twinkled with magic. It was the time of phosphorescence and the water was lit from below by millions of microscopic sea creatures, Mother Earth's way of revealing a promise. In darkness, there would always be light. He intuited the message, his instincts feeling blessed by a benevolent command.

A shadow emerged out from a dune. Scout observed a lone man, shirtless and in loose-fitting pants, strands of his hair hanging over his face, stagger onto the moonlit sand. The man went to where the beach sand met the scrub bushes at the forest edge, where the branches of a gnarled arbutus hung low. Beneath its branches, the man dropped onto one knee, reached down with one hand to touch the wet sand, and with the other, lifted his flask to the heavens. He cried out a word, his curse echoing, loud, and sharp with vengeance. The sound carried high and bright over the stillness, making Scout's ears flatten to his head. A low guttural growl rumbled from his belly as he pulled his lips back and up to reveal his fangs.

Scout held there, not moving, sniffing the stench of malevolence emanating from the man's voice and movements. He watched the man linger there, stoop, then snorting his anger, rise to make his stumbling his way back to the pier. Each of his staggering footprints glimmered with bioluminescent sparks, as if thousands of tiny shards of crushed marine organisms were giving one last light from their bed in the sand before flickering out. The man walked like a wounded animal, tripping and falling before clumsily negotiating the wooden pier steps that bridged to higher ground above, and disappear into the darkness.

Off beneath the tree, at the spot where the man had knelt, a faint surge of light energy remained in the depression. It held faintly. Then it began to sputter and flash, becoming faster in speed and intensity until twinkling light erupted and rose from the sand, twisting like a frenzied swirl of fireflies. It spun higher and higher until, at last, at its center, the shape of a human, a woman, appeared. The translucent figure broke from the light and stepped out onto the sand. So lightly, as though she were fog, she walked near the water with her arms embracing her belly. She threw her arms forward, outstretched to the gentleness of the wind, sand and air. From this gesture formed the spirit of a boy who began to run playfully beside her, his childish laughter ringing hollow in the darkness.

Scout's heart softened at the music of the boy's laugh. Scout's animal spirit ached to be released from his earthly form so he could dance and tumble alongside the unborn young soul. The mother softly crooned a lullaby, its melody sweeping up and over the ocean's breath blowing in off the waters of the bay. The spirits of the forest beyond joined in her chorus and smiled at the joyful exchange as the two spirits reveled in their play.

Soon, the mother spirit finished her song to call to her son. The child spirit returned to her and they absorbed into each other becoming a single transparent image that dispersed into twinkling fireflies. Together, they descended back into the earth, and were gone.

Scout knew that the animal beings of the earth, those who lived honorably by Nature's creed, had been bestowed with the power to witness such transformations. The woman was sending a message: she needed to be avenged. The man, Scout knew, if he had remained on the beach, would have seen nothing. Most humans did not possess the gift of sight, only the very few gifted and of pure heart. Scout knew of only one, a woman he had visited in a dream vision. Grace. Tomorrow, she was to arrive on the island on the morning ferry from Campbell River.

On the night beach, while the people of the island slept, a sacred promise had been made. Scout had heard the voices of the Ancestors, Nature and the elements that gave all humans and animals life. It called to him in the swish of the waves, the rustle of the leaves, and in the faint tinkle of light from the marine life. It was how the Ancestors embraced the creatures of the earth to summon their own powers to do the right thing, to right a wrongdoing, to bring justice to laws that were broken, to bring peace and balance back to the land. Scout arose from the underbrush. He knew what he had been called on to do. Guided by the Ancestors and the animal spirits, he began to run. He ran all night through the long distance of the old growth forest to the ferry landing where he would wait to reveal himself to her. He needed her humanness to bring the man to justice. Her empathic powers were strong. The Ancestors and Scout trusted her. He had already made the initial connection; the spell of retribution had been cast.

Grace

G RACE FINISHED THE TEXT to her mother just before the boarding call went out.

Taking off from Toronto now. See you this evening.

The tightness in her shoulders softened as she settled into her seat. The further she got away from Toronto and the ordeal at Danton, the electronics global manufacturing conglomerate where she worked as a communications expert, the sooner the bad energy would leave her alone. She didn't even care that she was seated between two strangers.

She pulled a book out of her bag and lost herself in the story, distracted herself from the boredom of her flight to Calgary where she'd change planes. Reading made the time feel shorter than the four hours it took.

The WestJet hub at the Calgary airport had shops and kiosks, so she could waste time wandering and perusing their shelves, maybe grab a donut and coffee at a Tim's before the next boarding call. But waiting was tedious so soon she settled into a seat by the window and watched the sky cloud over, the rain obscuring the view of the mountains from the airport windows.

Finally, the voice from the speaker called her flight number and boarding began again. It would take less than an hour before it landed in Comox but the rain was heavier now and crossing the Rockies was turbulent on the best of days, so soon after takeoff, the intensity increased. She'd grin and bear it.

The turbulence over the Rocky Mountains bounced and rattled the 737 as it hit one air pocket after another. Grace had flown this route once before just after her parents had settled into their home on Galliano Island. Her mother had warned her that this stretch of the trip could be turbulent, but this time, it was much rougher than the last one. An unexpected storm, known as a weather bomb, had blown in from the Pacific, delivering high winds and torrential rain, the kind that West Coasters were familiar with and usually took in stride. She imagined that her parents, Maria and Leo, were probably experiencing a power outage like most of their neighbors on Galliano Island, and using their backup generator to keep essential household utilities going while the wind from the storm battered their island home. Grace sat straight and tense, her seat belt pulled secure, tightly gripping the armrests of her seat, but also noting the alarm of the other passengers who were clearly panicked. Some lipped prayers in anticipation of meeting their Maker, some with tear-stained faces crying in fear, and others allowing a scream to escape their stoic expressions as they were jolted and thrown around in their seats. It was bad. Would the plane crash? Would they all die?

She closed her eyes and took long, slow breaths. As though in a fully conscious dream, she saw it. Grace watched the future unfold. The landing in Comox would be rough and traumatic, but the plane and its passengers, although traumatized with fear and somewhat battered, would be all right, leaving them with an exciting story to tell for years to come. Grace could read the energy around her, especially weather. She was fully engaged with the signals, sensing a difficult landing but with no causalities. Her senses assured her, but that didn't dispel her own fear. It sounded like the cabin would shake apart.

Ten minutes prior, the pilot had cautioned everyone to make sure their seat-belts were securely fastened and to secure loose objects and carry-on luggage away in the overhead compartments. He warned that the plane's descent into Comox would be "a bit bumpy.." His voice was anxious and abrupt, his brevity evidence that the flight was in a dangerous situation. It felt like the plane was hitting one solid barrier after another as it descended through the dark clouds and driving rain.

Then, without warning, the wheels hit the runway with the sound of an exploding canon, an ear-shattering bang, as the landing strip met the wheels sooner than the passengers had expected. The impact had knocked the wind out of Grace. Everyone breathed a great sigh of relief as the reverse thrusters engaged and the plane slowed to make its way to the terminal even as the wind pelted sheets of heavy rain against the fuselage, creating a barrier between it and the doors to the terminal. It came to a stop near the entry doors of the Comox terminal, but the wind and driving rain would negate the deplaning process. For now, everyone would have to remain in the cabin. The regional airport, part of the air force base, had no covered ramps to disembark into. Everyone waited as the storm raged.

Grace leaned back in her seat and closed her eyes. She had left early that morning from Toronto International with a two-hour layover in Calgary and she was exhausted. The trek to Galliano Island in British Columbia was always a day-long ordeal. Now they were holed up on a plane until weather conditions allowed the passengers to safely deplane without being blown off the exit ramp. It was 10:00 PM, with no indications that the storm would lighten any time soon. She had planned to stay at the Best Western in Courtney before heading to Campbell River in the morning where she would catch the noon ferry to Quadra. It would be only a short drive across to Heriot Bay where she'd take the forty-minute ferry ride to the Valdez Point landing on Galliano Island. She pulled out her cell phone to call the hotel, advising them of her situation and to ask them to hold her room.

She closed her eyes again and fell into a restless sleep.

A Dream

A DISQUIETING DREAM INVADED her unconscious mind. She knew it was a dream and not one of her visions because the feeling was distinctly different. This was a hybrid of the two, unique and telling. Dark figures were running through the aisles of machinery at Danton International, her workplace. What was she doing here? She felt the form of a woman closing in on her and knew who it was. She could smell the perfume: strong, pungent, penetrating the acrid stench of electronics being burned into circuit boards. The combination soured the air and stuck, burning, in her dream throat. Evelyn had found her. Grace tried to run but couldn't get her legs to move. She and Evelyn were now standing face to face, Evelyn directly in front of her, pointing a gun at Grace's heart.

Grace heard the click and closed her eyes, waiting for the bullet to explode into her chest. But, instead of the sound of gunfire, the howl of a wolf pierced her ears.

She held her hands over her ears to shield her mind from the piercing pitch as she searched through the dimly lit factory looking for its source.

Evelyn evaporated into the darkness to be replaced by the manifesting form of a ghostly wolf. Slowly, it pranced toward her from the end of the long passageway. She recognized the animal. It was the same wolf that had appeared in her dream the night before when she had decided to get away from Toronto. Away from Evelyn. Evelyn who was using her position and power to coerce workers to accept the implanted chip technology deemed to be for security purposes. It was not. Instead, it released nano organisms that controlled their minds, making them the most productive laborers in the world. Grace, Michael Rylie and Jim Heatherton had tried to stop her and had succeeded. But...

The wolf-creature padded silently toward her then stopped, dropping a dead rabbit at her feet. Blood still running from its neck, it landed with a splat on the hard, epoxied floor. This dark, red liquid snaked toward the tall machinery near the left wall where it was joined by an ever-increasing pool of crimson liquid gurgling up, each bursting bubble releasing the excruciating squeals that Grace knew were Evelyn's death screams. Evelyn had fallen from the catwalk into the moving machinery mechanism below.

An external screech jolted Grace awake. Had Evelyn followed her into the plane? A muffled cry escaped her as she grabbed the seat in front for safety, searching for the source of the scream.

Get hold of yourself, Grace. It's a baby.

A young child a few seats ahead was shrieking with a tantrum in the confines of her mother's arms.

"I know how that kid feels," the man beside her said. "I'd rather brave the rain than stay in here. Are you OK? You looked like you were having a nightmare."

"I guess the turbulence upset me more than I realized."

The captain came on the intercom and told them they could disembark.

"Oh, good," the man said.

Around her, passengers were standing and reaching for their carry-ons from the overhead compartments. The sudden din and crush of people crowding the aisle to wait for the doors to open made Grace's head hurt.

The man remained seated and bent forward in front of Grace, straining to look out the plane's small window. "He's right. It doesn't look as bad out there right now. At least they're letting us deboard."

Grace shivered as the man's eyes lingered on her. He made her uncomfortable yet nothing about him indicated any ill-omened intentions. Grace would have picked up on it. She could usually tell if there was something menacing about a person. She shook off her apprehension, deciding that her nerves had gotten the better of her. After all, she was tired and had just experienced a terrible nightmare—or whatever that had been.

His eyes were staring directly at her as he smiled warmly and held out his hand and introduced himself. "Rubin," he said. "My name is Rubin Machowitz."

"Grace." She cautiously accepted his handshake. She knew her hand was trembling and her palm moist. Grace stared back at him, waiting for a signal that would tell her what was amiss about this guy, but no sensations sprang from the hand connection.

As she continued to watch him closely, a ripple fluttered in her stomach. It was probably the nausea that accompanied her panic attacks.

He was a young man with strong, chiseled facial features, in his thirties perhaps. His bushy, dark brows framed his intense, brown, piercing eyes. Yes, there was something about him she didn't like. A tousle of his dark messy hair hung over his ears. He was probably much taller than she was but it was difficult to tell as they sat squeezed in the confined space of the plane's economy seats. He sat on the aisle side barring the entrance to the now very crowded narrow aisle where people pushed and tugged trying desperately to get space in a sardine-packed line that would soon start moving toward the door exit.

"We may as well stay seated," Rubin said. "There isn't even an inch of space to stand. Are you sure you're all right? You look pale."

"I'll be fine as soon as I get out of here." She shrugged, gasping for air through an open mouth, trying to appear calm, knowing her claustrophobia was evident by the perspiration on her forehead.

Rubin must have noted her distress. "Just breathe slowly," he said. "Breathe. You'll be OK in a minute." He looked around. "Where did they go? Flight attendants. Flight attendants. Where are you?"

The feeling of being trapped, being unable to move or get away from the crowded confines of the plane, exacerbated Grace's anxiety attack. It was like she was back in her dream, immobilized by fear. She took several long rasping breaths, trying to calm down. No, just claustrophobia, but this episode was full blown. Her head pounded and her ears buzzed and not just from the change in pressure. She put her head down to her knees as best she could in the confined space, trying to restore her equilibrium.

Rubin grabbed for the air sickness bag in the pocket of the seat in front, opened it and put it into Grace's hand.

"Hang in there, Grace," Rubin said. "We'll be outta here in a few minutes." He put his hand gently on her back trying to be reassuring. "This will just have to pass."

She felt violated at his touch and hurled into the bag. Grace looked up at him, both annoyed and embarrassed. *Did he have to touch me?*

He removed his hand. Was he feeling uneasy having to attend to a sick passenger he barely knew. Grace sensed that he was straining his neck searching for a flight attendant to help him, but that would be futile. Even if he could catch the attention of one, the attendant could never reach them through the packed walkway.

Awkward, thought Grace, almost smiling to herself. The last thing she wanted was to get another passenger involved in her malaise, never mind her phobia. But her smile faded quickly. How could this man know that this would just have to pass? Even Leo, her father, a family physician, couldn't make it better.

Rubin continued his reassurances. Grace could feel his worry for her—or was it something else that drove his attention and concern? This man had several energies emanating from him.

"Oh good," Rubin said after several minutes. "The line's starting to move. People are getting off the plane. Are you feeling any better? Will you need help to walk?"

His words and the fact that they would soon be off the plane made her feel a bit better. She took a deep cleansing breath and looked at this stranger who was being intrusive yet kind yet awkward and misleading all at the same time.

"I'm so sorry," she said. "This happens to me all the time. I just need a minute or so and I'll be as good as gold." She sounded like her mother and chuckled, trying to laugh off the incident. Several more minutes passed and the aisle was now clear.

Rubin got up and held his hand out to her. Grace accepted it and joined him in the aisle as he reached inside the overhead compartment.

"Is the black backpack with a Danton logo yours?" he asked. He pulled it down along with a carry-on of his own. They were the only two items left there.

"Thanks." Grace blushed at her frailty, hiding her embarrassment by bending over to pick her carry-on up from the floor. The action made her head spin again and she reached for the seat back to steady herself.

Rubin grabbed her arm in concern but she slung her bag over her shoulder and started moving away from him toward the open door.

✻ ✻ ✻

The cool damp air revived Grace as she walked down the plane's sloping ramp into the heavy rain. The terminal doors were another two hundred feet away and she quickened to a run. Rubin was in close pursuit behind her. The automatic glass doors slid open with a thud and they rushed inside, drenched and breathing heavy from their sprint. The other passengers were already crowded around the baggage conveyor where the first pieces of luggage rolled down a chute, popping into view through the flapping strips of vinyl hanging at the opening.

"I'm waiting until the crowd disperses," Grace said. "Don't feel like pushing my luck."

Grace walked over to a seating area by the windows and sat down and watched the rain over the airfield. She needed space, away from the hoard of people at the baggage claim area and from him.

Rubin followed. "Is anyone meeting you?" he asked, his eyes fixed on her again.

Grace gave him an irritated look but it didn't make him stop. *Is he hitting on me?*

All this somehow made her feel disloyal to Michael. Not that they were a couple, but she and Michael, and Heatherton, had worked closely together to thwart Evelyn's plans at Danton. When they realized the scope of Evelyn's deception and how it had harmed the workers in the Danton manufacturing area, the three of them banded together, became a team. In a bonded trust and friendship, they knew they had to stop her. Yet, with Michael, there was more than friendship, at least on her side— a great deal more. They had an attraction to each other. No, it was even more than that. Michael Rylie had saved her life. He had grabbed Grace firmly around the waist, negating Evelyn's attempt to pull her over the catwalk railing as she lost her own footing. You didn't do that if you didn't love a person. Grace was sure she loved him. But the word was never exchanged. She'd felt that electricity from his first handshake the day she started working at Danton a year and a half prior, but nothing more had developed of it so Grace doubted what she thought his feelings for her might be.

"I'm staying at the Best Western in Courtney tonight," she said. "Bad timing with the ferries. I didn't want my parents to drive all this way, especially through this storm. I'm renting a car in the morning to drive to Campbell River and from there I'll catch the ferry to Galliano. Anyway, it's nice to have your own transportation."

"That's a coincidence, I'm staying at the Best Western, too," Rubin said. "Let's share the cab." He paused.

Had he picked up the alarm bells that were going off inside her head?

"I mean we're both going to the same place. I see that makes you uncomfortable." He laughed and raised both arms in surrender and reached into the inside pocket of his jacket and pulled out a leather wallet with his police badge and ID. "I'm a police detective. I've been stationed out here to help investigate a missing Indigenous girl." He handed the badge to her for her inspection.

Grace frowned, uncomfortable at having to be polite. "Well, I suppose." What else could she say? He seemed nice and had been helpful. If she said no, would that be like resisting arrest or failing to comply with police orders?

The Cab Drive

IT WAS NEARLY 2:00 AM WHEN the cab dropped Grace and Rubin at the hotel. They hadn't spoken in the cab, both weary from the ordeal of a long and rough flight, but mostly because they didn't really know each other.

Grace had never seen a police badge before. For all she knew, it could have been fake. She regretted agreeing to share a cab. *No worries,* she thought. She would quickly check in, get to her room, and leave promptly in the morning, never to see him again.

Grace stepped out of the cab and paid the driver. She snatched the handle of her luggage the cabdriver had unloaded from the trunk and perused her surroundings. Inside, through the glass doors of the dimly building, was an empty lobby. Tired and desperate for warmth and rest, she proceeded to the check-in counter where a female clerk looked up at her in surprise.

"Are you Ms. Walker?" the clerk asked. "I didn't realize your husband was accompanying you."

Embarrassed, Grace turned to look at Rubin who was standing right behind her.

"Oh. No! No, you have it all wrong. This man was on my flight and when he learned that I was staying here too, we decided to share a cab."

Grace did not miss the amused snicker coming from her companion. The heat of her face told her it had turned red.

"The name is Rubin Machowitz," Rubin said, stepping ahead with his credit card between the tips of two fingers. "I have my own reservation. We're not together."

The grin on Rubin's face made the clerk pause and glance over to Grace again. "Is he joking?"

"No."

The unconvinced clerk checked the computer then looked up again. "My apologies," she said. "I thought that two of you were…"

"I'm exhausted," said Grace. "Would you check me in first? I want to get an early start in the morning."

The clerk quickly handed her a key card. "Room 210."

A young man in a porter's uniform with buttons bulging at the waistline, politely took the handle of her suitcase and immediately steered it to the elevator. He pushed the up button and waited.

Grace turned to face Rubin for a quick goodbye. "Thanks so much for your help. Best of luck with your investigations." Free from the burden of her luggage, she straightened, standing tall.

Rubin took her hand, holding it longer than Grace thought to be appropriate.

Uncomfortable, she pulled away and walked toward the porter who was holding the elevator door open.

❋ ❋ ❋

The elevator door opened with a ping at the second floor which was lushly carpeted and quiet. They didn't speak as the porter led her down to the end of the hall, the wheels of her bag swishing against the patterned broadloom.

The porter opened the door to room 210 and put Grace's bag on the luggage stand. "Have a nice stay," he said, pausing discreetly, looking for his tip.

Grace pulled a toonie from her pocket and handed it to him.

He looked at it, nodded with a huff, smiled, and left abruptly.

Alone in her room, Grace hoped she could sleep without nightmares. The nightmares were the main reason she'd given in to Heatherton's urgings to take a mental health leave from her job, to head out west. Setting it up as business leave, Heatherton had effectively convinced her to take time off. A sabbatical, he'd called it, though Grace knew it was because she was becoming unhinged from the pressures of the trial and the secrets she was keeping. It was starting to affect her work duties from the post trauma of it all. The investigation into Evelyn's fatal mishap in the Danton factory was over.

The Ministry of Labor, and the police, had deemed it an unfortunate accident even though the question of what everyone was doing on the factory floor at that time of night was still under consideration—and still looked upon with deep suspicion even though the trial had been over for several weeks. Jim Heatherton, head of public relations, had assured the authorities that late meetings were not unusual, that that night's meeting had involved a walkabout in the circuit production area. Forensics had discovered alcohol in Evelyn's system, indicating she'd been intoxicated, careless, had lost her footing on the catwalk, fell to her death directly into the machinery below. That's the way Heatherton explained it. No mention was made of Evelyn's diabolical misdoings toward the employees of Danton Global, or of Grace's special visionary powers.

Then the dreams—the nightmares—started.

She pulled back the thick white duvet on the queen-sized bed and tested the softness of the pillows that she'd doubled up. That's all she remembered before the hallway noise of other guests awakened her. A beam of light slivered through the side of the curtains and Grace realized that she'd slept soundly, without dreaming, and that it was morning. The bedside clock read 7:30. She'd barely slept five hours. Her eyes stung; her shoulders ached. She lay there hoping to fall asleep again but the hallway people were on the move.

Then silence in the hallway. Peace. She closed her eyes.

A sudden *bring-bring* from the bedside table brought her out of her half-sleep. She picked up the receiver.

It was Rubin Machowitz.

No. Please, no.

"Good morning. Did you sleep all right?"

Damn. He *was* hitting on her. How the hell did he know her room number? Would she have to register a privacy complaint with the hotel manager? No. The night clerk had announced her room number as she'd handed Grace the key. *Guess he took note! Maybe all police detectives paid attention to those kinds of details.*

"Like a log," Grace said, her head nestled snugly on the pillow and her voice nasal with sleep. She wasn't sure where this conversation would lead. "What's up? Is there something wrong?"

"Well, I knew you must be hungry because neither of us had eaten since the measly pack of peanuts the airline fed us on the connecting flight to Comox. You know, the flight that nearly killed us?" He chuckled.

He's trying to keep the conversation good-natured. What's he really up to?

"I wondered if you'd join me for breakfast. I hear the hotel dining room serves à la carte as well as buffet. My new boss tells me it's quite good."

Grace slid her legs off the bed and sat up, her eyes still closed. Squinting, she looked at the clock again: 7:35. What the hell was he doing calling so early?

Grace wasn't expecting to ever see Rubin again never mind have a friendly breakfast with him. Awkward. She was in love with Michael. Would accepting a breakfast invitation be... cheating? She yawned loudly enough for Rubin to hear and ran her fingers through her hair, tucking the loose strands behind her ear with her free hand as she paused, giving her time to think up an excuse.

"I'm not even out of bed yet," she said, then regretted her choice of words. He was probably picturing her naked or in a skimpy nightie. "You go ahead without me. It's going to take me time to... wake up."

She almost said, "make myself presentable," but decided not to further the excuses. And she certainly didn't want him picturing her in the shower.

"Oh, that's not a problem. I'm not ready either," he said. "Let's say nine? I'll get us a table. See you then."

Grace stared at the receiver, wondering how she'd allowed that to happen. She didn't know his room number so she couldn't call back and cancel. She flopped back down on the bed and closed her eyes, trying hard to fall back to sleep, ashamed of herself for accepting an invitation from a man she barely knew.

Grace went to her purse and pulled out her cell phone. She sent a quick text message to Michael. She would let him know about Rubin and ask that Heatherton run a background check on him. Heatherton knew the Crown Attorney from connections at the Toronto police department. He'd find out about Rubin quickly; probably be back to her before she got out of the shower. She hit send, put the phone down, then went to her suitcase to pick out another pair of jeans and a clean T-shirt and laid them out on the bed. She had slept in the clothes she'd been wearing.

The hot water regenerated her as it rained over her skin. As she relaxed, she realized that she was flattered by Rubin's invitation to breakfast and wondered if Michael would be jealous. She hoped he would be. She knew it would be inappropriate for Michael to show affection toward her at work where they both had important positions. What would that look like to the management and other employees? But couldn't he drop the professional attitude when they were away from the office? Heatherton saw it, too, she thought.

Grace had an hour before she'd meet with Rubin. The luxury of a leisurely shower had somehow settled her nerves. Here alone in a hotel room, she allowed herself to breathe. No one was after her here. She was away from Danton, where she never knew if one of Evelyn's minions might be watching her movements and reporting them back to Evelyn. No one was intent on harming her in this place. She could feel the tight knot that had been in her stomach ever since she'd left Toronto loosen its grip. After the harrowing flight over the Rockies, it felt amazing to unwind. By the end of the day, she'd be far away from the stresses of the Danton ordeal she'd endured. She could enjoy the peaceful retreat of a remote island where beaches, mountains, and old-growth forests were only lightly touched by civilization. She could regroup, restore her sanity. She'd be safe. And even if the now-deceased Evelyn had loyal followers still looking for Grace, they'd never find her on Galliano Island.

She finished drying her hair and went to check her cell phone. No messages or replies yet. *Strange. That's not like Michael.*

The phone in her room rang again, shattering its quiet and making her jump. She looked at the clock. Surely it wasn't Rubin again. It was only 8:30. No call display. She picked it up anyway.

"Hello?"

"So you don't trust this Rubin guy," an anxious voice said. It was Michael. "Did he follow you to the hotel?" Michael was usually to the point with his conversations, but right now he was being overly blunt. *Or was he jealous?*

"Michael. Hi. I think I'm still jumpy from the flight. We ran into very bad turbulence and I had an episode. An anxiety attack. This guy, Rubin, was sitting in the seat next to me and helped me. But somehow it happened that he's staying here, at the same hotel. And this morning he invited me to breakfast. I don't know what to think. As you know, I'm not exactly trusting anyone these days. Trust? More like paranoia. That's why Heatherton sent me away. Did you know that? It was Galliano or the Loony bin." Grace's attempt at easing the tension didn't work. "I'm not saying I don't trust him, but don't you think it's strange that all of a sudden I have a buddy?"

"I'm putting you on speaker," Michael said.

"Grace." It was Heatherton. His British accent was unmistakable. "Rubin Machowitz is with a special investigations unit with the Toronto force. His superior says he's been stationed by special request from the

BC missing persons unit to Campbell River. They've asked for help to investigate a missing Indigenous girl. Island Nation Band, they said. Galliano Island. I'd call that a bit more than a coincidence. Maybe you should come back home. At least Michael and I can protect you here."

"But that's exactly what he told me," Grace said. "I'm not picking up anything overly sinister about him except that he's a bit…"

"A bit what?" Grace heard Michael huff annoyance. *Or is it concern?*

"I don't know. Actually, yes I do. Michael, I think he likes me and I have a breakfast date with him."

"Bastard. Did you tell him you were going to stay on Galliano?"

"Shit! Yes. I told him I was renting a car and driving to Campbell River where I'd catch the ferry to Galliano. Damn it. I told him where I'd be staying, too. He showed me his badge. I wasn't feeling good and he was so kind. I just let it slip. I can't believe I was that stupid." Grace shook her head. "My parents are expecting me so I can't change where I'll be staying. They're really looking forward to seeing me so I can't stay anywhere else. And I really need this retreat."

Silence. Then Michael spoke.

"Maybe we shouldn't fly to conclusions," he said. "He checks out legitimately. All the same, tell him you've decided to fly back to Toronto. Make up some excuse about being needed back at work. Nothing major in case he decides to verify your story and finds out about Evelyn's accident. Then rent a car at the airport and head out to Campbell River from there. I'll arrange for the rental under our corporate account."

"Stay in touch with us, Grace," Heatherton said. "Call us before you board the ferry and let us know all is well. It's probably OK. But don't give Machowitz any more information about your background. Right?"

"Right."

"Grace." It was Michael again, his voice mellow. "Trust your instincts. Call me right away if you have any visions. Hell! Call me even if something doesn't feel right."

Check-out

G RACE GATHERED HER THINGS and packed everything back into her suitcase. She'd check out, leaving her luggage at the front desk in the secured room behind the check-in counter; she'd meet Rubin in the dining room for a quick breakfast; then take it from there. Although she didn't really think Rubin was any kind of threat, she would take Michael's and Heatherton's cautions to heart. Why take any chances? Anyway, after a quick breakfast, she'd never see Rubin again. One thought made her smile: Maybe Michael was jealous.

Grace was quite hungry, so the savory aromas wafting in from the dining room made her stomach growl. A sign at the concierge desk at the dining room entrance read, PLEASE WAIT TO BE SEATED, but Rubin called to her from a table draped in crisp, white linen situated by a window that overlooked a wet and rainy street.

"I took the liberty of ordering us coffee," Rubin said, a bright smile on his face as he stood up to pull out her chair. A lock of his unruly hair fell over his forehead. He pushed it back with his hand.

He seemed so nice. Was she being silly about her discomfort? Maybe she really *was* having paranoia issues. Still. How could he be a danger to her? Nonetheless, Grace would be cautious and do as Michael and Heatherton had advised.

"Thanks. I'm starving. Have you ordered?"

A waiter in black pants and shirt with a white chef's apron tied around his waist brought her a menu and filled a stemmed tumbler with ice water. He reached for the carafe of coffee and poured it into both cups.

She waved off the menu. "I just want some eggs. Scrambled with brown toast on the side."

The waiter smiled at Grace then nodded at Rubin. "And you, sir?"

"Oh. OK. Make mine over easy. Two, please. And with bacon."

The waiter noted it on his order pad and left for the kitchen.

"You seem like you're in a hurry," Rubin said. He looked at her questioningly, obviously noting something strange in her demeanor.

"Do you always notice everything?"

"It's the detective in me. Is everything OK?"

"Well. I got a call from my office this morning. Seems they're short staffed all of sudden and asked if I could fly back to cover." She didn't lie well and hoped it didn't show, although Heatherton *had* suggested that she fly back to Toronto. "I'm headed back to the airport to catch a 1:00 PM flight. I'm already checked out."

"That's kind of intrusive of them, isn't it?" Rubin's eyes squinted at her. "Can't they find someone else? I mean they're infringing on your... your vacation."

OK. So now he's asking leading questions. Grace shrugged and smiled but didn't say any more. *I'm not going to elaborate. Brevity is good.*

"Does it ever stop raining here?" Grace asked, attempting to change the subject, but sensing that this would only make Rubin wonder why she was being evasive.

"Another storm is moving in. You really plan to fly out under those conditions?" He looked directly into her eyes then laughed.

Grace fidgeted in her seat. Rubin Markowitz was a good detective. He could read people like a book.

"OK then. Don't tell me what's really going on. But I recommend you check with the airport before you go. All flights are likely to be delayed." He laughed again.

❇ ❇ ❇

Grace got her suitcase and backpack from the security area and walked out of the hotel where several taxis waited. She walked up to the first cab in line.

The driver put her luggage into the trunk and came back to the car.

"Airport, please."

"It's going to be a slow drive ma'am," he warned. "Weather's got traffic movin' real slow."

She watched Rubin who was watching and listening from the lobby door. "I have a plane to catch."

As the driver pulled away, Grace smiled and waved goodbye to Rubin.

Escape?

T HE AVIS CAR RENTAL COMPANY was expecting her. All she had to do was get out of the red-herring taxi. Michael had handled all the formalities so all she had to do was show her employee number and her driver's license, and sign the rental agreement. She was out of the air-port and on her way in less than fifteen minutes.

Michael must have been really worried that Rubin might be a threat. But then again, he always planned for contingencies. It was just the way he was. She decided she wasn't going to second guess the reasons for his reaction any more than that. It was just the way he was. Michael was the first person she met at Danton when she started there a year and a half ago. During her orientation week, she often caught him staring at her. Grace wondered if perhaps Evelyn had noticed it too. Was that the reason Evelyn had immediately taken a dislike to her? It didn't take long to learn that all the men at Danton were Evelyn's property. Michael had kept Grace out of Evelyn's line of fire—or at least he'd tried to. How was he to know that Grace's "powers" would expose what Evelyn's research team was really up to?

After a couple of Grace's strange episodes that looked something like epileptic seizures, she'd confided in Michael and Heatherton about her visions. She had picked up on the bad energy at Danton soon after she started working there. If Michael and Heatherton thought she was off her rocker, or worse yet, on drugs, she didn't care. They had to know that something was amiss at Danton. After a confidential meeting in Heatherton's office, she thought for sure it would be the end of her career. But, it seemed, they already had suspicions about Evelyn's microchip program. They, too, had witnessed the trance-like behavior of the plant workers.

That's when they'd become a team.

On the surface, Michael appeared stern and inflexible. Yet somewhere below that guarded personality was a gentle and caring man, even though it rarely showed. Once he knew about Grace's strange talent, and how Evelyn's microchip technology overpowered a person's thoughts and actions, he realized the whole organization was in danger. Grace in particular. Evelyn suspected that Grace knew things. Things that Evelyn believed were none of Grace's business. Nor anyone else's business, either.

Grace greatly appreciated that Michael micromanaged everything. He was part of Evelyn's project team even though she never fully disclosed what the implanted microchips did. Evelyn told her team it was for security, that it was a device to make it easier to badge in and out of the premises. That was all it was, she'd tried to assure him.

※ ※ ※

The weather had worsened again and the pummeling rain even drowned out the sound of the music on the radio. The wind, rain, and slapping of the wipers on the windshield was all Grace could hear. Water droplets pelted the windshield faster than the wipers could take them away. The drive to Campbell River was usually a scenic one, with mountains covered in coniferous trees and dotted with a crystal-clear lake here and there at their bases, but now, everything was obscured by clouds and heavy fog. It was like driving through a dirty slop of mud.

After half an hour on the road, her shoulders were aching from hunching over the steering wheel as she strained to see the lane lines.

Not that it mattered. As far as she could see, she was the only one stupid enough to be on this highway. She didn't know which was worse, the turbulence on the plane or the storm conditions she was driving through right now.

She should have listened to Rubin. "We were wrong about him," she muttered under her breath.

But Michael wasn't often wrong.

Rubin had been telling the truth about the storm conditions. Was he checking her flight out of Comox right now as she drove along this road in the exact conditions he'd warned her about? He was probably just trying to keep her at the hotel for his own interests. Or, perhaps, he'd truly had her welfare at heart. Had he gone to the airport to fetch her back to the hotel? *That would be creepy.* But if he had, he'd have learned that she'd deceived him, and this would trigger a whole new set of questions that might lead his trying to find her.

Grace breathed deeply and scolded herself out loud. Sometimes she could be such a wimp. Another half hour and she'd be in Campbell River. Would the ferries be running in this weather? No. They weren't running. Her special sense had kicked in again. She wanted desperately to get away from it all, not to have to worry about whether anyone would discover her unusual sensory abilities however she had come by them. She wanted to be secluded and safe with her parents, cocooned for a while to restore her confidence, to recharge her energy. She drove on, not so much because she was brave, but because she didn't have any other choice.

❋ ❋ ❋

Finally, forty long minutes later, she was at the outskirts of Campbell River. Usually a pretty West Coast town with its touristy shops, new Super Plaza, and picturesque marina, it looked sullen and dismal on this squally afternoon. The fog had cleared enough for Grace to see the waters of the strait, dark and choppy, with white caps bubbling. She definitely wasn't going anywhere until the weather settled. The ferries wouldn't be running until later in the afternoon. She'd still be able to catch the last one to the Galliano's Valdez Point landing. Knowing it would be too long a wait in the ferry line-up, she pulled her car into the parking lot of the harbor where the pleasure craft and yachts bobbed perilously against their moorings. She could wait out the rainstorm in the comfort of the restaurant, The Riptide.

The Riptide was one of her favorite eating places. It overlooked the harbor. She loved the marine atmosphere, the call of the seagulls and the briny smell of the air. On her last visit out here, Maria, Leo, and Grace had had lunch here on a grocery trip into Campbell River. But today, her car was the only one in the lot. People didn't venture out in these conditions. She pulled into the first spot closest to the building. Before stepping out and making a run for it, she zipped her Columbia jacket high to her neck and pulled her hood over her head.

The warmth inside The Riptide wrapped her like a blanket. She pulled back the wet hood of her jacket. Not another customer in the place. She saw only one server.

"Just sit anywhere you like," a spidery-thin woman with graying hair called from behind the bar. "I'll be right over to give you a menu. Nasty out there, isn't it?"

Grace nodded and chose a table by the window, the one, in her opinion, that had the best view of the marina. Instead of the usual tranquil sight of boats serenely tied at the pier, the scene was depressing and fierce, boats and yachts bobbing and bumping violently against the docks, those hollow thuds resonating over the wind and pelting rain. Cold radiated off the glass, making her shiver even though it was mid-summer. She moved to the table by the fireplace where the gas-lit flame danced as it spread its warmth.

The waitress approached.

"Just coffee for now," Grace said before the woman could ask questions. "I'm waiting to catch the ferry."

"It's probably going to be a while," the woman said.

They smiled at each other, nodding agreement.

"I'll brew a fresh pot but I'll leave the menu just in case you change your mind. My name is Sarah." She walked away into the kitchen, leaving Grace alone among the empty tables.

The Riptide

G RACE TOOK OFF HER JACKET, hung it on the coat stand. then settled back into her chair to unwind from the tension of her harrowing drive through the storm.

As her muscles relaxed, her mind drifted. Her thoughts bounced from the turbulence of the plane and her dream about the wolf, to Rubin, the stranger, the police detective who just happened to be from Toronto, to her parents, how much they might be looking forward to seeing Grace, and she them.

Opening her eyes again, the clutch of uneasiness about Rubin, the weather, and the ferry delay poked at her core. Her mind refused to go to the peaceful thoughts of being away from work and spending time with her parents whom she loved beyond measure. But like the weather, her thoughts couldn't be controlled. Childhood visions flooded in, troublesome "episodes" that had singled her out as the weird girl. Grace had always known she was different from her parents, different from her friends, unique in that she could not only sense things but actually *see* things that had happened, both good and bad. And those visions had always led to one of her episodes, one that would result in her teachers' calling her mother who would come and take her home. The weird girl.

The episodes didn't last long but they always left her shaken, drained of energy. She had little control over when or where one would creep in. Sometimes she could hide it. But only until the anxiety incapacitated her.

Why her?

She'd Google-researched clairvoyance and related visionary phenomena, fortune tellers, seances where mediums spoke to spirits. She'd found some interesting anecdotes, but this information was mostly conjecture so she didn't trust most of it. However, the phenomenon she dealt with, although rare, could be associated to families. This, she had discovered when reading about a remote Latvian village and a peculiar trait that the inbred villagers, rumored to be descendants of a fabled ancient oracle, displayed. If it were a family trait, then why didn't her parents also have that same ability?

Internet research had left her without adequate answers so she decided to ask her parents directly. Surely they would have done some research on her condition and would be able to explain the origins of the episodes to her. But the day she confronted them, what she learned was not what she wanted to hear. She wished she had never asked. That question had left her with more questions. How had she come by her powers, those "abilities" she wished would go away?

How could she forget *that* day?

She was twelve years old at the time, a child with just too much information to process. She could still hear her father's voice.

"Grace." Leo put one loving arm around her shoulders and with his free hand, he grabbed her hand tightly. "We are a family and nothing will ever change that."

She didn't need special senses to know something she didn't want to hear was going to be said anyway.

"Let me explain." His sigh was brief. "Your mom and I—Maria and I—tried for many years to have children. There were three miscarriages. Each one devastated us more than you can imagine. We went from specialist to specialist but were never able to carry a baby to term. Our hearts were broken at the thought of being childless. Then a friend…"

Grace remembered all too well that pause and the sideways glance he gave Maria.

"This 'friend' told us of an opportunity from a private adoption lawyer and you came into our lives. You were only a few days old. It was the miracle we had been wishing for. You have no idea how much happiness you brought us. But. We had to sign a legal agreement that the identity of your biological mother would never be revealed. I'm sorry, my darling. We always knew we'd have to tell you one day. I guess this is the day."

It *was* the day. It was the day Grace stopped calling them Mom and Dad. Why should she? They weren't her real parents. She was hurt and angry. She had never known, or even suspected, that the reason she was so different from them was because she didn't share their genes. She now felt even more flawed. So many questions. Had her real parents been mentally deranged? Was she some kind of alien? And now, whom could she ask about the reason why she was so very weird?

She had stormed out of the room, hoping to evoke an episode that might reveal the identity of the people she really belonged to.

None came. Ever. She cursed herself, disgusted because she would forever be an afflicted misfit, the weird girl, with no explanation of why or how she had come to be this way. But all the while, Maria and Leo never challenged her anger or tried to dissuade her from referring to them by their formal first names.

The anger diminished. They were, in every sense, her parents and she loved them dearly, but she would continue to call them Maria and Leo, never Mom and Dad.

"It's going to be a while before the ferries run."

Sarah's voice made Grace jump.

"Just let me know if you get hungry."

Sarah set down a coffee pot on the table in front of her but before Grace could start a conversation, one that might bring her out of her dark space, her cell phone pinged with a text message. "Sorry. I have to take this."

Everything OK?

Grace laughed. Maria had an uncanny ability to come to her aid when she needed it. Sometimes she thought that Maria had a kind of ESP of her own. Grace was tired and bored from the weather and the interminable wait. Maria always seemed to know when Grace needed attention or diversion.

She texted back.

Just hangin' out at the Riptide—ferries not running.

Another ping.

Well then, here's my grocery list. You don't mind picking up a few things for us at Superstore—would you?

Grace perused a multi-item list. The list made her smile. They were baking supplies and, in particular, ingredients that went into her favorite muffins. She could almost smell the spicy baked goods coming out of the oven.

NP—see you tonight.

Grace looked out the window then back to Maria's message. The restaurant was quiet and warm, comfortable. She didn't really want to face the cold rain again. The ferries wouldn't be running until late so she had time to eat, time to let her jacket dry, too.

She called over to Sarah. "What's the special?"

"Didn't really plan one for today. Didn't expect many customers. But our burgers are the biggest and the bestest in town."

Grace ordered and returned her attention to the conditions outside. She'd eat, pick up Maria's groceries at Superstore, then put her car in the ferry wait lines.

Windows seemed to elicit Grace's sensitive intuitive powers, especially when she was tired and when the outside atmosphere was fierce. Weather elements had an energy they shared with whatever they came into contact with. Like windows. Like Grace. Weather was like a record keeper for Grace, keeping records she beckoned to herself like a gossipy woman might. She now remembered a time in grade school when a particularly distressing vision had caught her totally off guard. She was taking a mental break from her lessons, daydreaming, and looking out of the classroom window. She saw a car speeding as it approached the school's slow zone and she saw her friend Amy start into the crosswalk. She heard tires screeching. She heard Amy's scream. She felt the panic in Amy's heartbeat and a sudden and intense second of pain. She had stared, transfixed, out of the window that day, so long ago, as she saw Amy's body lying motionless on the road as the vision melted before her eyes. But Amy was sitting in the desk directly across from her. She looked over for reassurance that her friend was safe, and breathed a sigh of relief. This episode had gone unnoticed by Grace's teacher and although Grace's heart was beating rapidly, and she felt that familiar dizziness and nausea that occurred in the aftermath, she was able to calm herself.

She was only eight years old but knew what had happened. Just another episode! But this was the first time it had gone unnoticed by a teacher or by anyone else, so she decided to keep it a secret so no one at school would know. She remembered feeling smug, satisfied that she could conceal her "fit," as she called it. She could brag to Maria when she got home from school that she had conquered and kept control of the affliction. She had been certain that Maria would be proud of her for handling it on her own.

Grace had shrugged it off not realizing that her vision had been a forewarning. Energy didn't have a time signature. It could leap to wherever it wanted to go.

The school bus dropped her off in front of her house at 4:00 PM.

Grace waved cheerfully at the remaining children still on the bus as she leaped triumphantly off the last step. She skipped happily to greet her mother as she usually did. But Maria's welcome home held a worried smile, her body language tense and rigid.

When their eyes met, Grace knew immediately that something was terribly wrong. The atmosphere became thick, ill-omened. She felt it so strongly that she thought she might be having another incident. No words would come out of Grace's mouth to ask the question. She already knew what Maria was about to tell her.

"How was your day, Grace?" Grace could tell that Maria was trying her best to sound calm and controlled.

This was real and Maria had something terrible to tell her. Suddenly, Grace's mind returned to the phantom accident she had witnessed earlier. She knew exactly what Maria was trying, as gently as possible, to tell her.

She also knew that Maria was watching the distress in her face. Grace didn't want her to say the words so Grace struggled to find her own voice to tell Maria that she already knew.

"My teacher didn't know. I saw the car hit Amy but then the vision faded. I looked over to Amy's desk and she was sitting right there doing her work." Flooded with guilt for not warning Amy of the danger, Grace's voice stuttered in despair. "I didn't tell her. I didn't tell anyone. This is my fault." She could barely catch her breath as she sobbed into her mother's breast. While she understood she had some kind of extra-sensory ability, never before had she realized that this might also endow her with great responsibility. She remembered trembling as Maria drew her tightly into a protective hug, trying to shield her from the guilt and confusion raging through her delicate psyche.

"No. No," Maria whispered, trying to assure Grace. "It's not your fault, Grace. Don't ever think you had any responsibility for this. That car never should have been speeding in a school zone."

Thereafter, Grace kept her visions to herself. She learned to control the sick feeling that came afterward, so her teachers never suspected there was anything wrong. Grace knew that no one else could see or feel her visions. They might be able to see the fear and terror on her face, but she learned to hide that, too. As long as she could keep it secret from others, no one else would be aware of the situation. For all Grace knew, Maria and Leo had convinced the faculty that her condition had been brought under medical control. The teachers never questioned or mentioned it again. But Grace had to learn to tell the difference between visions of past and evolving energies; when she had to act; and when she need only observe. Of course, there were other incidents where she could see things before they happened. But none was ever as traumatic as Amy's death. Maria and Leo agreed that it wasn't necessary for Grace to tell anyone at school what had happened, but in future, she must always let Maria and Leo know when an episode occurred.

Maria and Leo were overly protective parents, yes. But then Grace was a particularly difficult child because of her unusual physiological issues. They were both doctors. Leo was a doctor of family medicine and Maria was a psychologist. In those days, they practiced out of a multi-disciplinary medical arts clinic in St. Jacobs, a small town outside Kitchener, Ontario, where they lived. It was a wonder they had time for their professional work at all because during her preschool and elementary school years, Grace was frequently under their professional care for "episodes." They explained to Grace that children sometimes have fears that manifest themselves as real events. Maria would call them "day terrors" except, she explained to Grace, "when you have them at night, they're 'night terrors'." They always chose to talk her through the terrifying events. They would lovingly and patiently console her until she regained composure from the frightening visions. Maria always had exactly the right words to explain what happened. As Grace grew older and started school, she was regarded as someone who was "different." Grace never understood why her parents chose to handle her episodes without other professional care. They certainly had access to expert child psychologists who, no doubt, would have dragged her into some kind of alternate reality. But it was never an option they considered. So, in Grace's own immature way, she considered herself somehow flawed, unable to distinguish a terror from a reality.

Her terrors were particularly problematic when they occurred at school. Grace didn't know what Maria and Leo had told her teachers, but when a troublesome episode occurred during school hours, the teachers would knowingly remove her from the classroom to a safe area until either Maria or Leo could come to collect her and take her home. Once home, they would discuss the vision and the fearful emotions that came with it. They wanted her to understand that this was just the way she was. It was part of her, and they would teach her to understand and accept that there was nothing overtly wrong with her. But sometimes, the episode was beyond explanation. It was during those times that Grace knew there was something extremely different about her.

✳ ✳ ✳

Sarah placed the platter in front of Grace with a clunk. It snapped Grace out of her wandering thoughts. The burger was huge. She looked at Sarah and they both laughed.

"I might need a take-home container for some of it," Grace said. "Can you bring me one? And a knife to cut it in half?"

"They are rather big," Sarah said. She turned and left to a workstation to get a Styrofoam take-out box.

Grace ate less than half of the enormous burger and slid the remainder into the white take-out container for later. The ferries had microwaves.

✳ ✳ ✳

The Superstore, only minutes from the ferry dock, was almost deserted. Grace walked systematically up and down the aisles, looking for the items Maria had listed: whole wheat flour, raisins, cinnamon, baking powder and sugar. Maria was probably going to make Grace's favorite, spice muffins, for breakfast tomorrow morning. Grace longed for the peace and remoteness of her parents' island home. She longed for the support and protection Maria and Leo gave. She needed time for her spirit to heal. Evelyn's fall from the catwalk haunted her, as did the clandestine efforts to stop the microchip program that had started the chain of events that had caused Evelyn to come after Grace in the first place, resulting in Evelyn's demise.

Before checking out, Grace visited the video section, purchasing a few from the bargain bin, then returned to the snack aisles. She loaded chips, cheese crisps and a bag of jujubes quickly into her cart. She decided that the distraction of movies and junk food would keep the demons at bay. Maria would give her that look of disapproval but then she'd put the movie into the PlayStation, snuggle next to Leo on the sectional, smile at Grace on the lounge end and take the first handful of chips, then hand the bowl to Grace with a resigned squint. She would know what Grace needed to distance her thoughts from the drama.

Ferry to Galliano Island

J UST AS GRACE HAD PREDICTED, the weather conditions cleared to a light rain by mid-afternoon. Grace had bought all the items on Maria's shopping list, adding several of her own. Galliano was not a place where you just went to a convenience store on the corner to pick up snack food. Snack food in the general stores was not as easily available, and sold for a premium.

Rather than wandering around without further purpose in the Super-store, Grace left and drove the short distance across the road and down the highway to the ferry landing and parked her car in the line-up.

Usually, the ferry boarding lines burgeoned with vehicles as they queued up in six long rows, often making the last arrivals wait for a next ferry, perhaps the next two ferries before there was room to board the vessel. Today was different. There were only twenty-four cars. Grace had counted them. The ferry had capacity for eighty vehicles. Lots of room, she surmised. While the water still bubbled with white caps, she determined that the Quadra ferry would start running again within the hour. Her stomach was in knots. On her one and only previous visit to Galliano, the ocean waters had been calm, the weather pleasant, but today was definitely not "good weather." Maria had told her stories about how rough the crossing could get.

Grace bolstered herself against her fears. She was looking forward to the peaceful atmosphere of Abalone Hideaway, her parents' home on Galliano Island even though it was a bit of an ordeal to get there. She rather liked the adventure. First, she'd take the ten-minute ferry crossing to Quadra Island. Because the Galliano ferry dock was on the other side of Quadra Island, she would have to drive across the narrow north end to Heriot Bay. There, she would board the second, much smaller ferry. Under normal weather conditions, it was a pleasant forty-minute sail past scenic islands with mountains painted against the horizon, perhaps see dolphins en route or if exceptionally lucky, a whale. Orca often hunted here. But that was in good weather. That wouldn't be the case today. The sky was still heavily shrouded in the dense mist of the waning storm. Grace took it in her stride. She focused on the welcoming site of the Valdez Point landing dock despite the clouds that would make it appear dark and mysterious. She loved the island even in the rain. While Galliano was remote, there was a spiritual quality about the place that hadn't been trampled by a density of people. It spoke to her. It told her to be peaceful and reflective. For Grace, the energy here was soothing and wrapped her in a protective embrace. Nature that was pure and in balance had healing powers.

The Quadra ferry loaded quickly. Despite the churning white caps, the crossing was uneventful. Ten minutes later, the cars unloaded.

This was the first time she'd made the journey alone. When Grace had last visited, two years prior, Maria and Leo had been there to pick her up from the airport and look after the transportation. Grace hoped she could remember the directions. Somehow, a voice in her head guided her to *Turn here.* She slowed her speed as the rain became heavier again. She was grateful that a few of the other cars on the ferry also seemed routed in the same direction. It didn't take long. Before she knew it, she was there, with the Heriot Bay Inn to her left, the ferry dock directly in front, and the Galliano ferry in the corral waiting for its run, again only a few cars in the queue along the roadside. No fancy queueing lot here. It was now 4:00 PM.

She parked her car along the side of the road where she waited for the horn to sound the boarding call. They were probably waiting for a more-significant load. She wondered if load size was a consideration in maintaining the regular schedule. She heard a few more cars pull up behind her. For the moment she could decompress so leaned back to concentrate on the patter of the rain on the car roof. She closed her eyes and allowed the rhythm to soothe her fatigue and uneasy stomach.

❋ ❋ ❋

Grace hadn't intended to fall asleep. It was two blasts of the ferry horn—loud, deep, mournful sounds—that jolted her awake. The suddenness of the noise made her heart pound as though there were danger all around her. The digital display on her dash read 4:27. The cars ahead were starting their engines. The gangplank boomed and thudded as each car drove over it onto the ferry. She started her car, the windshield wipers clearing her view to watch the process. She felt sorry for the ferry personnel in their bright yellow rain gear, hoods pulled forward over their heads, and a light baton in hand, guiding vehicles to the onboard lanes, the overspray soaking them as cars and trucks obeyed their direction cues. She followed the procession and found herself assigned to the center lane, about midway into the vehicle bay, sheltered enough that the driving rain wouldn't soak her as she got out of the car to make her way up the stairs to the observation lounge on the upper level.

She felt the pause and the forward pull as the reverse thrusters kicked in, pulling the ferry away from the dock into the choppy water toward the Valdez Point port. The windows were streaked, heavy with a cascade of pelting rain that obscured all visibility. Grace settled into the padded benches and checked her cell phone. There were no other messages from Maria, so Grace sent a short text.

Will be there in forty minutes. Could use a cup of Earl Grey.

Grace didn't like how the ferry lurched and dipped against the waves. She wished she'd brought Gravol with her. At least the ladies' room was close by in case she had to vomit. Her stomach was certainly giving her signals that it might happen. Feeling ill like this made her vulnerable to wayward energies. She tried to clear her mind and think of happy times.

She checked her Facebook feed then text messages again. Maria had replied.

Hang tight. The kettle is on. Damn the waves.

Grace chuckled. Maria was so in tune. It was like she was always watching Grace with her mind's eye. Maybe Maria did have a sort of sixth sense. Maria always knew how Grace felt. She could almost hear the conversation she was having with Leo. They'd be talking about what to say and what not to say to Grace: only idle banter, nothing leading. They were careful not to press for information. Maria was aware that tension or too much "fussing" made Grace uneasy. Leo would have Gravol at the ready if her nausea hadn't subsided as soon as she'd exited the ferry. They were probably watching the clock and looking out of their big picture window at the driveway. Grace thought of them running out to the car to greet her, despite the rain, and scooping her into a warm embrace. The thought made a lump form in her throat. Her head buzzed from the motion sickness and it happened.

The heavy sound of breathing indicated panic. She could feel Evelyn closing in her. Grace tried desperately to cling tight to the protective metal rail. She tried to run on the catwalk high above the factory floor, but it undulated like a roller coaster. Grace felt herself fall to the level two stories below, the impact painless but jarring. Lying prone on the cement, she raised her head and saw the wolf approach from the long aisle, passing machines on each side, carrying a dead rabbit in its mouth. It stopped in front of her and dropped the rabbit on the floor where it exploded into a swarm of fireflies accompanied by the rhythmic beat of drums.

The ferry horn brought her out of it again. A voice over the PA instructed the few passengers on board to proceed to their vehicles for departure. Grace rose from the seat she occupied, clutching her aching stomach, wiping sweat from her face. Though she felt unsteady, she started down the stairs. She couldn't wait to get off the bobbing ferry to stop the sick feeling. She cursed the vision. She was probably pale with frown lines deeply indenting the space between her eyes. They called it The Look. Leo and Maria would know the moment they saw her. They always did.

Grace felt the heavy thud of the car over the gangplank bridge, making her feel like someone had punched her in the gut. *Damn.* The road climbed for about half a mile before she needed to turn off. She passed by the few cars parked along the roadside, waiting for their turn to board for the return to Heriot Bay. She didn't count them this time; her primary concern was to get out of the rain and settle into a warm house. *Won't be long. It's only a few short minutes.*

She turned left on Seavista Drive and in less than a minute, she saw the sign for Abalone Lane. A quick turn and she was on the circular driveway that descended into the hollow where Maria and Leo's timber-framed house stood.

At the bottom of the driveway, she turned off the engine and rested her hands on the steering wheel. She took a deep breath. Tears welled. Finally. She was here.

As she studied the familiar details of the house, she could feel relief as her muscles unclenched.

Two people with black umbrellas over their heads came bounding from the wraparound porch.

Grace opened the car door and ran toward them, flying into their arms. They huddled there in the rain, umbrellas askew, Grace getting wet but feeling warm and secure in their company.

"We're so happy you're here, darling," Maria said, pulling back to arm's length to appraise her daughter.

Grace didn't miss the subtle exchange of glances between Maria and Leo. Leo had her clutched at the waist.

"For heaven's sake. Let's get out of the rain," Leo said, pulling them both toward the covered porch.

As they jaunted awkwardly toward the shelter of the porch, a dog—no, it was a wolf—ran across the driveway into the treeline at the end of the property.

Grace froze, staring as though she'd been gripped by a vision.

Leo spoke up. "This kind of wildlife isn't unusual here on the island of Galliano, Grace. Though I've never encountered a wolf this close." He smiled at her. "*This* close. But I've heard they're a problem this year. People are finding scat everywhere. Must be good feeding on Galliano this season."

Grace's eyes were wide with disbelief. The dark ears, the white spot on the forehead, the rich brown of the wolf's fur… She knew this animal. Its markings were unmistakable. It was the wolf in her dreams. She even knew his name: Scout.

Abalone Hideaway

$\mathbf{M}$ARIA HAD BEEN COOKING. The house smelled like spicy chicken soup, one of Maria's specialties, one of Grace's favorites, comfort food that settled her at times when the wayward energies came calling and took residence in her thoughts. The flames from the wood-burning stove in the corner glowed and danced and the wood crackled, taking the chill off the cold and dampness brought on by the storm of the last couple of days. She inhaled the security. Grace immediately felt protected, the walls cocooning her from the creeping messages beyond its barriers. Maria and Leo had taken care to set an atmosphere they knew would calm the anguished feelings Grace fought against.

"You must be hungry. You should eat something." Maria reached her hand out to Grace's face, brushing away an unruly strand of hair, tucking it behind her ear.

Grace shook her head. *No.* "My stomach still isn't good from the ferry ride." The confession made her acutely aware of the motion sickness that still cramped her belly.

"Got just the stuff for that," Leo said, producing a blister package of Gravol and popping out two of them. These, he handed to Grace with a glass of water.

Grace smiled and obediently popped them into her mouth, taking a long slug to wash them down.

Leo nodded. "That should do the trick. Give it twenty minutes and you'll be feeling better."

Grace could see his concern and she didn't want her first evening on Galliano to be all about her malaise due to her vision's aftereffects. It would take only the slightest comment for Leo to insist on more medication to make her feel better. The doctor in him always prevailed. Evasively, she turned to gaze out the windows at the wet property below, the heavy drizzle of rain hanging solemnly in the air, the mountains of Quadra obscured by white, mistlike clouds, the deepening gray falling into darkness as evening approached.

"Leo and I are going to have soup," Maria chirped. "I'll put out a bowl for you in case you think you can manage to get it down."

Grace shrugged and watched Maria, meticulous, as she set the table with steaming bowls of soup and a basket of hot crusty bread. "At least... come and sit with us."

Grace acquiesced, humoring her well-meaning mother. She took a roll from the wicker basket and tore off a piece, nibbling tentatively lest her stomach balked.

"Have you heard from Michael?" Leo asked.

"He called me after the plane landed in Comox," Grace said. "I'll call him in the morning to let him and Heatherton know I've arrived safe and sound." Hearing Leo mention Michael's name made her wish he were there with her. Michael was difficult to describe. Grace felt a bond that she wished was a romantic one, but he'd never made a move on her. He protected her, and Grace loved him for that, more than a friend, though less than that of boyfriend. It's not how she wanted the relationship to go. She felt something for him even though he didn't reciprocate, at least not in the way Grace would have liked. The Gravol was kicking in, she was feeling drowsy, but decided to tempt her queasy stomach and took a spoonful of chicken soup.

"Mmm. This is delicious."

Maria beamed, and Leo squeezed her hand.

"Take little sips," Leo said, obviously assessing his daughter for signs that she might be sick from trying to eat so soon. He nudged an empty wastebasket closer to Grace.

"I'm OK," she said, grinning at Leo's assessing gaze. "My stomach seems to be settling. But I feel quite tired."

"Just the effect of the medicine," Maria said. "I'll turn down your bed as soon as we finish eating."

Grace tore away another chunk of bread and dipped it into the soup, letting it soak up the succulent broth. Though she didn't really feel like eating, she needed to ease Maria's worry that Grace could read by the glint in Maria's eyes and the frown lines that creased her forehead. The sodden bread dripped down Grace's chin as she scooped it into her mouth. Luckily, it went down without objection from her stomach. Her eyes felt heavy. Leo was right, the Gravol was working. She scooped the last two spoonfuls from her bowl and pushed away from the table.

Maria looked pleased as she got up from the table and headed for the stairs to the second floor.

Grace followed.

Her room was on the back side of the lodge and had a large window looking over Maria's gardens below and out over a short stretch of water where the trees opened up to show the view of the ocean against the mountain backdrop. Maria had put a new bedspread on the queen-sized bed, a mottled mixture of green colors that imitated the color of Nature against pale-blue walls and soft-cream linen curtains. Maria fussed, pulling back the spread, fluffing the pillows stacked two high. A new, white, cotton nightgown lay across the bottom of the bed. Maria had thought of everything. The room oozed peace and comfort. Maria went to the window and pulled the curtains shut before approaching her daughter and hugging her.

"Your father will get your luggage from your car in the morning. Get a good night's sleep." Maria's voice was soothing. "You'll feel better tomorrow." She paused briefly to evaluate Grace's face, then sighed deeply before releasing her embrace. Then she left, closing the door with the familiar click that defined the loose and wearing handle.

Grace could hardly keep her eyes open. She wobbled as she undressed, allowing her jeans and T-shirt to fall to the floor, not having the strength or will to hang them in the closet. She sat on the bed to pull the nightgown over her head. It was light as a feather and soft as silk, and an aromatic lavender smell told her it had been stored in the dresser drawer with a scented sachet. Grace slid under the covers and closed her eyes as her head sunk into the softness of the pillows.

On her arrival to Abalone Hideaway, the sudden appearance of Scout, the wolf that invaded her dreams, lingered in the back of her mind. She couldn't shake the image or the thought. It would be one of those nights where deep restorative REM sleep would elude her. She would sleep lightly, half conscious of her environment. Even with drugs in her system that made her drowsy, Grace recognized the pull, a niggling feeling of anxiety that often signaled the onslaught of an insightful vision. She was being prepared. For what, Grace was unsure. Half asleep, she moaned restlessly as transitory images of a beach with flickers of light that rose from the sand and swarming fireflies flashed through her subconscious to disappear into darkness. Energy signals. Galliano was supposed to be a haven free from these malevolent phantoms. Had Scout summoned her for a purpose? Perhaps. She had only been on the island for a few hours, but there was an unmistakable and strong energy that permeated the atmosphere. Grace hadn't detected this presence on her last visit. And along with the energy, there was something else: a mysterious feeling that there was something she had to do. It mingled, intertwined with the energy, and settled into Grace's core. It was shadowy and protective in the same measure. She had always worn her empathic gift like a burden but here, the presence lifted some of its weight. It clung and played with her mind as she slept.

❋ ❋ ❋

The harsh shriek of an eagle startled her to a sitting position, her eyes wide with alarm. It took her a moment to orient herself. A raptor, she thought. Grace recognized its call. She loved seeing them as she walked along the Galliano beaches and watched their skillful dives as they swooped to the water to snatch a careless fish that had come too close to the surface. She fell back onto her pillow and closed her eyes again, hoping to sleep longer, but the raptor's calls persisted. It was probably making a breakfast of the goldfish and koi residents of Maria's pond at the end of the fenced property. The noisy creature wouldn't let up. Finally, Grace slid her legs to the side of the bed, stood to stretch before going to the window to look out. The rosy glow on the horizon probably meant the sun was about to come up. She was fully awake now, so gathered her clothes from the floor, dressed, and went downstairs where the morning's chill filled the room.

Grace pulled Maria's fisherman's knit sweater off the hook by the door, slipping her arms into the thick wool sleeves. She was shivering in her tank top. The woodstove had burnt itself out and the air in the open-concept kitchen/family room felt damp, raising goosebumps on her skin. But it was getting brighter outside, and soon the sun would be up and the outdoor temperature would rise, warming the room, but for now, she needed the sweater's warmth.

Feeling out of place, she took stock of how she felt. Her nausea had passed but best of all, she felt remarkably calm. It was like a power fail where suddenly it became very quiet with the absence of the inaudible hum of electricity. Maria and Leo were still asleep. She stood at the island counter, wondering what she could do. It would probably wake Maria and Leo if she decided to make coffee; the grinder on the Cuisinart was like a siren. No, she would wait, even though she could have used a kick of caffeine. Too bad the Island didn't have a local Tim's close by where she could go out and get a coffee. In Toronto, a coffee shop was a five-minute walk, one on every corner. She sighed, missing the convenience of Toronto city life. She looked through the large picture windows to see if she could spot the raptor. No raptor, but something was moving beyond the fence line.

She stepped onto the upper deck that gave a panoramic view of the rough grasses and bushes beyond the fence. It spanned the back side of the property and from this vantage point, Grace could get a better look. The musky aroma of earth and pine was intoxicating. She took a deep breath of the sense-stimulating air. The bushes rustled. A doe and her fawn stepped out of the brush. *Foraging for food?* Grace loved that deer frequented the outskirts of the property. Maria sometimes threw the vegetable greens over the fence, always a treat for the wildlife, and it ensured that deer would be frequent visitors. But something else moved in the undergrowth.

Grace stiffened with anticipation. Was it the wolf she'd seen yesterday? Was it real? Or a vision? A day terror, as Maria used to call them when Grace was a little girl? She dreaded another vision, but she didn't feel the usual physical expressions that indicated the onslaught of a message. She had come to Galliano to escape all that but there was something here that commanded her attention. She could sense it.

Maria

G RACE HAD BEEN ON GALLIANO a full week, but she was still locked into her own fears and turmoil. Maria watched her daughter, helplessly knowing that whatever had happened in Toronto must have been more upsetting than Grace had let on. Typically, when Grace was like this, withdrawn and quiet, jumping at unexpected sounds, she needed distractions—ordinary distractions. Maria would help pull her out of that uncertain state. What Grace needed was contact with people whose energy was kind and soothing. Grace needed the tranquil environment of Galliano. For most visitors to Galliano, it was the kind of tranquility which, after about a week, was more peace and quiet than any city dweller could handle. But it was precisely what Grace needed at present, or for however long it took to bring her back to equilibrium. Maria guessed that this time it might take a long while. Maria had watched her daughter grow up with challenges that other children hadn't had to deal with: frightening insights, disturbing and vicious acts that played out in vivid detail and that manifested unexpectedly like ghosts, and at the most inopportune times.

Maria had heard of the accident at Danton, the company where Grace worked. Maria realized that Grace's visions had brought her into direct conflict with the woman in charge of operations, visions that showed the exploitation of innocent people. Visions were one thing, but that same woman had tried to kill her. Maria wondered if the woman had discovered Grace's empathic abilities. Grace had seen through the woman's misdoings and had put an end to the harm it was bringing down on the company's workers. Grace, for now, would keep those details to herself, Maria knew. The plan was illegal and posed a threat to the people who worked there. That Grace could expose the woman's manipulative plan would have been frightfully disturbing to the woman. The woman's name was Evelyn. Maria knew that Grace would never allow that kind of evil to hurt innocent people. Was she lucky to have found allies in Michael and Heatherton? Fellow employees who welcomed her unusual abilities however strange they appeared to be?

A week had passed and Grace's mood continued to be low. Grace was not exactly withdrawn, but quiet enough that Maria knew that Grace's mind was ruminating on events she wanted to forget. To ease some of the inner turmoil that Grace was trying to put behind her, Maria thought it would be good for Grace to go out to what Galliano residents called "town." Lewis Landing was nowhere near what anyone might describe as a town. It was a hamlet at best, one with a general store, the Sunset Restaurant, and it also had a community hall, the "Community Centre," that served as library, bank, police station and post office. Galliano's ultimate source of pride, the Medical Center, complete with helipad in case of dire emergency, was located one mile up the road from the Community Centre. Leo volunteered his services there two afternoons a week.

The full-time population of Galliano Island was around a thousand people, but it would swell to three times this during the summer months. The rugged beauty of unspoiled beaches, hiking trails and campgrounds held an allure that drew "mainlanders" to its shores. It spurred the growth of businesses catering to tourist and visitor needs. But this expanded population was temporary and depended largely on warm weather and good sailing conditions—safe ferry navigation to Valdez Point, Galliano's ferry landing.

Galliano

F ROM NOON UNTIL 3:00 PM, the Friday market at Lewis Community Hall was a cheerful and festive affair, bustling with friendly greetings and enthusiastic chatter as folks caught up with one another, sharing what had happened in each other's lives over the past week. They all knew each other in a collegial sort of way, not bosom-buddy friends, but close acquaintances, perhaps in a bit of an intrusive sense just short of meddlesome. Most of their homes were located outside the small hubs of island commerce. Lewis' artisans' market supported the local economy, such that it was. It was important to the locals in many ways. Resident craftspeople, bakers, potters and weavers offered their wares for sale, giving them extra income to support their peaceful though frugal lifestyles. The market was exceptionally robust from June through the end of September, the vacation season, bringing in patrons or tourists from Campbell River, Courtney, and sometimes as far away as Vancouver. Galliano was a favorite spot for day outings. The market also gave the locals a reason to hang out and socialize. Even on this small island, fifteen miles long and eight across, isolation was a problem, so on Fridays, the market was like a fair with joyful reunions, and after the market closed, a martini or two at the Sunset Restaurant bar extended the festivities late into the afternoon and sometimes the evening. It was a place where they could enjoy the music of a local singer or a group of musicians. It brought out the best—and the worst—of Galliano residents.

Galliano had a small population of Indigenous people who called themselves the Island Nation Band. They didn't mix well with the transplanted population. They especially resented the very affluent who came with yachts and built sprawling timber-frame houses overlooking the most scenic outlooks of Galliano, lands they considered sacred. Yet the Island Nation Band people were not restricted to reservation land at Little Deer Cove. They also lived near Smelt Bay, almost directly in line with Hollyhock, an exclusive wellness retreat. They had every right to make their home in any chosen location of Galliano Island—their ancestral lands—the same as any other resident. While the white folk truly thought of themselves as stalwart stewards of the land, it was clear that the Island Nation Band and Galliano's values clashed. It may have been the reason they didn't mingle socially. It was subtle, but tensions did arise.

Tamara

JOSEPH AND REBECCA were Island Nation Band and had a table at the market. They sold traditionally prepared smoked salmon, dried and smoked over an open outdoor fire. It was a favorite feature at the market. The locals, and especially the tourists, quickly bought up the prepared delicacy. The salmon was always sold out an hour after the market opened, leaving Joseph and Rebecca time to attend to errands, which they did with haste to avoid stares and judgment. The whispers about their family were palpable. People would stop talking as they walked past, offering only a strained grin as those gossips attempted to hide their opinions about Tamara, Joseph and Rebecca's daughter. "Tamara ran away." "Tamara was promiscuous." "Serves her right." "That's the way Indians are."

Although her absence had been reported to the authorities, neither the Galliano police nor the mainland police could provide any further information as to what had happened to her. Just another missing Indigenous girl?

❊ ❊ ❊

The traditional ways of Island Nation Band gave Rebecca some solace as she danced, secretly, on sacred ground near the shores of Lewis

Landing. Rebecca's grandmother was a healer. Rebecca's grandmother had appealed to the Ancestors to reveal what had happened to her granddaughter, with no success. This Full Moon Ceremony's songs and dance rose into the evening glow of the setting sun, making a powerful connection to the spirit world. It was a power that heightened at water's edge on the nights of phosphorescence. Although Joseph worried that Rebecca would be seen by the locals, made fun of for chanting and dancing around a driftwood fire, Rebecca didn't care. The old ways had served her people well for thousands of years.

Leo

W HEN MARIA STOPPED THE CAR at the door entrance to the Galliano Medical Clinic, Leo leaned over to kiss her cheek, but before he opened the car door to get out, he glanced at the back seat. Grace had been withdrawn since their last visit to the Lewis moorings. Something about the beach area seemed to have spooked her, but she wouldn't elaborate. He respected that she didn't want to talk about it, that's just how Grace was, so he assumed it was because she didn't want to risk an episode.

He smiled at her, not wanting to pressure her for a response.

"You can wait here if you don't want to be around the crowd at the Market."

Grace nodded and smiled back.

"Grace is doing fine," Maria said. "We're going to have a splendid afternoon, aren't we, Grace? I'll acquaint you with some of our friends and maybe with a few young people of the island, too."

"Here's a hug," said Leo, wrapping his arms around an imaginary Grace. "How about getting an apple pie at the Market? We'll have a feast of clams and then dessert. My mouth is already watering." His attempt at easing the malaise that hung over his daughter didn't seem to have worked.

"Have a good day, Leo."

He was happy to hear her talk, at least. Was she coming out of her funk? "You bet, honey." He felt his grin turn into a broad smile as Grace leaned forward to let him kiss her cheek before he exited the car.

"OK, let's see what we can find." Maria laughed then drove the short distance back toward the marketplace, Grace still sitting in the back seat like she was a customer and Maria a taxi service.

Lewis Community Hall

I	T WAS ONLY A FEW MINUTES after high noon and the Lewis Community Hall was crowded with market patrons and day-trippers looking for novelty items and home-baked goods. With Grace following, Maria pushed her way to Hannah's counter. The pies were selling quickly but Maria was able to move to the front and place her order. She noticed that Grace was eyeing the blueberry scones.

Maria called to Hannah's helper, "And how about six of the scones." She turned to Grace. "We'll need a snack on the way home after we pick up Leo." She licked her lips and raised her eyebrows to communicate the deliciousness of the pastry.

"They're my favorite too," came a voice beside Maria. Holly, whom Maria had hired to help with the gardening when it had become too big of a job for her, was like a second daughter to Maria, tough and rough around the edges but needy for attention. Maria offered the young woman a softer touch that only a motherly figure could. Holly ordered two of her own. "Who have you got here, Maria?"

"This is our daughter, Grace. She's here from Toronto. Maybe the two of you can hang out on your day off."

Grace exhaled softly. She didn't look to be exactly annoyed, just uneasy. Was she embarrassed that her mother was arranging her social life like it was a play date? Probably.

✳ ✳ ✳

Holly smiled, and her head nodded in greeting, but Grace saw tension in Holly's body language. Although Holly's attitude was frank, she didn't give off any negative vibes, just an edgy attitude that came with people who had a chip on their shoulder. Still, it was nice to meet someone younger, closer to her own age. Maybe they had interests in common. Though probably not. One thing was certain, Grace would keep her powers a secret and that was reason enough not to make friends here on Galliano.

The room was loud with chatter and the crowd was starting to annoy Grace, so she poked at Maria's shoulder to get her attention over the noise. "I'm going outside for some air."

"OK. I won't be long. I'll meet you at the car."

Maria's frown and manner told Grace that even though Grace was twenty-three and no longer a child, her mother didn't want her to be out of her sight. Did Maria know—or worse, feel—something Grace hadn't picked up on?

✳ ✳ ✳

Once outside the crowded community hall, Grace took a deep breath of relief. She looked up at the cloudless bright sky, squinting against the light. She cursed herself for not having brought her sunglasses The sun was high overhead and hot on her bare shoulders. She raised her hand over her eyes to shield against the glare coming off the many vehicles parked along the road that sloped downward toward Hague Lake. The lake was obscured by trees, but she could hear the joyful shrieks of children and the splash of swimmers, the thumping of a volleyball. From the sounds, it appeared that there was crowd also enjoying the frolics along the lake's inland beach.

Nestled in a hollow was the Sunset Restaurant where people sat at outdoor patio tables. Grace decided to check out that local hangout. The white umbrellas shaded the customers from the noon heat and glare. She spotted Holly heading to a table where a young man sat sipping a Corona.

Impossible Friendship

T HE PERMANENT INHABITANTS OF GALLIANO were a mixed bunch. It was hard to say what attracted the full-time residents to the remoteness of this island. Mostly, like Maria and Leo, they were retired folks looking for peace and quiet in this place of untouched nature, but there was also a small contingent of younger people, millennials, who found the cities overbearing with little opportunity to join the successful middle class like their parents had. They sought a less-demanding life, somewhere they didn't have to compete. They were pleasant enough, but when asked what had brought them to Galliano, they'd answer with a shrug and a blank expression on their faces, a look that commanded you to mind your own business. Perhaps they were runaways. Perhaps they suffered from bad family relationships. Or maybe they couldn't cope with others of their demographic in an urban society. Whatever the reason, it was not to be shared and the locals were laid back enough not to press their privacy.

It was different for Grace. She didn't mind the competition. She had graduated from the University of Toronto, majoring in Public Relations, and was the head of her class and had easily fit into the demands of corporate life. At the annual job fair held at the University of Toronto,

Heatherton had recruited Grace to her job as a public relations officer at Danton.

It wasn't the direct day-to-day issues of the job that were problematic for Grace. With her academic training and skills, she could easily handle the duties of public relations, keeping a clean and ethical profile for the company. But it hadn't taken her long to discover Danton's underbelly. Grace's empathic ability soon rooted out the lingering secrets that held a sinister and destructive energy. A peculiar characteristic surrounded malicious energy. It was like a gossipy person, a "know-it-all." It wanted to tell you everything. Once it was put into motion, it could not be contained and it sought out Grace for resolution. At Danton, Grace soon learned that Evelyn Loudon was the source of the agitated energy that scratched at Grace's awareness. She had learned that ignoring it would lead to outcomes with consequences. Evelyn had to be stopped from subjugating Danton workers. When Evelyn found out that Grace, Michael and Heatherton had discovered her intent behind the microchip program, Evelyn went on the defensive. On the surface it seemed logical that security cards would never be lost again. The security at Danton was high and workers often were late reporting to their stations as they badged in because they'd forgotten or misplaced their cards. The problem would be solved by implanting a chip into the palm of their hands. All they had to do was wave it over the reader. It was Grace who first noticed the change in the workers. Those who were implanted seemed to be almost hypnotized after the starting buzzer sounded. When she pointed the phenomenon out to Heatherton and Michael they started to secretly investigate. Something bizarre was definitely going on. But Evelyn was sharp, and after noticing their suspicion, showed the nasty side of her personality. Nothing was going to stop her even if she had to kill those who tried. But Evelyn had made a strategic error. She'd underestimated Grace's power.

Here on Galliano, there were few demands. You did your own thing. Grace loved the bustle of Toronto, and even after living there for two years, had only grown fonder of its demanding lifestyle. But for now, here on Galliano, this was exactly what Grace needed. She needed less stimulation, less energy. Nature was always therapeutic and restoring and she hoped that this time, she could count on those forces to calm her. She couldn't get over the difference between then and how she felt now, standing beneath the hazy purple of the towering mountains on the horizon, beside the sparkling glare of the sun on the ocean, and among the majesty of old growth trees that reached toward the sky. It was so peaceful compared to how she'd felt just a few days before in the city, it was like she had been transported to another world. It was like she had grown roots herself, the power of the forest and the land filling her. Toronto, like a festering wound, had dumped so much on her—stray negative emotions left behind from a myriad of bad actions and intentions—so much residual ill will. Whether people knew it or not, it lingered and infiltrated their thinking and actions without their even noticing, and all of the recipients in turn would leave their own traces to pass on to the next unsuspecting person who passed through its invisible orbit. The folks on Galliano had checked their ill wills back on the mainland.

Grace watched the unhurried movement of the island people. There was no urgency, no competing for space, and Grace briefly wondered what it would be like to live here, whether she'd be happy making a home on the island like her parents had, even for half the year. But she did love the city. It may have been rough around the edges, polluted, and sometimes overwhelming, but being here was the right thing for Grace right now, even if forces had drawn her to the Island for a purpose. And, she did feel that she had a larger purpose for being on Galliano than her own need for respite.

Holly and Hollyhock

ACROSS THE WAY, bending over a young blond man with a scruffy beard, Holly Anderson was laughing, twirling a lock of her shoulder-length, straw-colored hair around a finger. She was a petite five-foot-two, slender-built woman in her mid-twenties, the same age as Grace. Galliano had been her home for only the past two years, but she was the quintessential Galliano type. She looked and dressed like she'd been time warped from the 1970s, with a sloppy oversized T-shirt that she wore over a long, multi-tiered peasant skirt that stopped just above her ankles, and road-worn sandals strapped to the blackened bottoms of her feet. Locals knew not to be fooled by her appearance: her large blue eyes in her lightly tanned face could go cold in an instant. Enchanting as she was, Holly was hard to figure out, a peculiar sort. Happy at times, moody at others, occasionally lashing out with particular venom if someone had ruffled her own particular take on the world, Holly lived in the moment, enjoyed what she could afford, smoked the island's home-grown weed, free-loaded as much and as often as she could, and simply blended into the Galliano carefree culture. The island was well known as "that Hippie Place," so she didn't particularly stand out. She would joke that she worked for her namesake. Hollyhock was a spiritual and wellness retreat located on Sunset Beach, a pricey venue for the

105

elite who sought exotic spa treatments and organics to cleanse them of the toxicity of their wealthy lifestyles. She mused that the place had called to her, that it had magically beckoned her, convincing her that this was where she belonged. Intoxicated by Nature or weed, perhaps? But in truth, it was named for the prolific hollyhock flowers that over-towered most adults, and bloomed prolifically in Hollyhock's prize-winning botanical gardens. Holly worked there as a domestic, sometimes helping with the gardens to deadhead the fading blooms. During the summer months, she made her home in one of the ram-shackle bunkies along the beach road overlooking Smelt Bay; the winter months she'd house-sit a vacation home temporarily abandoned by owners who had returned to the city or to warmer climes like the Caribbean.

The locals regarded Holly with caution. She had a habit of making a scene, especially at the Sunset Restaurant. She had no qualms about telling a wealthy tourist to fuck off if they dared try to treat her like the hired help. She could be sweet but she'd also lash out if vexed. In spite of her temperament, Maria had taken a liking to her. For all the things Holly was not, she was a good gardener and hard worker. When the Walker's one-acre property, complete with flower gardens, pond and lawn became more than Maria wanted to look after, Holly was always willing to help bring Abalone Hideaway back to perfection. Besides, Maria made sure she had hydrating refreshments while working in the summer's hot sun, and always invited her to join her and Leo for a nutritious meal and a glass of wine at the end of a hard day. Maria would pick her up from Hollyhock which was across the island and drive her back home at the end of the day. Best of all, Maria paid well.

✳ ✳ ✳

The patio area of the Sunset Restaurant was busy with customers. Holly and the young man sat at the table near the road under the shade of a wide, white umbrella. Grace watched her from the seat she had taken at an empty table near the restaurant's door, waiting for the Coke she'd ordered. The sun beat down on the patio patrons, and even under the umbrella's shade, Grace could see the sweat beading on Holly's forehead. Holly waved and Grace waved back.

Holly's male friend moved like his bones were made of rubber. He was dressed in a camo T-shirt and baggy kakis. He had turned his head trying to duck low under the table as he dragged on a joint. This had made Grace laugh. He was really stoned.

He was now attempting to get up onto his bike, but his movements were uncoordinated so he knocked it clattering to the ground. Holly pulled him back onto the chair beside her. Grace wondered what else he was on or had taken, no doubt a cocktail or a hybrid mixture of intoxicants. The guy was in no shape to go anywhere. Grace noted how close they were sitting to each other. He held out his hand, offering something to Holly. It appeared to be a joint. Holly lit up, inhaled deeply and smiled back at her companion.

The odor wafted over to Grace. *Time to get out of here.* She rose from her chair, leaving money on the table for her drink even though it hadn't arrived.

To Human Ears

T HE LEAVES AND VEGETATION in the old growth forest rustled. To human ears it would have sounded like the wind, but Scout could hear the voices of the Island Nation Band's Ancestors whispering to him. The Ancestors needed his help. They needed Grace's help. This was their way. They called to earthly creatures of pure heart to help them guide a soul to the Sunset Land where those who departed the earth would remain forever in harmony with the elements of Nature. Scout had been selected for a noble quest. Together, they would guide Grace to discover the heinous crime that kept Tamara locked to the earth underneath the fireflies who danced on the beach on the nights of phosphorescence. Tamara's spirit and that of her unborn child were earthbound until her killer was brought to justice. She was a young woman thought gone of her own accord, but like so many of her Indigenous sisters, she had been murdered. Gone forever.

While Scout's pack remained close to the Galliano Island coast, near the water, stalking the small game of the land, or fishing for salmon in the shallows, Scout patrolled outside the wire fencing of the Walker property. Grace would feel the pull of his protection. Energy was governed by the laws of Nature, no matter the species. Every action, especially evil ones, left a residual imprint that lingered, however faint.

The wolf and Grace could read the energy left behind, energy left by ill intentions and violence. Scout felt her and he knew Grace could feel him. Her power was strong, but she resisted her gift. She would pick up on the messages even though she was trying hard to close off the empathic signals, trying to seal her mind shut against the turmoil caused by the events back in Toronto, events she'd come to Galliano to forget. She would try, but she could not deny her power any more than she could cease breathing. It was part of her. And it sought the truth.

Lewis Landing

T HE TIDE WAS OUT WHEN Grace's father went to check on his boat that was moored at Lewis Landing. They were going to have a day of leisure, sailing around the island, hoping perhaps to see whales. While he did his inspection, Grace would dig for clams in the inland cove where the basin emptied with the ebb, exposing the sandy bottom.

Two years prior, she'd found this place to be a refuge from the torrent of empathic messages that were bombarding her. Lewis Landing usually calmed her. But on approach to Lewis Harbor this time, Grace's muscles tightened. It had found her, the wayward energy that whispered and faintly called to her. It bristled, lingering, beseeching her attention. It was like electricity that prickled inside her body. Grace could feel it in her hands and feet. It shuffled into her ears like white noise, a low, barely distinguishable hum. She became aware of a song, ancient, an infant's lullaby. She fought the onslaught. There were times when Grace could push the signals away as if refusing to pick up a phone call. She concentrated, trying hard. She took an intentional, slow, cleansing breath and focused on the squawk of the seagulls, the splash of the waves on the pier supports, the briny smell of the air that she so loved, trying to stay in her place of peace, guarded from the world around her. *No, not here,* she pleaded. She considered this place an Eden, where heaven touched the earth and water, a place where God would cradle her within protective arms, safe from the evils outside of her control. *No. Not here.*

✳ ✳ ✳

Leo parked the SUV close to the boardwalk that led to the single lane of wooden decking at the water level below, where boats of various makes and sizes were anchored secure to their berth. The wooden gangway was steep, declining low to the deck, indicating the tide would be out for at least an hour yet. Grace would have ample time to fill her bucket to the brim with plump butter clams and blue mussels. It wouldn't take her long as mollusks abounded here in the rich, nourishing waters. When she'd gathered enough, Grace would take them to Leo to hang in his specially devised mesh sack that would hang over the side of the boat to purge for the day, allowing the sand to be expelled from the shells before they would make a feast of the succulent delicacies: a delicious West Coast seafood dinner, common to Maria and Leo, an infrequent delight for Grace.

"I won't be long." It was obvious that Leo knew that her empathic powers were being invaded. "I could help you dig and then we could check out the boat together. If you like."

Grace shook her head. "I'll just deal with… whatever." She pushed him gently toward the boardwalk. "I'll be OK. Go."

Leo hesitated, giving her an anxious look before turning to walk over the bridge to the harbor, looking back frequently.

No, Leo. I'm not going to change my mind.

Grace waited until he had boarded the *Serenity* before grabbing the bucket from the back of the SUV and heading to the sandy basin. With each step, the prickle spread, moving further up her legs and she knew she could no longer will the energy away. It was only a matter of time before the message would come through. She surmised that something ominous must have happened here and the enduring energy that remained wanted to give away its secret.

She reached into the bucket, taking out the little hand shovel Maria always used to dig weeds from her flower beds and crouched to the wet, exposed, basin floor. She plunged the little shovel in then scraped a narrow top layer of sand toward her, unearthing a cluster of fat butter clams. She picked one up. As it clunked into the metal bucket, the vision slammed her hard, momentarily obscuring her sight then slowly opening like a kaleidoscope on an event that once occupied this space. She watched as the horrific scene unfolded before her like a movie with her as a phantom watching from the sidelines.

It was dark and two people were on the Lewis Beach area in front of the harbor, waves swishing melodically on the shore, boats bobbing in the water. The silhouettes of the people wavered against the full moon that lit the beach. Frantic gasps of a female filled the space as she ran to escape the chase of a man. When he caught up to her and as she turned in profile, Grace could see her rounded belly. The man grabbed her by the torso, but she fought, resisted, fought again, finally pulling away with a burst of adrenaline. But he was too fast and strong. He caught up to her again. From behind, he hit her on the head with an object, a gun perhaps, and she fell helpless onto the sand. The impact made the sand sparkle ghostlike with the phosphorescence of the night. She lay there, face down and so very still. He stood watching for several moments before dragging her to the treeline, over to the arbutus tree that hung low to the ground. There, he started to dig. He buried her there, carefully raking with his hands over the mound when he had finished. The sand would be further smoothed by the incoming caresses of the tide.

And then... the vision was gone, releasing Grace as though she'd been pushed with great power from a cliff. Its force propelled her forward onto her hands and knees into the wet silt. Her body shook as she struggled to take in air. Sunlight slowly melted away the darkness, bringing her back to the present. She lifted herself off the sand, exhausted from what she'd seen and from having felt the trauma the woman had experienced.

As she regained her composure, she saw the wolf about a hundred feet away. They caught each other's gaze and she was instantly hypnotized by transference of thought. She knew this wolf. He'd been in the dream, the dream that visited her on repetetive nights.

The wolf pawed at the wet sand, unearthing a pile of clams, scratching the clams into a mound. The wolf looked Grace's way and flung a shell in her direction. Then another. He had found a much better cache over there than where Grace had been digging. This was the same wolf. Yes. She was sure. His name was Scout. Her vision and the animal were connected. She could feel it. And she knew with certainty that he would not hurt her.

She felt the need to reach out to him as if he were a pet dog. She crawled toward him.

Then a gun shot made her drop flat to the wet sand. The crack quivered like the uncontrolled strings of an electric guitar, resonating, splitting the air in the quiet of the afternoon. Where had it come from?

When she looked up again, the wolf was gone but a woman stood on the gravel lane with a hunting rifle projecting from her shoulder and aimed at the treeline.

Crack. A second shot echoed through the basin's low tide depression.

Then Grace saw Leo, up by the gravel road, running across the bridge that connected the pier to the land. "What the hell are you doing, Rebecca? Can't you see that Grace is down there?"

"What are you talking about?" Rebecca called back. "I was shooting at that wolf that's been hanging around here. Who the hell is Grace?"

Scout

K NOWING THAT GRACE WOULD BE GOING clam hunting, Scout had already been watching from the protection of the bushes. They had waited a long time for her to come and she was on the island now, where the act of violence had occurred. Today at Lewis Landing, the energy had overtaken Grace and Scout was relieved about that although he knew Grace wouldn't be. He felt the ripple of the violent vision as she was being drawn into it as witness. She saw what happened to Tamara, though not the face of Tamara's killer, only his silhouette, jagged and shimmery, indistinguishable from the shadows of her vision. Grace was a witness to a past murder. A murder that needed to be reported to the police. But Scout and the Ancestors knew that Grace was afraid to speak up because of what had happened in Toronto. Would anyone believe her? How credible is a woman who says she witnessed a murder in a vision? Would she dare go to the police? Dare open up an investigation and start interrogations for which she had no answers?

Scout understood her dilemma and had moved out into the basin to reveal himself to her. They had met before in a dream, but would she actually accept his guidance as he stood there on the estuary? Their eyes had met only briefly, but in her current alarmed state, would she trust that he and his pack and the Ancestors would protect her? He con-

121

centrated with all his might. He hoped the Ancestors would reinforce what he was trying to tell her. She had to accept. She had to understand.

Then Scout had sensed danger. A woman on the roadway was raising her hunting rifle. He heard her cock it. He bolted to the safety of the trees. A crack. Gulls screamed as they took to the air. A second shot made him shake his head with the loudness of it. Hunkered down in the salal underbrush, Scout watched the man he knew to be Grace's father run toward her and call out her name in fear.

"Grace!"

Rebecca

R<small>EBECCA WAS FEELING IT</small> more than usual today. During the past year, she'd been watchful, vigilant for any sign that might offer a clue as to her daughter's whereabouts. Ever since Tamara had gone missing, the heavens weighed down on Rebecca with a dread she could not explain. She feared the worst but also reminded herself that Tamara had wanted to explore the opportunities offered by the B.C. mainland. Perhaps that's where she was. Rebecca hoped so because their last time together had been spent in an argument about doing just that, leaving Galliano. She could still hear the slam of the door. Rebecca pushed back the memory before remorse plunged her, once again, into that very sad place of regret where she would be tortured by her emotions in a place where even a smudging ceremony on this sacred beach could not cleanse her guilt.

She pulled into the gravel area reserved for parking above the harbor and recognized Leo's SUV. He was probably down at the pier checking his boat. She scanned the harbor area. No one was there that she could see. Opening her car door, she stepped out to look toward the basin to check how long the tide would be out. That was when she spotted the wolf pawing at the sand, unearthing clams. It was a bad year for wolves because lots of small wild animals had repopulated the island since the last full invasion of these predatory visitors a few years ago. The cycle had come full circle and now they were back. It alarmed her. She knew that a wolf would kill if hungry or threatened. In the absence of rodents and deer, would they attack a human? She opened the trunk of her car and pulled out her rifle. "Not if I can help it," she grumbled. These creatures had already wiped out an entire cage of rabbits that her husband, Joseph, was raising on the Little Deer Cove Reserve. At least her laying chickens were still safe, enclosed in the new protective fencing Joseph had put up.

She checked the area again but saw no one, so raised the rifle to her shoulder and took aim, not directly at the animal, but slightly over its head. It was not her place to kill or wound an animal unless it was a direct danger to her or another person; though it was within tradition to take the life of an animal to use as food or for its fur. The Island Nation Band had title to hunt the land as their Ancestors had before her. But today she would be gathering clams and she was taking no chances. The sound of a gunshot would scare it away. She aimed at the wet shore of the beach, pulled the trigger and prepared to shoot a second time.

She heard a man shouting from behind.

"What the hell are you doing, Rebecca?" It was Leo. "Can't you see Grace down there?"

But Rebecca had already pulled the trigger. A second crack would ensure that the animal would not return.

She turned to see where Leo was, but he nearly knocked her over as he ran past her toward the basin. It was only then that she saw a woman down on her hands and knees in the wet sand. She didn't understand. *How could I have shot her? I aimed in the opposite direction.* There was no way she could have hit her.

The Basin

L EO REACHED GRACE and immediately began fussing over her. "Grace! Grace, are you hurt?" His voice sounded foreign in its near panic, his breath rapid.

Grace could only look up at him, her physical energy drained in the aftermath of the vision, her body shaking with fright from both the vision and the suddenness of the gunshot. She whispered, "Something terrible happened on the beach. Down by the pier."

"I don't see any blood," said Leo.

"I heard a shot, but I'm not hit."

"I was aiming at the wolf." Rebecca had rushed over. "Didn't you see it? They're hungry this time of year. It could have attacked you."

Seagulls screeched over the water, breaking the silence as Rebecca waited for their response.

Grace hadn't confided in either Leo or Maria about the significance of the wolf. She wasn't certain about the animal's intent, only that the wolf had meant her no harm. And here was this woman, a stranger with a rifle. She couldn't tell Rebecca that the wolf was special, that Scout had appeared in her dreams. But this was the first time he'd appeared in the flesh. Perhaps he was a sort of messenger. Considering the startling vision Grace had just experienced, perhaps he had guided her to Lewis

Harbor to learn about the crime that had been committed. The crime no one knew about. The murder. Did no one else know? *That's it. No one knows. I'm sure of it.* In some way, this wolf had wanted Grace to discover a secret. The dreams, the vision, the appearance of the wolf... It all made sense now. It wasn't just the trauma of the accident at Danton. While it was shortly after Evelyn's death that the dreams began, this wolf was connected to her ability, her special powers. How far did her empathic gift reach? Surely it couldn't reach across a continent. Her mind was racing with questions. Yes, she'd had a vision of a murder on this beach, but Scout had appeared in her dreams weeks before.

There was always truth in her visions. Someone was violently killed on this beach. It was nighttime in her vision. She saw the victim and the killer but not their faces. Grace wanted to ask Rebecca if there had been a recent crime here on this beautiful spot. But the woman standing in front of her had a gun. Grace felt there was more to her than just a local woman who had also come to Lewis to gather clams. Something about Rebecca stopped her from saying anything more than she already had.

"That wolf was acting strange." Rebecca pointed to the spot where Scout had been pawing in the sand, a scattering of butter clams still exposed to the sunlight. "They don't usually eat shellfish. Looks like it found a cluster of fat ones. I'll help you gather them. I see your bucket is empty."

❉ ❉ ❉

Rebecca had meant Grace no harm as she watched the apprehension on her face. She could make amends by helping Grace fill her bucket with clams. She considered Leo and Maria one of the few residents who bore no ill will against her people. Leo would understand, at least she hoped he would, hoped that this wouldn't change that. She looked tentatively at Leo who was now helping Grace to her feet.

Rebecca led the way to the cache and they knelt on the sand, plunging their digging tools into the wet silt. She was right. The area was brimming with succulent clams. Less than ten minutes later, their buckets were full.

"Let's get these beauties to the boat," said Leo. "I'll hang them over the side to purge." He turned to Rebecca. "I have an extra sack if you'd like to me to take care of your clams as well. I could bring them to your house. Have you heard anything from Tamara?"

Rebecca swallowed hard but it didn't stop her eyes from filling.

✳ ✳ ✳

The mention of the name Tamara sent a shiver through Grace, but she didn't know why. Her eyes bore into Rebecca's as they picked up their laden buckets. They stood, turned, and headed toward the pier. Grace could sense that she was making Rebecca feel uncomfortable because Rebecca turned around to face Grace. She must have felt my eyes on her back. They exchanged a deep stare for several long seconds before Grace averted her scrutiny to shift her gaze and her mind over to the beach where the sun sparkled on the water as the gulls squawked, as the swallows swooped to catch the bugs in the sea air, as the waves slapped against the pier supports and swooshed up and back from the beach sand. Rebecca must have sensed that she'd made Grace uncomfortable, too. She turned to answer Leo's question.

"Thank you, Leo. I'm sorry for scaring the two of you. Yes. It's always best to clean clams in seawater."

Little Deer Cove

G RACE HEARD THE SUV rumble up the grade of the driveway to the road and glanced at the digital display of her alarm: 6:00 AM. Leo had told her he planned to awaken early to retrieve the purged clams from the dock at Lewis Landing. He and Grace intended to take them to Rebecca, and Joseph, her husband, on the Island Nation Band Reserve at Little Deer Cove. It would take about twenty minutes to drive there. The Island Nation Band's houses nestled in the old forest area, off the island road that circled Galliano Island. Grace was looking forward to the early morning drive, when island wildlife could be spotted along the curving roads: raccoon, mink, and deer in particular; perhaps, if they were lucky, an elk would be feeding near the forest edge. Her mother had told her about a cougar that had been sighted by the islanders recently. Grace wondered if they'd catch a glimpse of it. Of course Grace knew there were wolves—the famous sea wolves of the Discovery Islands.

The drive would allow time for Grace and Leo to discuss what had happened the other day at the Lewis Landing. She hadn't said anything to Leo or Maria, but had withdrawn to her room to rest after the exhausting physical effects of the disturbing vision, a troubling side effect of dealing with malevolent residual energy. Her parents had hovered, but had said nothing. They knew Grace. She would talk to them when she was ready. It was best this way.

Leo arrived back at Abalone Hideaway about an hour later. He had come into the kitchen to check if Grace was ready, when the phone rang. It was the clinic.

The conversation was short and Leo hung up the phone, shrugged at Grace and Maria, and exhaled. Duty called. "The clinic doctor on call for today has a family emergency. I have to take his shift."

Now it was Maria's turn to shrug. "You're a doctor, Leo. These things happen." She raised her eyebrows at Grace. "Those clams need to be delivered. They don't stay fresh for long. Don't worry. Grace and I can look after that."

Leo looked worried. "Need I remind you of the gun incident? Rebecca and Grace didn't hit it off. It might be kind of tense. Grace, are you okay with this?"

Grace couldn't hold back her chuckle as Maria raised her hand in a familiar gesture that was meant to reassure Leo that all would be well.

"You're thinking she might try to shoot me again?" Grace asked, trying to hide her smile.

"Rebecca wasn't trying to shoot you." Leo frowned. "I have no choice. The clinic needs me. Take the clams to Rebecca. Her house is close to the General Store. Your mom can pick up a few things for her pantry while you're there. Good cooks always need supplies."

✳ ✳ ✳

Grace felt energized this morning. A drive would get her out of the house and change her focus for a while. The picturesque scenery along the Galliano Island roads had a way of refreshing her. The hazy purple of the mountains and sunlit the waters at Little Deer Cove were stunning. There was a peaceful reassuring energy that hung around the boardwalk to the pier where the locals moored their launches. She thought about Michael. He had texted her every day and asked how she was feeling. He didn't ask the question directly, but when he asked about the Island, the scenery, the people, he was checking on her to get a sense of how she was doing—if she was recovering. He would like this place with its breathtaking views. She missed him.

They planned to see Rebecca first, then fill Maria's shopping list at the General Store. While Maria shopped for her kitchen items, Grace would wander the shoreline along the wet rocks, breathe in the briny air and let the wind blow through her hair to erase the unsettled feelings that lingered from her vision at Lewis. It would give Grace a chance to decompress after visiting the woman with the gun. She couldn't figure out Rebecca's motive for carrying a weapon. Grace had found Rebecca rather intense and mysterious. Grace wasn't sure how to talk to someone who carried a rifle and used it when required. Something about Rebecca worried Grace. Rebecca kept things bottled up. Grace could feel the conflict in there. Somehow, Rebecca's repressed feelings had reached out to Grace. She could feel the distress. Would Rebecca answer her questions if Grace dared to ask what troubled her? She knew she would have to be subtle—not raise her curiosity too much. Yet Grace felt Rebecca had sensory ability as well. Many people did but denied or ignored it. Grace's empathic power was exceptional.

Grace wanted to learn more about Rebecca. But discretely. She wouldn't pry. Somehow, she was tied to the vision. Grace felt it. There had been a flutter of delicate communication as their eyes met the other day. Leo had told Grace that Rebecca's daughter had gone missing. Grace had dismissed the relevance, but it lingered, forcing her mind to work on it, like trying to solve a puzzle. Just thinking about it caused that familiar prickly feeling to scratch at her core. From experience, Grace knew, the only way to soothe the agitation was to find out the reason for it. Rebecca seemed filled with unresolved fear. Why else would she keep a rifle stowed in the trunk of her car and why would she so easily pull it out and use it? It was only a wolf. At a distance, no less. A loud noise, like a car horn, would have been all it would have taken to chase it off. Grace would try to draw out Rebecca's fears, perhaps let Rebecca vent to see what she could find out. Although reluctant to pry, she would learn more.

Maria started the SUV and then realized she had forgotten her list. She scurried back to her kitchen to retrieve it from the counter. As Grace tuned the radio, she happened to look out the front window of the car. Standing to the side of their vehicle was her wolf, Scout. He made eye contact. Why was he so present? This wolf was watching her. He didn't scare Grace, but he seemed to be with her wherever she went. They stared at each other for a mere moment before he vanished into the trees.

"Got it," Maria waved her list over her head as she hustled off the porch steps back to the SUV. "Good thing. I would have forgotten the raisins. Morning glory muffins are nothing without them."

Grace laughed at her mother's unspoken encouragement.

✳ ✳ ✳

Grace found it strange that they saw no deer or other animals on their drive. The road was isolated, as though evacuated for some kind of looming disaster. They drove for twenty minutes then turned into a tree-lined gravel laneway that led to a one-story, timber-siding house. They spotted a man and Rebecca further back in the yard. Maria parked the SUV and she and Grace got out and walked up to Joseph with the sack of clams.

"Hi there," Maria said. "I think you've been waiting for these." She held out the hefty sack of clams. "We're going to feast on ours tonight."

Rebecca had walked over from the fire pit where fish were drying on a spit over the smoldering embers, the pungent aroma wafting with the breeze.

"How have you been, Rebecca?"

Rebecca snatched the sack, looking sullen and uninterested. "How would *you* feel if *your* daughter was missing?" She peered into Maria's eyes and then at Grace. Her shoulders slumped and her bottom lip quivered. There was an uncomfortable silence as Rebecca tried to regain her composure.

Maria broke the silence. Gently. "Hugo hasn't gotten any information on where she might have gone?"

"Who's Hugo?" asked Grace.

Rebecca answered. "Our Island police force of one. He's a Band member but doesn't broadcast that fact. Most of the islanders aren't particularly keen on him being in the position of law enforcement."

Grace knew that Maria could sympathize with Rebecca's anger. Maria was a mother too. But Indigenous daughters often went missing, not so with the daughters of most islanders.

Rebecca continued. "Tamara wasn't happy with the limited opportunities here. I told Hugo that didn't have anything to do with her disappearance. But he still didn't appear, to me at least, to be overly ambitious on pursuing missing persons. Any missing persons."

"Do you think it was maybe because he and Tamara were once a thing?" asked Maria. "Maybe it was because they had that falling out."

"How do you know about that?"

Maria shrugged. "Small community. Big mouths?"

Rebecca nodded.

"Maybe he was happy to see her gone. They had been the talk of the island and everyone had their theories. Theories you and Joseph didn't want to talk about."

"He says he's filed a missing person's report," Rebecca said. She huffed and turned toward her husband, her anger showing as her lips pursed, her eyes going dark with disgust. Joseph put his arm around her shoulders.

"The police don't give a high priority to our people," Joseph said. "Even when they're one of us." Joseph swallowed hard.

"I heard that a detective who specializes in missing persons is being dispatched to Galliano," Maria said. "Maybe he'll be able to get more information for you."

Maria's news jolted Grace. She remembered something that Ruben, the man who had sat beside her on the plane, had said in conversation as she waited for her luggage at the Comox terminal, that he was investigating a missing woman. Had he said something about a case on

Galliano? Grace couldn't remember. She stared at Maria with unease, her mouth agape before catching herself, but already putting things together—and the conclusion was not good. She didn't have to ask questions now. How was she going to bring this to the attention of the police without arousing suspicion on herself? She had discussed this with Michael and Heatherton and they were adamant: visions were not admissible as evidence.

Guy and Annie

M ARIA HAD INVITED their neighbors to join them for supper. The Boisverts, Guy and Annie, lived about a kilometer down Seavista Road where the road started to slope downward toward the ocean. They were the first islanders to welcome Leo and Maria to the island when they bought Abalone Hideaway two years earlier. Happy to have people they could socialize with, Guy and Annie helped them adjust to the remoteness of island life. Guy and Annie had shown them where the local general stores were located, acquainted them with the beaches and nature trails, took them to where the best views of the ocean would take their breath away, and got them used to taking the BC ferry to Campbell River for what they termed "major shopping" or just to get off the island for a day's adventure. "The remoteness gets to you if you don't reconnect with civilization once in a while," Guy had assured them.

Maria and Annie had chatted about tonight's seafood feast. Annie would bring homemade bread and a variety of cheeses; Maria would cook up the clams and serve them with fresh garden vegetables. And if they were lucky, Guy would bring fresh prawns caught earlier in the morning when he'd gone with his friend Andy to check on his prawn traps. Seemed Guy spent a lot of time with this Andy person no one had actually met. Seemed he was always "out on the boat" as Guy coined the phrase. They would make an evening out of the bounty of the sea and friendship. Maria fussed to get ready and chattered on about what a lively evening they'd all enjoy. Grace just listened as her mother went on and on about having a dinner party. She surmised that it might be a very long evening listening to chatter that didn't involve Grace.

Guy and Annie were long-time residents. They had moved to Galliano five years earlier. They were originally from Saint-Lazare, Quebec. Guy had worked as an executive manager for a large manufacturing firm that made snowmobiles. Although he didn't disclose the real reason why he'd left corporate life for the seclusion of an island, Leo and Maria suspected he'd been fired for reasons he didn't want to talk about: misconduct or breaching company policy, perhaps. But they'd become good friends and it really didn't matter to Maria and Leo. Whenever they got together, there was lots of food and wine and friendly conversation, lots of laughter.

That's what they'd told her, yet Grace had picked up on something. There was a distinct bitterness that often came in through Guy's banter as the social evening progressed. As the wine or whiskey loosened his tongue? Leo, the doctor, could tell that Guy was an alcoholic and had told Grace that he feared for his physical and mental health but that he wouldn't press the point. Lecturing Guy about his drinking wouldn't make him stop, Leo had admitted. It would drive a wedge into their friendship. "Although I'm sure Annie would appreciate my intervention." Grace would say nothing. She would just watch. And learn.

Guy was a colorful character in more ways than one. He dressed in brightly colored shirts, plain, plaid, or sometimes with flower patterns, and always worn over his tight-fitting jeans to hide his beer belly. He often wore a fedora when he went to town. His most-distinguishing feature was his vintage car. Guy loved his 1952 Cadillac Fleetwood, a true classic that he'd bought for a steal. He spent hours every day keeping it polished and in good repair. An obsession, Annie complained, keeping it in top-notch condition. He worked on the engine constantly so it ran quiet and smooth. The paint on the dark-navy body was original and in pristine condition. The chrome sparkled bright, like expensive jewelry. The luxury interior was still plush, though slightly worn. He washed and waxed his Fleetwood frequently. It was the signature of his identity and islanders would often ask him to chauffeur for special occasions like weddings or parades. Though Guy wasn't rich, he had the air of a man of means. He carried himself like a man of prominence. Even with a detectable French-Canadian accent, he was well-spoken and everyone could see he was an educated man. His approachable nature and hearty laugh drew people to like him. And how he loved his status! On Galliano, he was sort of a celebrity, uniquely regarded, and that pleased him. He never showed his downside in public though. Annie often took the brunt of his depressive moods.

Annie was a devoted wife who, at first glance, appeared to adore her husband. He was muscular, tall, with broad shoulders, dark, wavy hair that the local barber kept well-trimmed, and a five o'clock shadow that showed up well before four in the afternoon. Even with his wide mid-section, Guy oozed masculinity like a movie star and it made him attractive to all the women of the island. At least that's what he told himself. When he was feeling up and happy, when he considered that the world was treating him right, he was the perfect husband. But Guy also had a moody side. Annie surmised it resulted from too much drinking, a hangover probably, she'd guessed. Annie tolerated his moods both when he was enjoying his fame and when he tipped into his darker side. She had supported his rise of status in Saint-Lazare, exhibiting the role of an executive wife, hosting parties and meeting the other wives at the country club. It was what was expected as their husbands rose to prominence as business leaders. When Guy had run into trouble, she gracefully accepted the move to the isolation of Galliano where Guy took them to disappear from the limelight they'd once enjoyed. Annie knew that it wasn't a choice he wanted to make. But, over the years, they came to enjoy the quiet life where there were no demands or the ever-increasing pressures once imposed by his superiors.

Annie was happy to have Maria as friend and may have disclosed more information about their past than she intended, knowing Maria would keep the information secret. Maria saw not only the hickies on her neck, but also the bruises she would try to cover with clothing. Maria listened intently as Annie poured her heart out when she came over to have a cup of tea.

Maria learned that Guy had had an affair. Annie didn't regard it so much as a real affair because Guy had told her about the advances from Juliana, his boss's wife. It happened on the company yacht, when her husband was called back to attend to emergencies at the plant. You didn't question the whims and wants of a neglected wife who could ruin your career with false accusations. Anyway, she was sophisticated, with expensive clothes, upswung hair and perfect makeup. So—Guy had indulged her pleasure. He regarded it as a career move. It made her happy and Juliana reciprocated by speaking well of him to her husband who promoted Guy for exceptional performance, that is until he suspected that the merit of his performance had more to do with his wife than with company matters. And behind his back. The scandal was scathing and Guy's fall was swift and merciless, though the severance package was lucrative. It ruined him. He couldn't get other comparable work.

Home Again

IT WAS ALMOST NOON when Maria and Grace returned from Little Deer Cove, Grace feeling relief when the SUV descended the downward slope of the Abalone Hideaway driveway. There was something protective about their home, situated there in the hollow, unseen from the gravel road on higher ground. She breathed a sigh of relief and she helped Maria carry the groceries up the porch steps and into the kitchen.

"I have loads of stuff to prepare for supper tonight," Maria said. "What are your plans for the day?"

Grace was still stunned from the information Maria had disclosed to Rebecca and Joseph. She was sure that the detective sent to Galliano was Rubin Machowitz, the man she had met on the plane, the one who had come on so strong and made her uncomfortable. Would he realize that she'd lied to him about being called back to Toronto on a business matter? Could she tell him she knew that a murder had been committed on Lewis Beach? Her dilemma churned in her gut.

She would call Michael later in the day and get him to find out more about Rubin's background; especially the assignment he claimed to have here on Galliano. It niggled at her that Rubin was in the same place as Grace was. After her call, she'd go to the Lewis Landing Community Centre—if you could call it that. She knew that the police station occupied a single room at the same place where other community activities took place. Grace was already formulating her story. She would pop in and explain that the business matter she had been called away for was looked after and that she heard through locals that Rubin was here on Galliano. She would say that she was here to welcome him, to say hello. Yes, he'd buy that story. Then with a bit of luck, she could get Hugo to start talking about Tamara and what might have happened to her. She would also get the gossip from some of the locals about why a city cop was here. Perhaps Holly would be around. If not, Grace would seek her out at Hollyhock, pretending to buy some herbs or one of the soothing lotions they sold in their gift store.

"I think I'll go into Lewis Landing. Is there anything you'd like me to get from the store?"

Maria looked at Grace with skepticism but didn't press her about why she was going into town. Grace was happy about that. She was here to decompress and didn't want to talk about her reasons for going anywhere. Grace could feel that Maria suspected her visit to town might have something to do with what Rebecca or Joseph had said earlier. Hadn't they just returned with the supplies Maria needed? Why would Grace need anything else from the Lewis Landing General Store?

"All right then. Seeing as you're going anyway, could you get some Perrier, please?" She smiled at Grace and went to pull some money from her purse.

"It's OK. I've got it covered. I'll be back in a couple of hours."

✳ ✳ ✳

Standing outside the Community Centre, Grace felt awkward and uncertain. She didn't know what she would say if, in fact, this "special investigator" was actually Rubin. But she had to find out so she could settle that uncomfortable feeling she got when her intuition told her she needed to face something she was afraid of. Not that Rubin was dangerous, but still… she had knowledge of a murder and if she straight out told him, he would ask her how she knew about it. Grace didn't want anyone other than Maria and Leo and Michael to know about her premonitions. But she also knew if she didn't take control, it would drive her crazy. Until she resolved the reason for the vision, she would be haunted by it. She had to find a way for the authorities to launch an investigation.

The sign read GALLIANO POLICE STATION. That made Grace chuckle. The Lewis Landing Community Hall seemed deserted. She hesitated as she stood in front of the door.

"You looking for someone?" The gruff voice had come from the doorway of the community hall.

She turned abruptly in the direction of the voice.

The badge on the man's uniform read RCMP. His tanned face had high cheek bones and a prominent nose; his thick eyebrows matched his dark hair. Was this the man Joseph and Rebecca had talked about? Was this Hugo? The officer who knew Tamara? Did he know her intimately?

"You startled me. I'm looking for Rubin Machowitz."

"He isn't here at the moment," the man said. "Can I help you? I'm Officer Hugo Sinclair. You must be new to the island."

"Grace Walker. I'm visiting my parents, Leo and Maria."

Hugo's posture softened as a smile spread across his face. He walked over and opened the door to his office. "Come in and make yourself comfortable. Rubin should be back shortly. Stepped out to get coffee. From the restaurant."

Grace could feel Hugo studying her as his smile dissolved into a glare. It felt to her like he didn't like anyone who was looking for this new person, a person he might have resented in the first place for imposing on his duties and territory? And here was this mainland gal asking after him. Could Officer Hugo Sinclair not handle any police matter that came across his desk?

Grace stepped inside. The office was small and smelled of old and damp papers and reports. There was an ancient wooden desk up against the wall, with two chairs—one in the toe opening for Hugo, she assumed, and another at the side for anyone else who might have need of his services. The scratched wooden surface of the desk was clear of paper and forms, just a blotter, pen holder, and a landline phone in the left corner. A bank of two gray metal file cabinets stood against the back wall. On the other side of the office was a small jail cell. Grace's forehead wrinkled as she looked at it. The thought of anyone being incarcerated in such a confined space made her cringe.

"What's your business with Officer Machowitz?"

Before Grace could think up an answer, a noise distracted them, the heavy thud of the Community Centre door banging closed.

And there was Rubin with a large take-out coffee in his hand, looking at Grace through squinted eyes.

"You said you were going back to Toronto."

Grace squirmed, but hoped that Rubin didn't notice. "Things had resolved themselves before my flight time so I came to Galliano as originally planned." *Whew. That came out well. So far so good.*

Rubin nodded before his face broke into a wide smile.

But what do I say next? "I remembered what you said. That you were investigating a missing Indigenous woman." She hoped the stare she gave Rubin was an ambiguous one. "You know the island folks are talking about you." She could feel one side of her mouth turning up. She knew perfectly well he wasn't at liberty to disclose any information but decided to push her luck. "So have you found out anything?" The other side of her mouth followed the other into a full-fledged but insistent smile, one that wanted an answer.

Hugo's eyes were moving back and forth to each of them, the wrinkles on his forehead furled, making his eyes squint.

Grace had noticed that Hugo had tensed, straightened his posture, when she'd said the words, "missing Indigenous women." Or had she imagined that?

Rubin shrugged, feigning annoyance. "I've only been here one day. Can I report back to you after I do some investigation?"

Now Hugo was looking really uncomfortable. What were these two strangers doing joking with each other over such a serious matter?

Rubin, too, picked up on Hugo's discomfort. Grace could feel them both.

"Grace and I met a week ago. We were on the same flight from Toronto."

"I needed to get some stuff for Maria at the General Store. I heard people talking and I wanted to know if it was the same cop I met on the plane."

Did Grace owe Hugo an explanation? Would he be getting curious and start asking questions? Would he begin searching for answers that she simply wasn't able to disclose? She didn't want him drawing any wrong conclusions. He would have to understand that they were two people who'd met by chance and wanted to reconnect.

They all turned with a start, as the Community Centre door slammed shut again. A short woman whose heavy breasts bounced in her loosely supportive halter top, entered, coffee in hand. Grace contained her amusement as the men assessed the woman's elastic halter top that strained to contain her enormous breasts.

Ignoring Grace, the woman winked at both men. Her eyes shifted back and forth between Hugo and Rubin before she sidled up to Hugo. She poked Hugo on his shoulder and looked back at Rubin to see his reaction. "I saw your replacement come into the Sunset Restaurant for coffee. Thought I'd bring you one, too. I guess Toronto cops don't have manners." The woman winked at Rubin before giving Hugo another playful punch on the arm.

"Excuse me," Rubin objected. "I asked him. He said he didn't want one."

"Savannah," Hugo said. "Stop making accusations. This is Detective Rubin Machowitz. He's here on special assignment."

"That's right ma'am," Rubin said in his official-sounding police detective voice. "For the record, no one is replacing anyone."

Hugo took a step back from the woman. "This is Savannah Trinn. She owns and operates the Sunset Restaurant."

She seemed pleased with the endorsement.

"A busy establishment throughout the summer tourist months."

Savannah walked up to Rubin, leaving only half a breast width between them. Looking up at the tall man, she smiled widely into his face and held out her free hand for a shake.

Rubin took a wide step back.

"Nice to meet you… Rubin."

Grace noted the amusement in Hugo's eyes. He must have been glad to have her focus her deliberate flirtations away from him.

Grace was happy to be leaving the men to deal with this frolicsome woman. "Ahem." Grace managed to break Savannah's focus. "I have errands to run and Maria is expecting me back at the house. Welcome to Galliano, Rubin. Maybe we'll run into each other again." A part of her wanted to tell him straight out about her vision, but she had no proof. She had only the vision which would have sounded like she'd been high on island weed. Her gift was never understood—or believed, for that matter. She shouldered past Rubin and Savannah who were blocking the door entrance. She would have to find some other way, one that would sound a lot more rational than a "vision" to lead Hugo and Rubin to the crime scene.

❋❋❋

She hurried to the Lewis Landing General Store, picked up a case of Perrier and returned to her car. As she pulled out of the parking lot, she spotted the young man she'd seen with Holly the other day. He was wearing a shabby-looking cross-body satchel that hung low on his hip and was walking almost at a jog to catch up with a group of people. When he reached them, he and the other folks moved to the side of the road and waved at Grace as she drove past them, friendly smiles on their faces, as if they knew her. She waved back as a courtesy, in case they knew Maria and Leo.

❋❋❋

Back at Abalone Hideaway, she spotted a well-polished, old-model vehicle in the driveway. Maria's guests had arrived. Grace didn't know how social she felt and considered pulling back out of the driveway and heading for the beach area where she could walk, taking in the peace and tranquility of the ocean. But that would not only worry her parents as they wondered why Grace was away so long, but it would also disappoint them. Maria wanted her to meet their friends.

Grace hefted the case of Perrier from the back seat of her car. The wind caught in her hair and a noise rustled the leaves in the trees. She felt a presence that tingled in her core. She wondered if the wolf was near, saw nothing, but felt eyes on her. She shook the hair off her face and headed into the house.

The case of Perrier was heavy so she struggled to open the door to the kitchen, her one hand able to turn the handle but not control the door. It slammed behind her as she entered. Leo came to her assistance taking the load to the counter in the kitchen.

"In here, Grace," Maria called. "Guy and Annie want to meet you. We've been talking about you. Are your ears ringing?"

Grace heard a round of friendly giggles.

That's the way Maria was, trying to sound lighthearted because she knew Grace would feel hesitant about meeting strangers. And she was. They were staring at her.

The woman, Annie, rose from her seat and walked up to Grace and hugged her. Grace bristled. Her intuitive power had immediately kicked in the moment Annie embraced her. Annie was full of worry. It made Grace's skin break into cold goose bumps.

"Bonjour, ma chérie. Your mother has told me so much about you."

Grace cast an anxious glance at Maria, wondering how much she had told their island friends about Grace's affliction, or why she had come to Galliano. "Nice to meet you, too."

"Leo," Guy said. "Your daughter is a grown woman. You talk about her as if she was much younger." He waved his half-full glass of red wine in front of him, pointing it at Grace. His glistening eyes and open-mouthed smile made it evident that this was not the first glass of wine he'd enjoyed this afternoon. Perhaps he'd had many more before coming to visit.

Guy's eyes lingered a millisecond too long. Was he looking at her breasts? She hated when drunkenness made men study her physical features. Why did they do that?

"What?" the robust man said, his voluminous laugh resounding into the room. "No hugs for me?"

His teasing laugh had missed its mark at sounding fatherly so Grace nodded a curt greeting and walked behind the kitchen island to help her mother. She would keep her distance from him.

Maria noticed this and diffused the awkwardness. "Grace, would you cut some cheese for the charcuterie?" Maria then put her arm across Grace's shoulder, smiled and nodded in the direction of the refrigerator. "And bring out the salami and olives."

Annie positioned herself between the women and her husband who had come up to the kitchen island.

"Relax, Guy," Annie said, waving at him to sit down. "Grace is busy at the moment."

Guy plopped down into the leather recliner and took another slug of wine. "So, Leo," Guy said. "How do you like my choice of wine?"

Leo held up his near empty glass and chuckled. "I'm not much of a wine connoisseur. I'd better say that your wine is good because you brought four bottles."

One bottle sat on the coffee table and the other three were lined up in a straight row at the far end of the kitchen counter.

"Wine and friends belong together," Guy said. "Especially since the ladies are preparing such a delicious feast."

Leo took his opportunity. "But your liver may not agree." He gave Guy an admonishing look and then winked at Annie who nodded in agreement.

Annie looked on, hopeful that Guy would take Leo's hint and stop drinking. He'd had enough for today, having started early in the afternoon.

Guy frowned and acquiesced or at least gave the impression that he would stop. "Maria, I am outnumbered. May I bother you to make coffee?"

"I make the best coffee on the island," Maria said. "I was going to put the coffee on for Annie and me anyway."

Guy's jovial expression turned sour. He glared at Annie.

The situation had become strained. Guy's mood had taken an abrupt turn. The pressure bubbled like expanding vapor about to explode from a tightly sealed vessel. Grace excused herself to the den and closed the door. She sat in the chair that was positioned for the garden view out the window, where yellow daylilies bloomed. She tried to center herself, concentrating on her breath, inhaling long slow breaths and exhaling. The exercise quieted the feeling that she knew often triggered episodes. Once she was assured that she was calm, she pulled out her phone to text Michael.

> Rubin Machowitz has come to Galliano. Problem on the island. I had another vision. There has been a murder here. Rubin is investigating. Don't know how to handle this.

She leaned back in the chair and resumed her breathing mediation, waiting for Michael to answer her text. She had come to Galliano to free herself from the bombardment of the ubiquitous negative energy that was of a bustling city. She didn't expect it here on Galliano where life was slow. But when Guy's mood changed because Leo suggested he stop drinking, the energy in the house changed with it. It weighed on Grace with a feeling as charged as the one she'd felt back in Toronto. How was she going to handle this? How had it followed her to a place she considered an Eden. Yet Grace knew that wayward energy was consistent. The only way to diffuse it was to resolve the problem that had caused it in the first place. As she let out another big sigh, her phone pinged. It was Michael.

> Will get more info on Machowitz. Hang tight.

Michael had signed off with a thumb's up emoji. Grace stared at it. It felt odd, distant, uncommitted. She would have liked a heart.

She wanted to run and tell Maria and Leo but it would have to wait until the evening's festivities were over. She should have told them sooner. Withholding a troubling vision inside only caused her distress. She should have known better. The dream, the wolf, her vision at Lewis. It was all connected. She couldn't ignore it any longer. The energy was calling to her, but this time it was more than that. The message came with voices, a sort of spiritual presence that beseeched, pleaded. Did it come from her inner power? Or was there also an external force leading and pulling her toward its revelation? It was something she hadn't experienced before and she had to admit, it was eerie.

The Evening Progresses

MARIA AND ANNIE were on the upper balcony enjoying the late warm summer day and the view of the ocean that opened up between a gap in the old growth trees. Grace could see the water shimmer in the distance like it was an illusion underneath white billowing cumulus clouds. The ladies sipped on their tea and nibbled at the cheese and savory meats that Grace had helped arrange on the wooden board. She sat down with them, not to join in their banter, to have company.

"Where are Leo and Guy?"

"They've gone out for a drive in the Cadillac," Annie said. "Leo convinced Guy to let him drive. He thought some air or change of scenery would calm him down. Men and their fascination with cars!" Annie rolled her eyes and shook her head but smiled as if she approved. Grace felt that she was probably content to be away from him.

Grace settled into a cushioned deck lounger, pulling her legs up into the chair and her arms wrapping around to hold them next to her body. Maria and Annie were locked in conversation about dry weather and the danger of forest fires. The word "forest" closed Grace's ears to their chatter as Grace's eyes were drawn toward the trees at the fence line. The undulating sway of the branches was hypnotizing her. It was as though they beckoned her to the old growth treeline. As she watched,

161

listened, she could hear it: muffled sounds—voices perhaps—beneath the breathy sound of the light breezes. It aroused that tingling feeling in her feet. Eerie as it was, she could not resist its pull.

"Excuse me. I'm going into the garden. I need to stretch my legs."

Maria nodded and waved her on, continuing to give attention to Annie's prattle.

The sun broke through the clouds and Grace shaded her eyes with her hand while looking up at the towering height of the sycamores. As she neared the trees, the whispers became louder, the rhythmic call sounding like a song, its beat like a drum, each repetition more discernible than the last:

"Follow Scout... Follow Scout..."

Grace's ears buzzed and she feared the onslaught of a vision.

The thick undergrowth seemed to come alive. The salal leaves whirled in time to the chant as Scout emerged from cover. He eased out into the open, cautiously, moving slowly until he stood directly in front of Grace on the other side of the chain-link fencing. They held each other's gaze, linking their thoughts together. This was no vision. He was real—here and now. But how was she to follow him? The message was compelling. But "follow him" where?

"Grace!" Leo yelled from the house.

They must have returned from their joy ride but Grace hadn't heard the return of the vintage car.

"Get away from there. That's a wolf, not a dog."

Grace turned to see Leo running toward her, waving his arms and shouting at Scout. "Get out of here! Get out of here!"

Then Guy reacted as well. "My pistol's in the trunk." He took off.

When Grace turned back toward the forest beyond the fence, Scout was gone.

Leo was by her side now. Grace looked up at him. He had startled her and now she was trembling.

He approached her slowly. "Grace?" He took her hand. "Are you OK? Let's go back to the house."

Grace let out a gasp as the trance released her.

"What's happening, Grace?"

A tear formed in the corner of her eye. She could feel it. "They want me to find a murderer." The tear slid down her cheek.

"They?" Leo looked confused.

Before Grace could answer, Guy came running up to them, skimming the trees line with his pistol, like a sharpshooter.

"Put that away, Guy," Leo commanded.

"Wolves have been overtaking the island this year. They're a dangerous menace. I can go to the other side of the fence and hunt it down." Guy smiled. "There is a bounty for wolf pelts. Did you know that?"

"No. We have to live in harmony with them," Grace shouted. "No killing. Don't kill it."

Guy cocked his head to the side and then looked at Leo before lowering the weapon. Grace felt the scowl underneath the look of compliance on his face. She looked away as he stared at her.

"It's gone now," said Leo. "Let's go back to the house. Help Maria and Annie prepare the clams and prawns."

Holly's Folly

I T WAS NEARING DUSK and the air in the hollow of the Sunset Restaurant's outdoor patio hung heavy, pungent with the smell of cannabis. Hugo and special investigator, Rubin Machowitz, strained against gravity as they walked the steep downward slope of the road from the police station to monitor the activities of the tourists who would linger through the night, enjoying the lax enforcement on the Island.

Hugo checked over his shoulder, searching Rubin's expression for signs of disapproval. He couldn't read his neutral face. Frustrated, he turned to watch Elia who, he assessed, was having a lucrative evening, cordially—though obviously stoned—making his rounds, visiting the tables, reaching into his backpack to hand something to the person he was talking to, and then pocketing cash without counting or giving change. Hugo usually ignored the illicit transactions, but Rubin would take notice, so he wasn't taking any chances. He would wait until Elia joined Holly at the community picnic tables on the roadside, with the intention of catching them in the act of solicitation or possession. He would arrest them only to dismiss the charges later due to a technical matter, an oversight on the paperwork, or something like that. They'd forgive him. Anyway, they were both high and likely wouldn't even remember. The important thing was that to Rubin, it would look like he was keeping the law. No need for Rubin to file a discrediting report. He looked back again as Rubin watched his every move.

❊ ❊ ❊

Even though Elia was often stoned, he always kept a keen eye out. A cop's body language was unmistakable. Elia had intuited the intentions of Hugo and the new cop. He'd caught their intent. At their first move toward him and Holly, Elia had taken off with haste into the trees, leaving Holly sitting sprawl-legged and all alone at the picnic table.

She, too, had been watching Hugo and his companion, but not for the same reason. As Hugo and Rubin approached, she sat up straight and smiled at Hugo in anticipation. Hugo and Holly had had a "thing" before Tamara had stolen his affection. She hoped he'd take an interest in her again now that Tamara was gone. *Good riddance,* she thought. *Some friend!* Holly still liked him. A lot. The spark of attraction was still there and it made her forget that she still had the remnants of the joint between her fingers.

❊ ❊ ❊

"Holly." Hugo pointed to the contraband.

She giggled, shrugged, and flicked it onto the gravel.

He followed its flight into the dirt. He wrinkled his brow, paused, and looked at his counterpart before reaching for her arm to pull her to a standing position. "You know better. You're not supposed to be using that in public. Or buying it from a dealer, especially. You're under arrest." He read Holly her rights because Rubin was a cop of protocol. *Shit.* This was not what he wanted to do. Holly wasn't doing anything that wasn't usually overlooked on a touristy Friday evening. Hugo liked being that near to her. Gauging by her mesmerizing smile and her fixed stare drilling deep into his eyes, he guessed that she didn't object either. Her sigh at being handled by Hugo made him smile. He had to admit that he still had feelings for her even though he didn't dare show them. At least, he hoped his feelings didn't show. If anyone from the Band were here, they'd notice. The Island Nation Band was always watching. As were the town folks.

Rubin cleared his throat. "Are you going to arrest everyone on the patio?" The one corner of his mouth lifted in a smile while the other corner tightened with his squinted eyes, disapproving. He made an exaggerated sweeping arm gesture that Hugo would understand. It was obvious that most of the patio patrons were clearly in violation of the law. No one was trying to hide their actions. "Any lawyer could make a case that you're targeting her in particular. Anyway, I wouldn't arrest someone for smoking a single joint." He rolled his eyes, while shaking his head. "Even an illegally purchased one. Right?"

Holly flopped back onto the picnic table as Hugo released her arm. "Heh," she said, "Wanna join me and Elia at Lewis Beach? It's a nice evening for a swim." Her moves were rubbery as though her body had no bones, just loose and fluid, her muscles so relaxed that she wobbled to stand, her face within inches of his. Holly reached for his hand, but Hugo stepped back so she couldn't touch him. He knew she'd try to get affectionate. She'd fawn all over him, snuggling and hanging her head on his chest. He liked that, but that's not what Hugo wanted Rubin to see.

"I'm on duty," Hugo said. "But Officer Machowitz is right. I'll let you off. This time!" His voice softer than he wanted it to be, he had a hard time concealing a smile. She was high, kind of funny, and even in her intoxicated state, attractive. But all the more vulnerable. It made Hugo remember how they'd felt about each other before his relationship with Tamara, and he wanted to protect her, but Rubin was watching.

❋ ❋ ❋

Holly watched them make their way down to the patio where they sat at an empty outdoor table and ordered Cokes. She longed for Hugo's attention. Then realizing the folly of her attempt, she decided to hitch a ride to meet Elia at Lewis Beach. Elia's friend—his supplier—had offered to let them spend the night on his boat, the Auriga. It would be a nice change from the boring bunkie they shared, platonically. Neither was romantically interested in the other. It was simply a matter of convenience.

Responding to Holly's outstretched thumb, a white Jeep, top down and with a noisy exhaust system, screeched to a stop.

"Going past Lewis Beach?" Holly asked.

The bearded driver, his long hair tied back in a ponytail, nodded: *Sure.* She hopped into the back seat and they took off, the wind making her shoulder-length hair fly wildly. She sat back whooping her delight as she enjoyed the sensations of the turbulent air. *Lewis Beach is a short drive, so no worries,* she thought. Yet after the first bump that sent her flying off the seat, she hung on for dear life as the driver sped over the poorly maintained Island road. She clung tight to the roll bar as the wind and bumps jostled her body around. Minutes later, the Lewis Road sign came up, indicating the approach of the roadway to the harbor. The driver responded with a screeching stop and Holly jumped to the pavement calling back her gratitude.

"See ya around. Thanks a bunch." She waved her arm as the throaty rumble of the vehicle sped off, the dust and loose gravel kicking back from the oversized tires. She turned and walked the half mile to the harbor where she saw Elia waving to her.

The sun was slipping below the watery horizon making the sky dim like a roller blind was being pulled down. She loved Lewis Beach in the evening, especially if the phosphorescence glowed. She and Elia would smoke another joint, or maybe consume a brownie or two as they watched the beach sand sparkle with the touch of the waves.

She felt the movement of the ocean on the floating boardwalk as she approached the *Auriga.* It was moored off the end because other boats filled the leased spots. She wobbled as she navigated the plank board. Elia held out his hand to steady Holly as she climbed aboard. The *Auriga* swayed as Holly jumped into Elia's arms. Unsteady, they fell onto the padded seating in the bow, laughing at everything and nothing. There, they enjoyed the smooth wavering of the vessel as the evening waves kissed the shore. They listened to the melody of the gulls, the snort of the harbor seals stealing a glance at the activity of humans in their personal playground.

They laughed as they consumed the intoxicating pleasures Elia offered, delighting in the beauty and distortion of reality in this hypnotizing place. But they couldn't sit still in the comfort of the boat. Everything seemed magical. Drawn, they disembarked to the boardwalk and into the darkness of the night. They stepped onto the beach sand where their footprints sparkled with each step.

Holly ran further down the beach, deliberately stomping her feet to further excite the sand. She twirled and sang "Twinkle, twinkle little star." She was no longer aware of Elia who had climbed the ramp to the bridge and disappeared into the darkness of the trees. She was mesmerized by the breeze that caressed her skin and the twinkling phosphorescence at her feet. She picked up a branch from the sand and swished it in the shallow water, lighting it up as if electrified by her action. She was the magic, a witch perhaps. It was enchanting.

From the corner of her eye, she noticed movement in the darkness. Her delight dropped, spooked by an apparition. No. It was dark. Menacing. More like a daemon. It seemed to creep, floating toward her with malintent. Her stomach knotted.

"Elia?" No. It didn't look like Elia. She remembered Tamara's stories about Apotamkin, the east-coast "vampire" from Passama-quoddy, the creature who stalked people to their death at water's edge. Did Lewis Beach have one, too? The creature's gait increased, frightening Holly as it gained on her. Then she noticed there was something—an object—in its left hand.

The glorious buzz faded, replaced by terror. She turned to run for her life, her lungs uncooperative, the sand slowing her speed. She looked over her shoulder to assess its distance. It was closer, running now. She stumbled, falling into the wet sand, immediately trying to get to her feet. Close enough now. She could hear the oppressor's snorting sounds as it neared. It grabbed her arm, lifted the object in its free hand.

She felt the crushing blow to her head, the dizzying disorientation. She fell backward to the sand. Then nothing, just empty darkness.

Did she feel the crushing weight of its body on top of her, its hands pulling her shorts down her legs?

Questions

G RACE AWOKE TO A VERY QUIET HOUSE. While she was still asleep, Leo and Maria had caught the first ferry to Campbell River. They called it their "monthly supply run." The Superstore offered a large selection of groceries, hardware, and items not available at the two general stores on Galliano.

Grace stretched as she entered the open concept kitchen.

Maria had left a note on the counter.

Get free range eggs—two dozen from Rebecca.

Maria liked supporting the local economy. Yes, she could buy them at Superstore, but why, when she could get them farm fresh?

The house was cold, empty. It felt odd. She wandered around, trying to relax as an undefined energy poked at her. Maybe if she prepared some breakfast; just toast and coffee would do. She would enjoy it on the upper deck that overlooked Maria's garden and the ocean beyond. She hoped to see deer wandering around the perimeter. She loved that. If not, there were always birds, eagles, waterfowl, and maybe that chattery kingfisher that woke her this morning. Then, after a leisurely morning, she'd head out to Little Deer Cove and visit Rebecca for eggs. The thought of encountering the woman who'd shot at Scout pinched at Grace's stomach. *Damn it.* She tried to push the incident out of her mind. She would focus on a pleasant morning drive. Perhaps she would see wildlife on the way. Yes. It would be a peaceful drive, one that would sooth her and fulfill the purpose of her coming to Galliano. The thing about Galliano Island was that here she had no timeline, no pressing responsibilities that tugged at her inner secret power. No Evelyn trying to kill her. Yet there was the vision, the whispering voices. As the morning evolved, Grace listened and waited for her body to signal that something was about to happen.

❋ ❋ ❋

Rebecca was hanging laundry on a clothesline. She heard the crunch of stones signaling the approach of a vehicle and turned to see who was coming up her gravel driveway. She recognized Grace and walked toward the car to greet her.

"Hi," Grace called as she got out of the car. "Maria sent me to pick up eggs."

Would she hold a grudge? Why did she call her mother by her first name? "I'll go into the house to get them. Maria phoned me yesterday. I have her order ready." She nodded and offered Grace a weak smile.

❋ ❋ ❋

Joseph was nowhere to be seen. Being alone with Rebecca made Grace nervous. She wondered where Joseph was. Maybe he was hunting. Joseph hunting made her worry about Scout. If he came across a wolf, would he shoot it? Would Scout sense her apprehension? They seemed to have a type of thought connection. Hadn't Rebecca tried to shoot him the other day? Would Joseph do the same?

Grace stayed close to her car, but looked around, taking in the layout of their property. There were several outbuildings around the timber-clad, one-story house. A porch wrapped around two sides, the one side looking like an outdoor kitchen with a wood-fired, old-fashioned cooking stove. The small structure by the trees looked like it might be the rabbit pen where, Rebecca claimed, wolves had wiped out her entire colony. Further along by the forest line there was another pen with chickens clucking and scratching in the dirt, fenced in and secure, with a roosting coop at the center. There was no fire in the fire pit or salmon being smoked today. The place looked well-maintained and functional.

Rebecca returned with two cartons of eggs and handed them to Grace. "Your mother likes the brown ones," she said with a pleasant grin.

Grace handed her the money Maria had left.

"They're in Campbell River today, right? When are they expected back? Leo is picking up padlocks and gate latches for Joseph. I'll come over later to pick them up."

"They said the ferry's often full in the summer so couldn't say when they'd be back. I could bring those things over to you when they get back. Where's Joseph?"

"Out in the boat checking his prawn and crab cages. Sometimes he casts his line and does some fishing, too. Ling cod is in season. Very delicious." Her face brightened. "I will let Leo know if Joseph has a good catch today. Your dad loves seafood."

"Thanks. I'll tell him."

As Grace opened the car door to leave, Rebecca stepped toward her. "Can you stay for some iced tea?" She tilted her head toward the house. "I'd enjoy some company. Your mom likes my special blend." Her voice was sweet, almost pleading.

Grace put the eggs on the seat and smiled back at Rebecca. "Special blend?" She chuckled. "How can I say no to that?" Grace read a hint of sadness in Rebecca's expression.

They stepped onto the covered porch and around the side to the outdoor kitchen that was well shaded from the rising morning sun. Rebecca pointed to the lawn chair where Grace should sit, then stepped into the house returning several minutes later with a pitcher of iced tea and two tall glasses. She poured and they sat in silence, looking out toward the now-empty rabbit pen.

They're hungry this time of year echoed in Grace's memory.

"I think that detective from Toronto is messing with Hugo's authority here on Galliano."

Her blunt disclosure confused Grace.

"There's something about him that isn't honest. I have this... feeling." Rebecca looked at Grace, their eyes connecting, as if she were trying to read Grace's mind.

"I know the person you mean," Grace said.

"Hugo says he is investigating missing Indigenous women, but I feel he has some other agenda. More than trying to find Tamara."

Grace knew all about these kinds of feelings. She wondered about Rebecca's empathic ability. Grace had felt it in Rebecca that day at Lewis. Did her own ability reach out to Rebecca somehow?

"You mean Rubin Machowitz. That's his name." Grace studied Rebecca's face again.

Rebecca's forehead wrinkled. "You know him?" Rebecca's eyes went wide, her mouth agape.

"Not personally, but he was on the same plane on my flight here from Toronto. In the seat beside me." Grace took a sip of tea. "Hmm. Good. He kind of tried to come on to me after we landed." Grace huffed her disapproval. "I was shocked to see him here a few days later." Grace cringed thinking about it and Rebecca's face told Grace that she had picked up on that. *I'm not wrong about her.*

"Funny he hasn't come to us to talk about our daughter. I wonder if he knows that Hugo and Tamara were together. A couple." Rebecca looked sad again. "Joseph and I expected them to get married. Did you know?" She didn't wait for Grace to respond. "Then they had this big fight and she left the island telling nobody where she was going."

Grace's heart sank. She suspected that Tamara hadn't left the Island. Grace's intuition told her that she was dead. Tamara was probably the woman she had watched being murdered in her vision at Lewis Beach. But she couldn't just tell Rebecca. Her mind filled with guilt. Rebecca was suffering like any mother would if her child had disappeared. Grace hated her power. It put such an onerous responsibility on her. Honoring that responsibility had almost killed her back in Toronto. She had come to Galliano to escape that obligation. But it had found her again. It had sought her out and drawn her to this place. She swallowed hard as Rebecca stared at her. When she got back to Abalone Hideaway, she'd call Michael. He'd gotten her through the crisis at Danton, so maybe she could convince him to help her now.

Grace looked at her watch. "The 1:00 PM ferry should be docking soon. I want to be home when Leo and Maria get home. Thanks for the tea." Grace stood and hugged Rebecca and then turned and walked briskly to the car.

❋ ❋ ❋

Grace took out the tuna salad that Maria had left for her in the refrigerator and made herself a sandwich before going up to the second floor deck to watch the ocean. Soon she'd see the ferry on the way to the landing dock. When she heard the ferry horn, Grace sensed that her parents were on it. Now if only Michael would respond to her messages. She looked at her phone. Still no answer to the numerous texts she had sent. Agitation was building up inside her. It had to do with Rebecca's intuition about Rubin. It made her fretful. Somehow the wolf, the vision, and Rebecca's suspicions were all tied together. The problem was that Grace was the only one who knew about Tamara's death. And the call for help to find the killer was getting louder. She really wanted Michael's support. Needed it.

Half an hour later, Grace heard the SUV rumble to a stop on the driveway. She breathed a sigh of relief and hurried outside to help carry in the numerous bags of groceries that Maria would have bought at the Superstore. To her surprise, Maria and Leo had brought a guest. She stopped in her tracks, not believing her eyes.

"I've been texting you for two days," Grace said. "Why haven't you answered?"

"Your texts… had a tone of desperation to them. But I could go back to Toronto if you want." Michael flashed a crooked smile. "Anyway,

Leo confirmed my suspicions. I can tell when you're being invaded by empathic messages. That always leads to trouble. So instead of useless text chatter, I decided to be of real help." Michael walked over to Grace and embraced her. Grace's heart thumped as she clung to him. She was so glad he was here. "By the way, I have news about that detective from Toronto."

Grace pulled back. Maybe Rebecca was right. There was something Rubin wasn't telling anyone about his reason for being on Galliano.

With Michael's Help

GRACE DIDN'T EXPECT to be as relieved as she was that Michael had come to the island. She finally had the opportunity to unload her fears, to tell Maria, Leo and Michael exactly what she had seen. They knew her. Grace knew they wouldn't judge her or think she was crazy. She could rely on them to help her through this. With them, she didn't have to hide what she was seeing, hearing or experiencing anymore. Best of all, they would help her decide what to do. One thing was sure: she had to do something or the energy would drive her out of her mind.

They sat in the family room and, her parents listening, she told Michael about the vision. They hung on to all the details she disclosed about the man—at least she thought the figure was a man—chasing Tamara, hitting her and burying her. She told them about Scout and how the wolf had been in her dreams and was always watching her here on Galliano Island. Grace told them about Rebecca's deepest fear, Grace knowing it was true. Talking about it helped Grace make sense of all that had happened. Having the information about the murder out created a different path for the energy to flow. She worried because, just like at Danton, there would be complications. Energy was fluid, changeable, and easily altered its paths. It would want to find the killer.

Michael winced at the thought of a killer on the loose. Just as Evelyn had done, if the killer suspected Grace knew something, he or she might want to come after Grace if he felt threatened. This particular killer had gotten away with a crime and wouldn't want anyone to throw suspicion on him after all this time.

"Machowitz was on the Danton investigation team. It's on record that he doesn't think Evelyn's fall was an accident. I don't think he believes your testimony, Grace."

Grace gasped. "Rubin Machowitz is watching me?"

"I think that's why you were drilled so hard on the stand. Machowitz was responsible for those questions being asked. I think he asked for this assignment to follow you here. And, he'd be right. We weren't at the plant that night to finish a safety report, we wanted to pull Evelyn into a situation where she'd have to admit to the real intent of the chip implants. Unfortunately, we didn't anticipate that she'd have a gun and try to kill you."

"Is he hoping I'll be involved in something else? Like another murder? But there has been another murder. One that I had nothing to do with. So if I come forward and tell them I had a vision, Machowitz might suspect me." Grace was panicking, hyperventilating. She clasped her arms around her chest and rocked back and forth.

Leo rushed to her side and put his arm around her shoulder. "Calm down, Grace. You had nothing to do with it. You did nothing wrong. Machowitz won't find anything."

"But I saw the whole thing. I know now that I can't just let that go. Rubin already thinks I was involved in Evelyn's accident. If he finds out that I have this power—these visions—he might have grounds to reopen the Danton investigation. I didn't mention anything about it in my testimony."

"How on earth does a murder go undetected?" Michael demanded. "There must be some evidence. Somewhere." Michael's face brightened. "We could try to find evidence but make it look like we happened upon it by chance. If we find something tangible, we could report it."

"Rebecca said that Hugo, the one-man police force here on

Galliano, was romantically involved with Tamara. She and her husband, Joseph, thought they might even get married. What if he had something to do with it?"

Maria shook her head. "Hugo is a great guy and a good police officer. Everyone on Galliano thinks he's doing a great job. We have no proof. No reason to accuse him."

"Maria has a point," said Michael. "First, we have to find evidence. Grace, could you handle the trauma of another vision? We need a starting point."

"Not today."

Michael came close, knelt in front of her and took her hand. "I'll be right there with you. You don't have to be afraid."

"I'll do this." Grace said, straightening her posture. "I'll look for clues this time. There has to be something. It's just a matter of where to look."

Leo's concern was evident. What she'd experienced through that vision had left her exhausted and introverted for days to come. He gave Michael a cautionary look. "Visions find Grace. I'm not sure she should try to force one. They're traumatic for her. Maybe I should go to Lewis Landing by myself. Look around. See if they are any signs of violence. Maybe I'll find a weapon."

"That's it," Grace said. "The killer brought something down on her head. It happened at night so it was dark, but I think it was the handle of gun. If we find the weapon, there might be forensic evidence left. I think I can try to center in on the weapon if I can provoke the vision back to life."

Leo looked at her in surprise. "A blow to the head wouldn't have necessarily killed her. A concussion maybe but unless there was a massive bleed, she should have survived."

"But he buried her."

"Maybe she wasn't dead," Michael said, grimacing.

"… because the vision wasn't complete. I only saw part of what happened." Grace rose from her chair. "We need to go to Lewis Landing again. There's got to be more. The vision will show me."

As hesitant as they were about how another vision could affect Grace, they now had a plan. Once they could bring evidence to Hugo and Rubin, if he really was investigating a missing Indigenous woman, maybe Grace's empathic energy would settle down. But for now, her fingers tingled as she mentioned going back to Lewis Beach.

The phone rang and Leo answered. It was the clinic. Leo's eyes went wide, his mouth dropped. "I'll be right there."

"That's the clinic. Holly and Elia have been attacked at Lewis Beach. Seems they're in critical condition. I have to go." Leo gathered his things.

"We should go with you." Michael said. "Lewis Beach is where things are happening. Maybe we'll learn something."

Hugo

HOLLY'S INVITATION TO JOIN her and Elia at Lewis Beach played over and over in Hugo's mind. Wanna join me and Elia at Lewis Beach? It's a nice evening for a swim? He didn't like that she was spending the night on a boat with the local drug pusher. This punk was always high. Holly maintained that they weren't "together" as such, but he didn't buy Elia's intentions. After all, Elia was a guy and Holly, however unkempt, was pretty. What guy wouldn't want to get lucky with her?

It weighed on him all night, so the following morning, before Rubin showed up at the station, Hugo decided to go to Lewis Harbor to make sure she was all right. He hoped she would be sober by then and he could give her—and the punk—a ride back to Hollyhock.

Later, he wished he'd taken Holly up on her offer.

***

First, he found Elia lying face down in the gravel at the entrance to the bridge, hair sticky and matted with blood. Elia was moaning, mumbling incoherently, the words that did come out, making no sense. At least he was alive, and as much as Hugo disapproved of Elia, he was relieved that he was breathing.

Hugo rushed to him, turned him over and asked, "Who did this?"

Elia struggled to talk. "Holly... Where's Holly?"

Hugo took out his cell phone and called the clinic to send out the ambulance. Thank goodness there was always someone on call and the island had been allocated a refurbished ambulance the previous year. Then, as much as he hated his interference, Hugo called Rubin for backup.

"Do you know how to get to Lewis Beach? There's been an assault. I could use your help."

"On my way."

"Elia, help is on the way. Where's Holly?"

Elia struggled to raise his hand. He pointed in the direction of the beach.

"The paramedics will be here in a few minutes. I'm going to find Holly."

Elia nodded and lay his head back down on the gravel.

Hugo didn't want to leave Elia but Holly was his priority.

"Find Holly." Even though badly injured, Elia must have known she was in danger.

Had Elia seen who attacked him? Hugo dreaded what he might find on the beach. As he crossed the bridge to the decking, he heard the sirens. He was happy that the clinic was only minutes from the beach.

The ambulance arrived and as paramedics attended to Elia, Hugo drew his pistol and crossed the bridge, scanning the stretch of beach. The tide was coming in. Then he saw something. Off in the distance was a body, the shallow waves washing over it. *Holly!* He ran to her, fearing the worst.

As he ran, Hugo called out to the volunteer paramedics as loudly as he could. "Over here. Hurry. Hurry!"

He lifted her out of the seawater into his arms. The water was already washing over her face. Her head, bashed, was still bleeding, a good sign that she was merely unconscious, not dead. Her bottom half was unclothed.

"Holly? Holly? Are you all right?" No answer. He felt for a pulse at her neck. Yes, her heart was still beating. She was alive.

The paramedics joined Hugo on the beach, quickly put her onto the stretcher, carried her to the ambulance and raced off.

As Hugo picked up what was no doubt Holly's underwear from the water's edge, Rubin raced to his side.

"What happened here?"

"Holly… and Elia. Someone attacked them. Holly was right here. Elia over there." Hugo swallowed hard. "She wasn't able to answer me and…" He turned away, unable to say the words describing what had probably happened to her.

"What were you doing here? How did you know?" Rubin looked suspiciously at Hugo.

"Last night, Holly told me she was coming here. I didn't like that she was here with Elia."

"You've got a thing for her?"

An uncomfortable silence passed before Hugo answered. "Yeah. We used to be together. Before Tamara left." Hugo hung his head. "Yeah. And she's still important to me." The anger flooded in. "I have to get to the clinic. She's hurt. Bad. I need to go find out if she'll be all right. Would you mind sticking around? See what you can find? Anything that might identify who did this?"

Emergency at the Clinic

B Y THE TIME LEO ARRIVED, there were several cars already in the parking lot. He spotted Hugo's police cruiser and that detective from Toronto who was leaning against the cruiser talking to Hugo. The conversation appeared tense but Leo ignored it and rushed inside to see what had happened and how he could help.

The on-call doctor greeted him. "I've called for an airlift. The woman needs more attention than we can give her here. Elia has a head injury so he needs to see someone more specialized, too."

Leo scrubbed up and went to see what he could do in the meantime.

An hour later, a medical helicopter arrived and everyone helped get Holly and Elia on board for a hospital in Victoria. It left Leo feeling inadequate for the little that he and the other doctor could do. Holly's condition was critical.

※ ※ ※

Grace and Michael had watched the airlift activity from the parking lot.

Michael said, "I'm going to go talk to those officers. I'll be 'a curious visitor' wondering about a bad happening."

Grace smiled her approval of this tactic.

Michael approached Hugo and Rubin. "Wow. I didn't think things like this could happen away from the big city. Did you find the guy?"

"And you would be…?" Hugo's eyes penetrated Michael's. "And why are you asking?"

"I'm visiting the Walkers. Grace and I are friends."

"Of course," said Rubin. "You're Michael Riley. I recognize you from the Danton trial." Now Rubin's eyes bore into Michael's.

"The Danton case. Terrible accident. Grace is still suffering from the trauma of it all. That's why she came here to Galliano. She needed a respite."

Rubin's gaze moved to where Grace was standing. "She looks OK now."

Michael made no comment.

"Why is she here in the middle of another violent crime if she's so traumatized?"

"She's supporting her father, Dr. Walker. And where did that question come from?" Michael sensed an ulterior motive lurked behind Rubin's question. Dare he push for more information? "I remember. You're the one who tried to badger Grace about Evelyn's fall. The jury ruled it an accident yet you pushed the Crown Attorney to keep the line of questioning going on. And on. For a very long time. Why did you do that? You could see how upset she was." Had he managed to push Rubin's button? By the look on his face, he had.

Rubin shot back. "She didn't tell the whole story. And what she did say, doesn't add up. There's more to it. I'm sure of it." Rubin's look was cold. "So… may I ask why you are here? The real reason?"

Michael had to consider his answer carefully. He cocked his head, his brow wrinkling as he stepped closer to Rubin. "Grace is a good friend." Michael wasn't about to tell Rubin how he felt about her. He didn't even know how he felt about Grace, or if she felt the same. Anyway, it was none of this guy's business. The trial was over.

Michael could tell by the look on Grace's face that, although she couldn't hear their words, she knew she was the topic of conversation and didn't want to be. It was no surprise to him when she walked over to join the group.

She looked directly at Rubin, her annoyance obvious in her voice. "If you want to know something, why don't you just ask me?" Her assertiveness surprised Michael and, it appeared, Rubin, too. She was usually mild spoken.

Hugo looked on, obviously confused by the tone of the exchange.

"So," Rubin said. "Exactly what do you think we were talking about, Grace?" Rubin's partial smile told Michael that Rubin found it interesting that Grace was uncomfortable.

"The detective said he thought your testimony at the Danton trial wasn't complete," Michael said, pretending for Grace's benefit that this had surprised him. Michael wanted to see how far he could intimidate Rubin. Had it worked? Yes. Rubin looked like he had been caught in a trap. "He says he's here to investigate a missing woman, but it seems to me he has more on his agenda. He keeps asking about you and the Danton trial." Michael continued to stare at Rubin with that oh yeah look. This was setting in nicely. Michael hoped that Grace would play along, maintain her confidence. There was a lot they could glean from how Rubin responded. If Rubin's intention for coming to Galliano wasn't the investigation of the missing woman, but instead was an attempt to follow Grace for some personal vendetta, they could lay charges against him, perhaps even a restraining order, especially if Rubin continued with his accusatory questions. For now, they couldn't prove anything, but confronting him might make him back off, give them some room to find that evidence they'd talked about, something that proved Tamara was murdered. In the interim, Rubin was probably going to watch them like a cat sneaking up on a mouse. Although... perhaps they could use that to their advantage if Rubin continued to question Grace. That was harassment.

"I was under oath," Grace said. "I answered everything the Crown asked. Truthfully! The judge and the jury were satisfied. So what's your concern?"

✳ ✳ ✳

Grace was being straightforward and confident and her friend Michael was right there in her corner with her. Rubin realized that he had to be careful. They were right. He had asked for the assignment only after he'd learned that Grace had bought an airline ticket to Comox. Investigating further, he learned that Grace was going to Galliano. The assignment would allow him to watch her. He'd had a bad feeling about the entire trial. Maybe she, and her friend Michael there, had a connection to this current assault as well? Rubin couldn't prove that either, but it seemed strange that things seemed to happen wherever she went.

"No concern, really," Rubin said. "I apologize. This conversation has veered off in the wrong direction. I'm just helping Hugo with this case." As he stepped away toward his car, Grace called after him.

"Well, we're going to Lewis to check on Leo's boat," she said. "I trust that's okay with you?"

Sarcasm noted, Grace. Is she baiting me? Just to see what I'll do?

Lewis Beach

"I TOLD RUBIN WE WERE GOING to check on your boat," Grace told Leo. "He has no plausible reason to think I might be involved in this so if he follows us, it'll be clear that he isn't here about a missing woman."

Michael and Leo had shrugged it off, but Grace feared the scrutiny of Rubin's prying eyes. They got into their vehicles, Leo in his SUV, Michael and Grace in her rental car, and Hugo and Rubin watching through the parking lot's billowing dust.

It took only minutes to reach the area where Holly and Elia had been attacked and Lewis Beach was charged with an agitated energy that called to Grace as soon as they arrived.

She got out of the car and her feet and hands felt like they were on fire. Another vision was imminent, but this time, she would look more closely at what it showed her. They had discussed this carefully. What they were really after was physical proof of what happened. However, Grace knew that if they found that proof, Rubin would be even more suspicious of her. No. She had made up her mind. She was being called by forces beyond her control and she had to accept that responsibility or it wouldn't leave her alone. Her confrontation with Rubin had shored up her courage. She could do this.

Today, she'd call to it instead of trying to push it away. She proceeded onto the bridge. Michael and Leo followed and Grace knew they would be worrying, with more than a small level of certainty, that she was about to have an "episode," one that would leave her at first disoriented, disconnected, then drained and moody. It was always the same when a vision overtook her senses. She was glad to know that Michael, and especially Leo, were scanning the area to ensure that no one was around to see that they were looking for something, or that there might be something very strange in Grace's behavior.

The vision hit her as soon as her feet touched the beach sand at the bottom of the steps from the boardwalk. The vision wasn't of Tamara and her pursuer. It was of a boat, one she didn't recognize. Two people were exiting a boat. The name *Auriga* flashed momentarily on the stern. She saw Elia wave to someone on the bridge then stagger up the gangplank to join him, melting into the dark night. Oblivious to Elia's visitor, Holly ran to the beach where the phosphorescence twinkled. Grace heard her laugh and sing the nursery rhyme, "Twinkle, twinkle, little star..." The melody echoed as the vision enclosed her.

Grace looked for where Elia had gone but saw only a dark figure shifting in the shadows, walking across the sand, heading toward Holly. In the dark night, he seemed like a phantom, no distinguishable facial features, only footprints marking his approach on an unsuspecting Holly. His left hand held a long object, the butt of which reached his armpit, the barrel ending at his knee. A rifle. Yes. It was a rifle. Grace was sure of it. He reversed its orientation and plunged the butt end with great force at Holly's head. She fell to the sand where she lay still. He carefully laid the weapon on the sand, and dropped his pants. Holly must have regained consciousness. Grace heard her screams as she lay on the wet sand, just out of reach of the waves. The man restrained her flat to the sand as he had his way with her. Holly struggled and pleaded, flailed and kicked, but wasn't able to overcome his weight and strength. Grace heard his laugh—lewd and coarse—as he pulled up his jeans. He reached for his dropped weapon, aimed it, swung it against her head again and stepped away. This time she lay still.

Grace watched the boat leave the harbor, the name *Auriga* still on its stern, as it headed out of the bay, gliding out of sight, then swallowed by the darkness of the ocean.

Then as suddenly as the vision had appeared, it faded, and the darkness filled with sunlight again. Grace staggered, unsteady from the release, turning toward the steps where she would be able to sit and recover.

Michael and Leo waited until Grace regained her composure.

"It was a man," she said. "He had a rifle and knocked Holly on the head with the butt end. He raped her." Grace put hands over her face. The terror of the moment would hang on her conscious mind for a long time.

Michael touched her shoulder. "Think carefully. Did you see anything unique about the rifle?"

Grace tried to step her memory back into the vile scene. "It was long. From his shoulder to his knee. But it was dark so I couldn't see any markings. I saw a boat. With the name Auriga on it and it headed out of the harbor into the night. The darkness. Dark."

Leo spoke up. "I've never seen a boat by that name moored here." He looked back at the pier. "Did you see where it was moored?"

"At the end of the dock. Because I saw the rest of the boats behind it as it headed out of the bay. Is that important?"

Leo and Michael walked to the end of the pier to see if the *Auriga* had left any telltale signs of impact: a scrape of paint, discarded debris, anything. But they found nothing. They walked back to Grace and all three decided that each of them should walk a length of the beach, try to recreate the scene, picture where the *Auriga* had been tied to the dock, and where the perpetrator and victims had walked. Perhaps it would spur other questions that would lead them to further clues.

Grace headed directly to the arbutus where the killer had buried Tamara.

As she got closer to the spot, the wind picked up, gently at first, then stirred deliberately around the area. The rustle of the leaves sounded almost like a whisper.

Yes, it was a whisper.

What was it saying?

Grace closed her eyes and listened intently. *Au. Ree. Gah. Au. Ree. Gah.* The whisper kissed her ears, blending with the swish of the waves. She knelt on the sand and touched the ground with her hand. *This is where the body should be. But it's not here. There is no body.* Had the tide grabbed Tamara and washed her out to sea? *Au. Ree. Gah.* Grace's eyes popped open. *Of course!* Tamara had been moved onto the boat which went out to sea—with a purpose. Whoever had killed her had put her body on the *Auriga*. Or maybe, she wasn't dead yet.

Truth in the Wind

T HE ANCESTORS WERE PLEASED. Grace was moving in step with the laws of Nature, but her power would make others nervous, thus put her in danger. Grace knew what had happened and now she was acting to bring the perpetrator to justice. A grievous wrong had been committed and the energy sought justice. She was strong, but afraid. She had to be careful. If the killer's suspicion were aroused, he would come for her. Right now, no one but her family and Michael knew about the visions. To the law, she would appear to be mentally unstable. To the killer, her visions would be a threat. Grace knew that the dark person in the vision would do whatever was necessary to prevent her from getting too close to information that might lead to the discovery of the truth. The wind carried the whispers, chilling her skin. *Au. Ree. Gah.*

The Ancestors' spirits lingered in the sand, the air, on the water, and they surrounded Grace, too, with their subtle presence. All she had to do was listen and feel. The energy had absorbed it all. They would guide her. Scout and his pack would protect her if the killer got too near. They sang the song of courage and strength. It would vibrate in her being, constantly reminding her of what she had to do.

❋ ❋ ❋

Scout envisioned what was happening at the harbor and alerted the pack to be on guard. He knew the man, but had no way to tell Grace who he was. She would find him. They had to protect her. Scout, too, felt the impending danger.

Scout would wait for her at Abalone Hideaway. They would be back there soon and, with the help of Leo and Michael, would figure out what to do next.

The name *Auriga* made Scout's ears hurt as the Ancestors sang its syllables. Someone had to find that boat, find out who owned it, take the next step.

He saw two vehicles approaching the house and crouched below the salal. How brave she was. Her courage scented the wind.

An Emerging Plan

B OTH CARS PULLED TO A STOP on the driveway and Leo, Michael and Grace got out and walked toward the waiting Maria.

Grace did her best to walk tall, back straight, steps direct but knew her mother would see only trance-like eyes. Her mother could always detect the strain of Grace's exhaustion following one of her episodes. Grace went for Maria's outstretched arms, allowing her mother to cradle her within her embrace. There was comfort in the warmth of her touch and Grace needed that right now.

"It's okay," Grace whispered. "I've got this."

Maria hugged her again and with her arm around Grace's waist, led her into the house.

Leo and Michael followed.

Maria had made coffee and had laid out a tray of sandwiches. Food would relax them and provide a comfortable setting for problem solving. Everyone, including Maria, dug in with gusto.

"Was the weapon the same in both visions?" Michael asked.

Grace did her best to revisit the scene, back to where Tamara had been hit on the head. "No," she said. "Tamara's killer had a smaller weapon in his hand. A gun, I think. It looked like a handgun. I didn't see it very clearly. Holly's attacker had a rifle. That, I know for sure."

"I suppose," suggested Leo, "that even if it was the same person, he could have had two weapons. "Clearly, a handgun and a rifle are used for different purposes."

Michael looked thoughtful, his eyes moving from side to side, as he struggled to understand. "Although… Isn't it strange that both attacks were on Lewis Beach? I wonder what the connection is."

"I'm sure it has something to do with that boat," Grace said. "The *Auriga*. I saw two people getting off the boat and then I saw the name, and then the vision focused on it again. I saw it as the boat left the harbor. I'm sure the two people getting off the boat were Holly and Elia. Why were they there?"

Grace lowered her head, not sure if she should disclose what she was wanting to tell them. They'd think she was crazy. She wasn't sure if she believed it herself. "I kept hearing the boat name in the air. Like the wind was talking. Chanting it. That's what made me look out to the water." Grace looked up to see the reactions of Leo and Michael.

"Trust your instincts," Maria said. "Wherever they come from."

Michael said, "Let's say Holly and Elia knew the owner of the boat and he let them hang out for the evening or night."

Leo and Maria nodded. Grace searched Michael's eyes.

"We know there was a third person on the beach and that person likely is the one who assaulted them. I would wager that the same person is the owner of the boat. But why would he hurt them?"

"It's no secret that Elia sells cannabis," Leo said. "Maybe other recreational drugs, as well. When money's involved with illegal drugs…" Leo smiled. "I bet it's about paying his supplier. Not to mention they were probably both impaired, so easy targets. Both."

"You think Elia might have been withholding money from his supplier?" Michael asked.

"Right now, we aren't sure of anything," said Leo, "but I think it's a good supposition."

"Then it makes sense to find out who owns the *Auriga* and what kind of boat it is," said Michael. "Pleasure or illegal trafficking. We should be able to search something about that boat online. If not, I have someone who can."

"I haven't seen a boat by that name around here," said Leo. "At least not moored at Lewis. I've had the *Serenity* there for almost two years. You'd think I would have seen it."

"In my vision, I saw the *Auriga* off the end of the dock. I assumed it wasn't from here or it would have had a berth."

"Perhaps it's moored elsewhere on Galliano," Michael said. "Who can we ask about it?"

"Asking questions would arouse questions," said Grace. "I think it's best we keep all the information to ourselves."

Savannah

ALMOST IMMEDIATELY after Elia had been taken to hospital, the Sunset Restaurant's patronage dropped to its lowest level in ages. Savannah had always counted on Elia to supply the outdoor patio with recreational drugs; the Sunset's reputation attracted many tourists because of that. No repercussions. No prosecutions. The Sunset had developed a "name." Without a consistent supply of "recreation," Savannah knew, her customers would dwindle and she needed customers to keep her business thriving. She couldn't stand idly by and watch her thriving restaurant flounder. No way. She would have to do something.

Savannah found the contact on her cell phone. She pressed a button and the phone rang numerous times before it was picked up.

"You can't do business without customers, and neither can I," Savannah said.

"The kid's doin' fine. He'll be back in a few more days," the voice said. "The girl... Well she's not necessary, but will probably be OK too. I'll get back to you."

The connection dropped, leaving Savannah dumbfounded, standing there holding her cell like some duped idiot. Annoyed, she snorted her disapproval and slapped her cell phone onto the counter.

Probably OK, he said. She liked Holly. A bit rough around the

217

edges, yes. A quick temper, yes. But Holly was basically a good person. Her free and happy presence at the restaurant encouraged the customers to spend their money. She was good for business.

Savannah would make a phone call to the hospital. Ask about Holly herself. Maybe send flowers. The dealer was jerk. He didn't know anything. He just spouted off his mouth. The product of an impaired brain. What could he know about Holly's condition, anyway?

Coffee pot in hand, Savannah headed over to where Hugo and that Toronto detective were having coffee, trying to ensure her breasts were bouncing with each step. Savannah had taken a liking to... Rubin. That was the guy's name. Rubin. She liked his thick burly body and dark, unkempt hair. He looked tough and strong. Stereotypical of a police detective—from what she'd seen on TV, at least—he never smiled. Even his questioning eyes were sexy to her. And the way he looked at everyone like they were a prime suspect made him so attractive. As far as Savannah was concerned, he could interrogate her. Anytime he wanted. The thought made her smile. She wondered if he needed company tonight. *No harm in trying, is there?*

"Coffee's on the house." After filling their mugs, she slid into the booth on the side where Rubin was sitting, making him shuffle closer to the wall.

"You fellas found out who attacked Holly and Elia yet?" She fixed her eyes on Rubin's face.

"You know we can't discuss police matters with you," Hugo snapped.

His cold response irked her, but she wasn't giving up.

"How well did you know the victims?" Rubin asked.

"They're just... They're just regular customers." Savannah winked at Rubin, moving her face closer to his.

"Elia isn't just a regular customer. Is he?" Rubin shot back, making her bristle.

Savannah had understood Rubin's attempt at intimidating her and it excited her. "Humph. Everyone knows Elia. But what he does is none of my business. He doesn't cause me any trouble and the customers like him." Pleased that she had evaded the intent of the question, she snuggled closer to Rubin making Hugo snicker at Rubin's discomfort.

"Tonight's martini night at the Sunset. Why don't you join me. Drinks are on me."

"I'm afraid we have another engagement," said Hugo. "We've been invited to the Walkers. For coffee."

"Well, maybe next martini night." Disappointed, she got up and returned the coffee pot to the serving station.

Rubin

H UGO AND RUBIN made a quick exit from the Sunset.

"Thanks," said Rubin, relieved to get away. "But when did we get an invitation from the Walkers?"

"Just for you, I made that up." Hugo stopped walking, grabbed Rubin's arm and looked directly at him. "You said you know the Walker girl."

Rubin was instantly on guard. An answer might open up more questions, ones he didn't want to talk about. Ones that might reveal his ulterior motives.

"You seemed aggressive when you talked to her boyfriend at the clinic," Hugo said. "What was that all about?"

"Guy rubbed me the wrong way."

"Why were you interrogating the Walker girl like that?"

Rubin didn't want this conversation with Hugo—no, this interrogation *by* Hugo—to go any further. "Nothing in particular. I guess it's just the detective in me." Rubin forced a chuckle. "Like me, you've got yourself some kind of suspicious streak. I like that."

"Actually," said Hugo. "It might be a good idea to talk to the Walkers. What do you think?"

Rubin liked where that was leading to. He could get more infor-

223

mation out of Grace. As far as he was concerned, she'd crack sooner or later. "Yeah. Maybe Dr. Walker could add some information about the injuries. That might help us identify who assaulted the victims."

"I'll call them to see if they're home."

"How about we just drop in? I prefer information that's spontaneous."

Interrogation at Abalone Hideaway

T HE POLICE CAR DESCENDED the driveway of Abalone Hideaway. A Pacific wind had cooled the heat of the afternoon sun. The trees on the property swayed in the breeze off the ocean. The wind rustled the leaves and swished with a harmony-like chorus, singing with a voice unique to the West Coast. The sun broke through the clouds to cast phantom tree branches on the driveway, arms with spindly fingers ready to grab you. Something about this place spooked Rubin. In spite of this, Rubin had to admit that the location was enchanting. They were close to the water yet yards above ocean level. It was, as the name stated, a hideaway, a place no one could see if they didn't know how to find it. Obscure. Beautiful.

They stopped at the bottom of the driveway. An SUV and a small compact were parked in front of the board-and-batten house.

Good, Rubin thought. *The Walkers are home. They're going to be surprised by this unannounced visit from the local police and this visiting officer. Just what I wanted! Will this throw them off guard? That girl, Grace, has something she's hiding. I'm sure of it. I have a feeling about Grace Walker. There's a hesitancy about her that makes her seem less than forthcoming.*

From the second-floor veranda, Maria called down then exited the front door to greet her unannounced guests.

"Hugo! This is a surprise. Come and join us for an afternoon beverage. Who's your companion?"

"This is detective Machowitz. He's on special assignment."

Maria and Hugo nodded to each other. *She knows very well who I am,* thought Rubin.

"So he's the one that Michael has been talking about," Maria said, her smile turning to a frown and eyeing Rubin with distrust. "I have iced tea chilled. I assume you're both on duty and don't want anything stronger?" She stared for a moment waiting for confirmation.

Rubin shook his head as did Hugo.

Maria led them into the house and out to the second-floor deck where Leo, Michael and Grace were enjoying a glass of Cabernet. They stood as Maria announced them.

"We have guests. Seems the police are after us." Maria laughed. "I hope you haven't run afoul of the law when I wasn't watching. Have a seat, gentlemen. I'll get you some iced tea."

Rubin and Hugo took a seat, Rubin momentarily admiring Maria's garden before he squared his chair to face Leo and Michael.

Rubin's eyes fixed on Grace, then moved to Leo, to Michael and back to Grace, hoping to catch the slightest indication of insecurity in anyone's body language. "Lovely place you've got here," he said, attempting to make polite conversation.

"Maria has a way with plants," Leo said. "But it's a lot of work."

"Well I have help," Maria said, returning with two tall glasses of iced tea. She handed them to Hugo and Rubin. "I hired Holly to help me when it gets to be more than I can handle. She works at Hollyhock and tends to the flowers there so has experience with what grows here on the Island. Sometimes she teaches me stuff to make them grow better."

"Then you know the girl?"

"Oh yes. Holly is my botanical expert." Maria took a seat beside Leo.

"Dr. Walker." Hugo paused, shifting to look directly into Leo's face.

"At the clinic, when you examined Holly, did you find any evidence that might help us identify who did this to her? And Elia?"

Leo's smile turned to a frown. "She was raped. And yes. We have samples."

"And what about the young man?" asked Rubin.

"He had a deep gash on his head which we stitched up. He'll be all right in a few days. We sent him to the hospital just to be sure it's not a concussion. Or worse. The clinic doesn't have the diagnostic imaging equipment to make a positive diagnosis."

Rubin's quick shift back to Grace seemed to startle her. *Good.* "Ms. Walker, do you know the injured girl? And…" Here, he smiled at her. "Do you not find it strange that you're in a place where someone is hurt—again?"

Michael shot in with "Detective Machowitz, I find it strange that you're here on Galliano, on exactly the same island as Ms. Walker. Galliano is not exactly a hub of police activity. We could ask the same question. Why are you here and why are you grilling Grace? Or should I ask why are you harassing her? Do you have some reason… or evidence that is suggesting something?"

Then Leo jumped in to defend her. "Detective, my daughter is here to recover from a tragic and traumatic experience at the company she works for, Danton International in Toronto. Michael tells me you were involved in the investigation? Here on Galliano, it's quiet, and environmentally beautiful. Exactly what she needs. She is here to take a break from everything that happened. To restore herself."

"The Walkers have a point, Rubin," Hugo said. Then to Leo, "We just wanted to get some medical information from you, Dr. Walker."

Grace's posture had gone stiff. Rubin had upset her and he knew it and he was happy to see it. *Sometimes you have to push the boundaries.* No doubt, this friend of hers—boyfriend?—would be digging as deeply into why Rubin was here as Rubin was digging about why Michael was here. What Grace knew.

"Dr. Walker," Rubin said, maintaining his smile as best he could, "if you think of anything else or get any further information, we'd appreciate it if you notified us."

"Don't worry, Detective. The clinic knows its obligation in criminal matters. We will cooperate completely." Rubin could sense Leo reading him. And he could also sense that Leo was not only hiding something but was feeling defensive about it. Like daughter like father?

Rubin didn't miss the look that Hugo gave to Leo. He even rolled his eyes. Toronto detectives weren't welcome in tight-knit communities by anyone—residents or law enforcement.

"Thanks, Leo," Hugo said. "Any information would really help us. I can't imagine who would want to hurt them."

Rubin crossed his arms and leaned back into the lounger, wanting to press for more information, but Hugo snapped to his feet, ready to leave, and making it apparent that Rubin was taking an inappropriate line of questioning.

Rubin stayed where he was. "You have a boat moored at Lewis?"

"I bought the *Serenity* about two years ago," said Leo. "Just after we moved here. Lots of interesting marine life to see there, especially in the lagoon."

"When were you there last?"

"Enough," Hugo said. "We're done here."

He pulled on Rubin's arm to get him moving but Rubin wasn't about to be challenged.

"Let me walk you out to your cruiser," Maria offered. "I'm sending you off with fresh-baked muffins. Baked them this morning. Sound good? I think we're done here."

Rubin reluctantly acquiesced but as they walked to the driveway, he noticed movement in the bushes. A wolf suddenly ran out to block their path. It growled then crossed into the bushes on the other side.

Rubin reached for his revolver. "Wolf!"

"Relax," said Hugo, almost laughing. "It's run off. We startled it. It's probably more afraid of us than you are of it."

But Rubin continued to scan the bushes with the barrel of his gun.

Scout

S COUT LISTENED TO THE SONG of the wind. It was strong with voices calling out for truth and wisdom. The heart of the message was inspiring, full of power. All that had to be done was to seek justice. The smallest bit of evidence would be enough. Then the two men would make the connection, would know how and what had happened and then make an arrest. When the killer was convicted and incarcerated, Tamara's spirit would be released to the Sunset Land as would the innocent spirit of her unborn son. The process had begun but malicious motives always clashed with justice. It would not be easy for Grace.

The Ancestors and Scout knew that Hugo and Rubin were important to the quest. They were of the law, man's law, and they had the means to bring about justice for Tamara. But they were hostile. The Toronto detective, the one named Rubin, had an evil streak. His heart was not pure. He might even harbor some danger for Grace, believing she had a motive other than the sacred quest she had been chosen for. Scout knew this stranger to the Island was bad. Scout could not allow a personal grievance to come anywhere near Grace or Grace might suffer the same outcome as Tamara had.

Scout and the Ancestors would have to send out messages of support and comfort. Grace had to see this through. Scout growled from the bushes. He could feel Grace's anxiety about the man. He would have to be watched. Grace needed to be guarded.

Suspicions Arise

G RACE, HER PARENTS AND MICHAEL sat silent, trying to understand what had just happened. Detective Machowitz had been more than unpleasant. Why would he take that attitude? It didn't make sense.

"I suspected something about Machowitz when you called me the night you landed in Comox," Michael said. "Although, I didn't realize at the time that he was involved in the Danton investigation. There's more to his aggression than he's letting on."

"I don't understand why he's so antagonistic toward me. He wasn't like that at first. He actually tried to come on to me. What do you suppose he's trying to get at?" Fear was gnawing at her insides. "It feels like he's trying to get information that will throw suspicion on me. Does he actually believe I was responsible for Evelyn's death?"

"He seems to be taking this personally," Leo said. "Did he have a connection to Evelyn? Possibly to Tamara?"

That would make sense, thought Grace. "Good point, Leo. I'll get Heatherton to check that out. I know Evelyn had 'relationships' with a lot of men. Maybe Machowitz was one of her lovers?"

Nervous snickers flittered from all four of them.

"But we can't have Heatherton making any waves, though," said Maria. "Grace wants to forget about that awful experience. Heaven

237

forbid that investigation be opened up again."

"I think you're right," Leo said. "Maybe Machowitz is trying to get Grace to admit to something so he can open the case again."

"I can't exactly tell him that Evelyn was after me because I could expose her microchipping plan," Grace said, wanting to scream with frustration. "She turned those workers into the equivalent of zombies." Grace shivered at the thought of what else nano technology could do to a person's mind.

Maria patted Grace's knee. "It's over, dear. It's done. It's over."

"But what about my vision at Lewis? Tamara's murder?" Grace said. "I can't just let that go. My mind won't let me do that." She wanted to curl into herself, rock back and forth, transport herself to a place where she didn't have to think about anything anymore. "If we keep showing up at Lewis, if we appear to be looking for something, and if Rubin finds out, that will only make him more suspicious of me. He is sure to ask what we're looking for. And why."

"He won't find out," Michael said. "When we get the information about who owns the *Auriga*, we'll know what to do next. Grace, someone owns that boat and that person is involved in the assault on Holly and Elia. I would bet that the same person was involved in Tamara's murder, too."

"I wonder why her body wasn't found on the beach," Maria said.

"Maria's right," said Leo. "The reason her body wasn't found on the beach? She had to have been moved,"

Michael leaned forward. "If the killer's the same person, he must have taken her out by boat and dumped her far out at sea. Maybe there's still evidence on the *Auriga*." He took out his cell phone and started thumbing. "Heatherton can find out anything. We have to give him a bit of time."

"Well then," said Leo, slapping his thighs and rising from the chair. "Let's go sailing." His smile was wide. "It'll relax us. And who knows, maybe we'll see the *Auriga* out there."

"But what if Rubin's out there," said Grace, "watching things at

Lewis Harbor? He'll see us. He'll think we're up to something."

"We won't be up to anything at all, dear," said Maria. "We're just going out for a sail. Showing Michael the waters around the island."

Placing his arm over Maria's shoulder, Leo smiled proudly.

"What the heck," continued Maria. "If we see the detective, we'll invite him along."

"That doesn't even start to get funny, Maria," laughed Grace in spite of herself. "No way!"

The Plan

As head of Public Relations, Jim Heatherton had free reign to investigate anything. Grace worked for him, and was always impressed at how efficiently he could find out information about companies and the people who worked for them. He was a man of protocol and knew how to get information. His British background and mannerisms made him appear very proper and disciplined but that was a disguise. He was, in fact, a very shrewd investigator. Michael was right. There wasn't anything Heatherton couldn't uncover. It hadn't taken him long to learn about Grace's empathic ability and when Grace disclosed the details of her vision at the Danton research center, Heatherton found a way to get around computer security, giving them what they'd both wanted and feared: the evidence that would expose Evelyn Loudon's scheme to subjugate her workers.

That was why he, Grace and Michael were at the Danton plant that night. Evelyn had caught them hacking the system. One of her zombies must have given her a head's up because she knew they'd be in the plant that night. She knew this might be her one and only opportunity to foil their attempt at stopping her plans.

They knew she would stop at nothing, even if it meant she had to kill all three of them.

✳ ✳ ✳

Maria quickly assembled a picnic lunch, sandwiches, muffins, fruit and beverages. They would spend the rest of the afternoon on the water, maybe longer if they were lucky to spot the mystery boat. If not, they could always hope to see whales. Any day on the ocean was an adventure. They would certainly see the colony of seals that always hung out at Seal Rock. And Sutil Point, where playful sea otters were often spotted, was a favorite area for both residents and tourists. One way or another, they'd have an enjoyable day.

✳ ✳ ✳

While the Serenity bobbed gently, waiting in the water that sparkled with the afternoon sun, they looked around, half expecting Rubin Machowitz to be watching like a Peeping Tom. His questions and scrutiny still hung over all of them, Grace knew, like the smoke of a forest fire. They were relieved to find him not there although, for Grace, the residual energy of the assault was dawdling in the sand and on the boardwalk. Her feet tingled as they touched the harbor decking. The assailant had been there though she couldn't tell if that person was also the one who had murdered Tamara. She paused to allow the energy to give her clues. The anxious energy crept into her core.

Michael called to her. "Come on, Grace. Hop aboard." He held out his hand to support her and with a clumsy jump, she was on the *Serenity* and rather awkwardly also in Michael's arms. He laughed. "You certainly don't have your sea legs yet."

Grace pulled away to sit on the padded benches in the bow, not only to hide her reddening face, but also to think.

The second she'd landed on the boat, the electrical impulse had stopped. She stared back at the wooden harbor decking, her mind troubled by the subtleness of the energy. But the rumble of the engine drew her out of her thought process. She felt the pull of the boat as it headed out to sea. She would try to piece that puzzle together later.

✳ ✳ ✳

The moist briny air calmed Grace like a tonic. The ocean rocked the vessel as though it were a baby's cradle. Out here on the Strait of Georgia, there were no distractions, no threats, just the soothing sounds and smells of the ocean.

They sailed past Marina Island, Seal Rock, and then north to waters she didn't know. Leo and Maria sat back in their captain seats with Leo at the helm as the *Serenity* hummed through the glass-like ocean water. Even Michael, who had a tendency toward sea sickness, had tilted his head back, enjoying the ocean breezes. Life out here was serene. It was a place where Nature caressed one's soul, where spirits rejoiced in the beauty of the day.

Leo sailed north to explore Von Donop Inlet, where cliffs displayed ancient Indigenous rock drawings. It was something the wealthier Galliano seasonal residents often pointed out to visiting guests. There, the waters of the ocean cut inland to expose expensive homes on the scenic cliffs that dotted the shoreline of Galliano, homes in complete juxtaposition to the modest homes of the Island Nation Band.

Leo slowed the *Serenity*'s speed when they entered the inlet. Today, the inlet was deserted except for two vessels, one, an older-model speedboat that had just pulled alongside an anchored fishing boat. The larger vessel was well-maintained, and its exterior paint was bright and clean. The speedboat bumped gently into its port side where a tall, broad-shouldered man, features darkened by the onward sun, tied their crafts together. He then helped a woman board the vessel and the two disappeared into the cabin of the boat. Leo stopped, not wanting to get near.

Michael and Grace joined Leo and Maria at the helm.

"What's going on there, Leo?" Michael asked.

"No one does that. No one boards a boat like that."

"Did you recognize them?"

The disbelief on the faces of Maria and Leo was obvious.

"That looked like Savannah," said Leo. "The man... I'm not sure. Their boats are anchored like they intend to be there a while. And... Doesn't look like they're fishing."

The *Serenity* was drifting. Leo had to be quick. He reversed the boat to head out to sea again

"Wait. Wait," said Michael, pulling out his cell phone. "Pictures. I can enhance them back at the house. Maybe get the boats' names." His cell phone clicked several times. "Damn this sun. The backlight's making them dark. At least we have some. We might identify who they are."

Leo sailed further around the northernmost tip of Galliano, then south toward Little Deer Cove. The back side of Galliano was mostly raw nature, but shores were beautiful and the waters pristine.

"If we're going to see whales, this is where they would be," said Maria. "But it doesn't look like it today. Sorry, kids. I'm sure you would have loved that."

They stopped at the Government docks at Little Deer Cove where they moored and had their onboard lunch. It would give them the opportunity to discuss what they'd seen and possibly to assess what was going on and what it meant.

"Why would Savannah be out there?" Maria asked.

"I don't know," said Leo, frowning, "but it certainly seems odd. I know she does regular trips into Campbell River for supplies, but I didn't know she had a boat or went out on the water. By herself."

"From what I understand, her customers count on contraband? Yes? So perhaps with Elia not being around, she's doing his job? Meeting Elia's supplier? Even I have heard about the Island's wide-spread reputation. Galliano. Hippie Island. Clients don't just come here to eat at the Sunset."

"Hippie Island?" muttered Maria. "Really? Galliano is renowned as a place for Hippies?"

Eyebrows raised, Michael shrugged. "Well that's the gossip."

"That might explain it then," said Leo. "Elia isn't here right now so there's no one for the restaurant's customers to buy it from. Very bad for business."

Michael laughed nervously. "I think we should stop into the Sunset tonight for supper. Let's see if anyone else is on the job tonight." He winked.

"Should we let Hugo know what we saw," Maria asked.

"Absolutely not," laughed Michael, more loudly this time. "We were just out for a day of leisure and stopped in at the famous Sunset Restaurant in Lewis Landing for a quick evening meal and entertainment. They usually have a band, right? Locals?"

"Why not?" said Leo.

Grace wasn't so sure it was a good idea at all.

✳ ✳ ✳

The Serenity was back at Lewis Harbor by 8:00 PM and the evening sun spilled golden across the water all the way from the horizon. The evening air was intoxicating, moist and briny. Seagulls squawked and harbor seals snorted as they searched for the meal that would sustain them through the night.

Leo steered the *Serenity* into its slip where it bumped gently against the dock. Michael jumped to the decking to catch the rope and tie the vessel to the deck cleats. Leo finished securing the *Serenity*, and locked down items that might be stolen and closed the hatch. It took about twenty minutes before the *Serenity* was secured for the next time they would sail.

Michael and Leo lugged Maria's food containers with them as everyone ascended the plank to the bridge.

Grace looked back at the ocean. It seemed to pull her attention right into it. She didn't know what she was feeling or looking for, but the water's swish on the shore called to her.

Grace. Find me.

Her feet seemed planted to the boardwalk even as the others stepped lightly to the SUV. Something made her shiver. She scanned the beach and the bridge to the parking area. Lewis Harbor was making her feel uneasy even though the tingling she'd felt earlier still evaded her. She was worried that another vision might be waiting.

Sunset Restaurant

T HE SUNSET RESTAURANT was almost empty; only two tables on the patio had patrons. They were enjoying a beer.

Grace contemplated how unusual this must be. From what she'd heard, summer evenings—even on weeknights—had always drawn in customers.

Leo led the way inside and they sat at a booth, Leo signaling to the server that they would like a menu. Savannah was nowhere in sight.

"Great burgers tonight," the server said. He looked to be about seventeen, with unruly blond hair, and his shirt was open to the waist exposing his six-pack.

Maria and Grace grinned at each other. Maria whispered, "Not your usual sort of restaurant server but certainly one that Savannah likes to hire."

"Exactly what we came for," said Michael.

A little too enthusiastic, Michael, thought Grace. *Let's not bring too much attention to ourselves.*

"Burgers all around?" the server asked.

Michael said, "Very unique... this place."

Maria agreed with a smile. "Galliano has freedoms and charms all of its own."

Grace chuckled along with her mother but there was a look of dis-approval on Michael's face. Was he jealous because Grace had noticed the lad's abs?

✳ ✳ ✳

Hugo was making his rounds. The exterior French doors of the Sunset Restaurant opened to the outside patio so the Walkers, and their guest, Michael, were easily noticeable at the booth. He decided to smooth over the drilling that Rubin had inflicted on them the day before. He walked over to their table and pulled up a chair, blocking the aisle.

"I just heard from the hospital in Victoria." He wondered if Leo would appreciate the update. "Elia's being released tomorrow. Savannah says she's going to pick him up. Bring him home." Hugo paused, waiting for any reaction from them but they all seemed to be nervous. Were they hiding something? "You know. With Holly still in hospital? Savannah offered Elia her guest house."

"That's great news," Leo said. "Where is Savannah, by the way? Has she left already? That's unusual. Isn't it?"

Hugo looked around. "That is strange. She's usually here. She said she was leaving on the first ferry tomorrow morning." Hugo raised his hand to signal the buff-bellied server who promptly came over to the table.

"I'd like to talk to Savannah. Know where she is?"

"She said she'd be late. She's getting supplies." He pulled out his cell phone then put it back. "It's almost eight. She should be here soon."

A bell dinged from the kitchen and off the server went to return with four plates, two in each hand.

"I'll have a burger, as well," Hugo said. "Hope it's okay that I join you?"

"We'd be delighted," Maria said, a little too enthusiastically.

✳ ✳ ✳

This was their chance to subtly leak information to Hugo. He'd no doubt be curious about why they were here, like tourists, at the local pub. He never said much, but he was sharp and much more pleasant to deal with than that detective from Toronto when it came to extracting details.

"We were out in the *Serenity* today," Leo said. "Saw something kind of strange in Von Donop Inlet. Two boats stopping abreast of each other, right out there in mid-water, and a person—a woman—boarding from the water. I've never seen anyone do that." Leo stared at Hugo. waiting for a reaction. Hugo returned the stare with apparent interest.

"Hmm. Did you get the names of the boats?"

Michael cut in. "They were too far away. What do you suppose they were doing?"

Hugo harrumphed. "What do *you* think they were up to?"

The server placed Hugo's burger on the table.

"Sounds unusual, yes, but then who knows what people do when no one can see them. In Von Donop Inlet, you say?" He reached for the ketchup. "Were you able to recognize anyone?"

"No," said Grace. "But the woman was wearing a red halter top."

A commotion from the kitchen caused Hugo to turn toward it.

"Help me carry the boxes in from the car," a female voice bellowed along with a jingle of keys landing on a counter. The door to the kitchen thumped open and Savannah appeared in the dining room.

She was wearing skintight shorts and a transparent nylon blouse that hung unbuttoned to her thighs. The blouse flew open behind her as she walked, exposing a red halter top underneath. Everyone at the booth, even Hugo, sought each other's eyes. The mystery woman had been positively identified.

"Hello, Savannah," Hugo said with a mouth full of burger, ketchup at one corner of his mouth. "How's your day? What have you been up to? Your customers have missed you." Hugo put down the burger on his plate, wiped his mouth with a napkin and gave her a scrutinizing grin.

"Well, aren't you full of questions today." She returned Hugo's smile and came up close to him, thumping him on the shoulder. "The burgers are on me today and I'll have Six Pac bring out pie for dessert."

A nod of her head indicated the young male server.

Maria and Grace exchanged one raised eyebrow each. *Six Pac?*

"Pie all around, please."

"Business is slow, it seems," Leo said. "What's with that?"

Savannah shook her head and frowned. "Seems the customers miss Elia." She winked and walked back to the kitchen.

"Where's your sidekick?" Grace asked Hugo.

"You mean, Rubin? He said he had to go into Campbell River for a meeting. Police business stuff. He didn't elaborate. Actually, it's nice not having him around. I'm sorry he was so rude at your place yesterday."

"Savannah seems to like halter tops," said Michael. "Red ones."

"Yeah," said Hugo, rising from his chair, "the Sunset has the best burgers. Well, folks, thank you for the company. I have to get back to work."

✳ ✳ ✳

"Okay!" said Michael. "At least he knows. I wonder if he'll say anything to your detective friend, Grace."

"He's not my friend."

"I know." His laugh did little to reassure her.

"I guess we wait and see what develops. Meanwhile, I'll try to enhance those photos. Heatherton should have some information on both Machowitz and the owner of the *Auriga*. Then we can decide what our next move is."

Heatherton Has News

FROM THE UPPER DECK of Abalone Hideaway, Grace noticed that the sun had sunk below the horizon with only the remnants of the sun's glow along a narrow band of the waterline. It had been a long day with a puzzling discovery. It looked like Michael and Leo couldn't turn their brains off because they continued to exchange theories about Savannah's motives. Why the hell had she been in Von Donop Inlet? Grace tuned out their conversation. She wanted to be alone in the peace of Maria's garden. She wanted to process the tingling sensation she'd experienced on Lewis Harbor's decking and what had happened.

"I feel like enjoying the evening in the garden," Grace said. "I need some time alone." She opened the gate and walked to the pond and sat at the bench, leaning her head back to allow the cool air to wash over her face. She closed her eyes and listened to the crickets.

It wasn't just crickets she heard. She heard the whispers that were now becoming familiar to her. *Find her… Find her… Find her…* But the message was something Grace already knew. She'd heard Tamara's plea from the water as she stood on Lewis bridge. But how was she going to find her in that vast ocean? She guessed that her body had been taken aboard the *Auriga* and dumped somewhere at sea. In her vision, the *Auriga* was going out to sea. Perhaps the violent energy remained as she was dragged over the harbor decking to the boat. There was no indication of a body at the site where Grace had seen her buried. But voices told her to look out to the water. They had to find the *Auriga*.

She opened her eyes and heard a rustle in the bushes. Scout was watching her again, guarding her, and she felt at one with the spiritual power all around her. Grace considered going closer to the fence line. Maybe Scout would come out and give her a telepathic message.

A noise behind her.

Michael had broken the connection just as Grace had heard the wolf's approach.

"It's getting cool out here," he said, sitting beside her. "I thought you might need your hoodie." He placed the fleece-lined garment around her shoulders and left his arm there.

Grace wondered if it was so he could capture some of her warmth or if it was affection. He was wearing only a T-shirt on the upper part of his body. She hoped it was the latter but Michael's messages were usually mixed. She didn't dare ask him what it meant. Grace wanted him to leave his arm around her shoulder.

"I didn't notice the cold until you mentioned it." She paused and turned to face him. "There's more happening than my visions."

Michael's eyes moved to her brow so she knew she had to be frowning.

"I feel... and hear things from around me. And the wolf in my dreams? He's real. He's here now. In the bushes. Watching. Protecting. I've seen him several times since I got here."

A twig snapped and Michael startled.

Something was moving beyond the fence. Scout. Scout came to the fence.

Michael dropped his arm from around Grace's shoulders.

Grace put her hand on Michael's bicep to stop him from scaring the wolf back into the forest. "He won't hurt us. He's like a sort of animal friend. Don't laugh, but I feel he's guiding me. I feel forces that I can't see. It's like I'm supposed to do something to help find Tamara. It's crazy." Grace sighed with acceptance. "It felt right today when we tried to find the mystery boat."

Michael restored his arm to Grace's shoulder and pulled her closer. "You have remarkable powers, Grace. That's what helped us stop Evelyn from harming the workers at the Danton plant. I've seen what you can do. I believe in you." Michael faced her, head on. "But I also see how you struggle with it. The Universe works in extraordinary ways. I think that's why we were brought together." Michael pulled her close and kissed her forehead.

Grace's heart pounded. She wanted more, so she lay her head on his shoulder. They sat there in the stillness as the darkness surrounded them. Until now, their relationship had been professional, but here in the garden, with the soft sounds of dusk surrounding them, they enjoyed a closeness.

Maria called from the balcony. "Michael. You have a phone call."

"It's probably Heatherton." He grabbed Grace's hand to indicate that she should come with him.

❋ ❋ ❋

"Michael," came Heatherton's voice on speaker. "I have interesting news. The Auriga is registered to a man by the name of Levis Hardcastle and it is currently moored at Campbell River. It was a fishing boat, but it's been remodeled and is now registered as a pleasure craft. The Auriga's previous owner was a company out of St. Lazare, Quebec, Cartier Recreational."

"Why would a boat from Montreal be out here in B.C.?" Michael asked.

"It was shipped out there at Cartier's cost about five years ago."

"The plot thickens," said Leo in the background.

"There's more and it's very interesting," came Heatherton's voice. "You were right about Rubin Machowitz. For a short time he was assigned to a Danton special security detail, and seems to have had a close acquaintance with a certain Ms. Evelyn Loudon. I'm sending you a photo of the two of them, together, at a fundraising gala two years ago. Before Grace started working there."

The photo showed them together, arm in arm, then stepping into a limo.

"I checked the HR records," continued Heatherton, "and he was never on the payroll."

"Not surprised," said Michael. "Evelyn always had a collection of lovers. I knew some of them. But Machowitz? That one is a surprise. Could you try to confirm the nature of their relationship?"

"Will do," said Heatherton and the call ended.

"Hugo said Rubin's in Campbell River on police business," said Grace. "Do you suppose he's here for some other reason?"

"Like what?" asked Michael.

"Maybe he's wondering how Elia gets his supply. Thinks it may come to Galliano by boat and that's the reason Elia and Holly were at Lewis that night. If that's how Elia gets his cannabis, then maybe the *Auriga* is also involved in other illicit drugs."

Leo said, "This new information about Machowitz is making me nervous. He's up to more than he's telling. He was over the top hostile to Grace the other day. I don't like this. Drug dealers don't like people snooping into their business. Grace may be in danger."

"The question is," said Michael. "Why is he harassing Grace?"

"I think he blames me for Evelyn's death, but I don't understand why he thinks that. Evelyn was targeting me because she knew I could expose her microchip program."

"We know you saw the *Auriga* in your vision. But Rubin doesn't know that."

"That's true," said Leo.

"Let's find out how it ties in with everything and where and why the *Auriga* is in Campbell River and why it was at Lewis the night Elia and Holly were attacked."

"I agree, Michael," said Grace. "Do you think Rubin knows about the *Auriga* somehow? That there may be evidence on the boat that could lead the police to solve Tamara's murder? That's all we'd need. My part in this would be done. Once the killer is apprehended then the visions will go away."

Michael tucked his phone away. "We should go to Campbell River immediately. How does the ferry work?"

"There are no more ferry runs tonight," said Leo. "Let's put the SUV in the ferry line-up. There's always a long line-up for the first morning run. If we can leave on the first one, we'll be able to get home the same day."

Looking for the Auriga

A s EXPECTED, THE FERRY'S GATE OPENED at 7:00 AM sharp. They noticed that Savannah was in the priority line reserved only for the Galliano shuttle and ambulance service.

"How did she manage to get priority boarding?" asked Grace.

"Maybe she made arrangements," said Leo. "If she's picking up Elia from the hospital in Victoria, she could have gotten special permission. But she always seems to get preferential treatment, come to think of it." Leo pointed. "What's this?"

Savannah high-fived the ferryman. They shook hands and the ferryman, smiling, immediately put something into his pocket.

"That explains it," said Grace.

It would have been more comfortable in the ferry's lounge on the upper deck, but Leo, Michael and Grace decided to stay in the SUV so as not run into Savannah. They weren't in the mood for her this morning, nor did they want to let anything slip.

✳ ✳ ✳

The morning's sailing was smooth but foggy. The horn hooted often as the ferry made its way to Heriot Bay. They ate the muffins and sipped coffee from thermal cups that Maria had packed for the journey. It made

265

the confined conditions of the SUV more tolerable as they waited. It would be forty minutes before they arrived at Heriot Bay, then crossed Quadra to the ferry landing to Campbell River.

For Island residents, the trip to Campbell River was a slow ordeal, but for Grace and Michael, it could have been a quaint West-Coast experience had they all not been looking for the drug-smuggling *Auriga* and trying to find out how Rubin was involved with it.

The bump of the ferry into the coral indicated they'd docked at Campbell River. It was now 9:00 AM and they decided to head straight for the marina, ten minutes out of town. The road off the highway had several side roads and the signage was vague with only the street names, no pointers toward a marina. Leo had taken a wrong turn twice, but his third attempt on a potholed gravel road led them to their destination.

The marina wasn't what they expected because it was well hidden away from the roads and looked rather exclusive with its marina office, rental cabins and a diner overlooking the channel. It had about twenty slips for boats to moor.

"How convenient," muttered Leo. "Way out here, out of town, where it won't stand out against the luxury vessels that frequent the more-prestigious marinas along the main Campbell River highway. Smart move."

They squinted against the bright morning sun as they walked along the boardwalk to view the boats bobbing in the still waters of the pro-tected cove. There was one empty slip. It was still wet. This vessel had recently left. They looked out to where the cove entered the strait. A gray-sided vessel with a raised helm was nearly out of sight. They couldn't tell for certain, but it looked like the same vessel they'd seen in Von Donop Inlet. Perhaps the marina had information about the boat that had just left, though they supposed that boats freely moved in and out of the marina.

The marina office was still closed but the Dockside Diner patio was open for breakfast. They decided to have coffee and wait for the office to open. They hadn't come all this way to leave empty handed.

Michael smiled at Grace and took her hand as they walked up the stairway to the diner's deck that overhung the water of the harbor, offering an open view of the strait. Hand holding was not something that Michael did. It surprised Grace, but she didn't object. In fact, his touch made her stomach tingle and this was not due to the onset of a vision. It was protective. Perhaps loving. She wouldn't make a big deal of it. But it was nice.

If they had to wait, this was as perfect as it got. The tables were all empty so they chose one close to the railing where they sat, waiting for a server to offer them coffee.

"This is the life," Michael said. "I could get used to this."

Grace noticed that Leo had leaned back in the patio chair and was watching the two of them. It seemed to please him that Michael and Grace were enjoying the west coast atmosphere.

The server came and Leo and Grace ordered coffee.

Michael said he was still hungry and ordered the breakfast special. "What the heck? A guy has to keep up his energy and who knows what we might run into. What if that boat out there is the *Auriga*? What if it returns? What if we encounter an illicit drug deal going down?"

Both Leo and Grace were laughing by now.

"Oh, stop," said Grace.

✳ ✳ ✳

At 10:00 AM, a portly man in cut-off jeans and a polo shirt with a logo at the pocket, unlocked the marina office.

With his cell phone, Michael took several photos of the boats moored close to the empty slip then asked Leo to take a photo of him and Grace against the marina background.

Grace wondered what had gotten into Michael. He was acting so touristy.

✳ ✳ ✳

A chime signaled their entry into the marina office and the man who had unlocked the marina entered through a door behind the counter. The name on the man's badge was Porky.

"Mornin' folks. How can I help you this fine day?"

"We were supposed to meet someone here," Michael said. "The person told us to meet at slip number twelve but there's no boat there."

Porky scratched his head. "Seems the *Auriga* is getting lots of interest these last couple of days. I thought it was a privately owned boat. I guess Mr. Hardcastle is taking tourists out for tours. Lots of whales out there this year. I don't blame him. It helps pay the bills."

"Oh?" said Leo. "Did someone else ask about tours?"

"He didn't ask about tours directly. Just about the boat. You know it's a good size for up to eight passengers. It's good money at this time of year. Most of the boats do it, you know. This guy didn't say his name but he asked a lot of questions. Wanted to know how often it went out and when it came back. I suppose he wanted to be sure it was legit. You know not all the boats are licensed to take out passengers. There are safety regulations."

Michael then asked Porky if he'd do him a favor. "Would you mind taking a photo of the three of us outside the office? With the marina's name in the picture?"

Porky obliged and they stepped outside.

"Glad to be of help," he said. "That man—the one who asked all the questions—probably's from out of town because he didn't seem like a local. I offered to take his picture, but he got kind of huffy."

"Maybe he didn't like how his hair looked." Grace laughed as though she were making a joke.

"I don't think so," Porky said. "Dark, wavy hair. Looked very well-groomed. And that white shirt of his with the blue tie under his sports jacket would have looked real nice in the picture."

They looked at each other. Tourists didn't wear suit jackets. But Rubin Machowitz did.

"Want me to tell Mr. Hardcastle you were asking? You probably have to reserve a spot. Seems he goes out quite often."

"Well," said Leo, "as much as we'd like to take his tour, we have a name of another tour operator at another marina. Sorry, but we're only here for the day. But I will pass on the name of your marina." Leo helped himself to a couple of business cards.

✳ ✳ ✳

Leo pulled his cell phone from his pocket and checked the time. You never wasted a trip to Campbell River. Maria insisted that her pantry and freezers were always fully stocked. Tonight, she wanted to barbecue steaks for dinner. She'd get prawns from Rebecca, fresh from Joseph's traps. It would be a special meal after their stressful day of investigation.

After they'd finished shopping for the items on Maria's list, they ran, with loaded bags of groceries, back to the ferry terminal where the SUV was already parked in the line-up.

They weren't so lucky at Heriot Bay. They'd missed the 1:50 PM sailing slot. Already, the line-up at the roadside exceeded the twenty-car capacity limit for the smaller ferry to Valdez Point. The next sailing would be at 3:50 PM. It was going to be a long afternoon of waiting and already, the open patio deck at the Heriot Bay Inn was full of tourists. With the deck patio full, they would enjoy a glass, or maybe two, of wine at the inside tables. It wasn't the worst way to spend a sunny summer afternoon. Leo would text Maria of their arrival by 5:00 PM.

They ordered their wine and Leo took out his cell phone. He couldn't get a phone signal inside so he excused himself and went out to the patio.

✳ ✳ ✳

"Well. Fancy meeting you here." It was Savannah and sitting beside her was Elia. "Doing a grocery run in CR?"

Elia sat there quietly, sporting a large bandage on his head, and looking out of it.

Leo couldn't tell if Elia were stoned or sedated.

"I didn't expect to see you back so soon, Elia. You should come into the clinic to have the wound checked out tomorrow. Just to make sure it's healing okay. It's nice to see you back."

"Join us at our table." Savannah moved her chair over indicating that Leo should slip in a chair from a neighboring table.

"Grace and Michael are with me. We've already ordered beverages inside. But thank you anyway. Right now, I'm trying to catch a signal." He held up his phone. "I have to text Maria to let her know we'll be catching the 3:50."

Savannah looked taken aback. She wasn't used to people turning down her offers, especially men. She watched Leo as he held up his phone, moving strategically around the grass area looking for a signal.

Out on the lawn, Leo glanced over his shoulder at Savannah; he wanted to alert Michael and Grace that Savannah and Elia were at a patio table outside, and to stay clear of them. He found a signal and texted them and then texted Maria.

Maria responded almost immediately.

> I'll have everything ready for an early evening meal. BTW. Hugo and Rubin were here again looking for the three of you.

Interesting, Leo thought. *They're still after information.*

He went back to join Grace and Michael and let them know that Rubin was back on Galliano and asking about them again.

❇ ❇ ❇

"At least we know Machowitz wasn't watching us at the marina," Michael said. "I don't think he can be in two places at the same time." Michael placed his hand on Grace's.

"The harbormaster only gave us a description. We don't know for sure that the sports jacket guy was Rubin," Grace said. "Although …" Michael's hand on hers was warm and made her feel comfortable and safe.

"Are you sensing that it was him?" Michael asked. He searched her face, his eyes tight on hers.

"It's not like a vision. Just a feeling. But, if I were to bet on the odds…" Grace took a sip of her Chardonnay as a voice crackled in her head, *It's him… You know it's him.*

The 3:50 was right on time. They were the fourth car to load on the ferry. Savannah and Elia must have been much further down the line-up of cars. Maybe they wouldn't even make the 3:50. They felt safe to go to the upper lounge and then go outside to the open deck and enjoy the scenery. Grace knew that Michael hadn't experienced the splendor of the islands this way before, a peaceful yet exhilarating feeling only the Canadian West Coast offered.

The breeze rippled the ocean waters, an occasional whitehead breaking against the light of the late afternoon sun. The three of them leaned on the chest-high rails, the wind blowing their hair, the ferry's engine rumbling. Michael put his arm around Grace's shoulder, neither of them saying a word. They simply drank in the atmosphere and enjoyed the moment. This felt so right, the two of them here together. What it meant didn't matter, only that they were together and could rely on each other just as they had during the Danton incident. Yet, it felt like more than that. If they weren't investigating a murder and assault crime, Grace would have found it romantic.

A Change of Heart for Elia

ELIA'S HEAD HURT. He took some Tylenol and Buspirone to help with his withdrawal. He'd stay at Savannah's guest house which was just a short walk from the Sunset Restaurant. He was well aware of the reason that Savannah wanted him close by. Her clientele enjoyed what he had to sell, and Savannah certainly benefited from a full house of customers, most of them lingering and buying food and alcohol throughout the evening. She had confided in Elia that she'd taken things into her own hands, that she'd met with his supplier, picking up his weekly supply. Savannah was pushing Elia to get back to supplying weed to her customers. She said she'd give him a few days to recover from his concussion and withdrawal, but expected him back on the job. And soon. How bad could it be anyway? She would promise to look after him as long as Elia looked after her, and her business.

But Elia wanted to get clean. He'd already been offered a job as a ferry attendant as long as he maintained his sobriety. *Holly would like that,* he thought. He could understand that Holly didn't take him seriously when he was stoned but maybe he could show her his better side. It was an opportunity he wanted to try. Holly was important to him.

He cursed at his discomfort. These withdrawal symptoms were annoying, but he had to hang in there. He had no intentions of getting beaten up again because he didn't sell enough. *Bastard! Levis can kiss my ass if he thinks so. And if he comes at me again, I will be prepared.*

Elia had purchased a revolver. Also, Elia would avenge Holly. Coming after Elia was one thing. Coming after Holly was quite another. The guilt that Elia felt because Holly had taken the worst of Levis's rage, was almost overwhelming.

Elia had checked in on Holly before he left the hospital. He had slipped past her hospital room and had seen that her face was bruised and her spirit was broken. He feared that she might never recover emotionally. How could she? And why would she? The beautiful free spirit that she was lay there tarnished now. The thing about Holly was that she learned from everything that happened to her—good or bad. After all, she could look after herself and she would survive, though she'd be different now. She would certainly be more careful about whom she hung out with. Elia would certainly not be on her list of favored friends.

But that wouldn't stop him from trying to make amends. Elia knew she still wanted to be with Hugo. *Humph. A cop who has no regard for her feelings.* Elia knew how much Hugo had hurt her when he gave in to Tamara's flirtatious attention. Holly would not forgive Tamara's manipulative ways. Holly had thought Tamara was her friend, had confided in her. But then Tamara had gone after the man Holly loved. Tamara knew how to attract a man. Hugo was no exception and he'd easily fallen for her moves. She flaunted her body in front of him, making sure that Holly saw it and making sure, too, that Holly had caught them in the act. An act that had left a miscalculated consequence.

As the weeks passed, Holly was sure that Tamara was pregnant. Her otherwise flat belly on her skinny frame was rounding as the weeks went by. Tamara knew Hugo would do the honorable thing. Tamara had stolen Hugo from her deliberately just to show Holly that she could. Tamara had always been jealous of Holly's beauty. Elia had never heard Holly speak so disrespectfully to another person. They had a vicious verbal exchange right on the Sunset patio, one that everyone heard. In a rage, Holly had threatened to kill her. That's when Holly started toking up. But that was also when Hugo started to realize that he'd been manipulated and his attention started to wander back to Holly. That started another round of anger. Tamara was furious and started flirting with other men to make Hugo jealous. She even came on to drunken Guy, the town's unofficial and flirtatious mayor. Hugo didn't like that and tried to rescue her from his lewd attempts. Guy, although personable and gregarious, had become verbally abusive to her when he realized Tamara's flirtations weren't for him. It was all for show—for Hugo. Elia knew that Guy thought of himself as a catch for any woman. The drunker he was, the more he thought that way. It got Guy into trouble often as women tried to get away from him when he went too far. Hugo would intervene. Hugo sometimes drove him home, back to Annie on those occasions, leaving his vintage car at the Lewis Community Center which he would pick up the next day.

The prescribed drugs to ease Elia's withdrawal didn't offer the euphoric feeling cannabis did. They rendered Elia sleepy and lethargic. It was good not to crave the cannabis that nagged him in the background. He spent the rest of the day reclining on Savannah's couch, not quite sure how he felt. But even in the stupor of it, he thought constantly of Holly and wished she were back on Galliano. He hoped that she wasn't going through the same thing he was. Withdrawal was a bitch. He felt awful that he was the reason for her distress. If she hadn't been with him that night, she wouldn't have been attacked. Raped. He teared up thinking of it.

✳ ✳ ✳

Savannah brought Elia food: soup and a sandwich. She figured he wouldn't feel hungry because of the drugs he was on and because of the withdrawal he'd told her was happening. She assessed that he was pretty much out of it either way. She didn't know how she felt about that. Would he make as many sales if he wasn't obviously high? He was always happy, laughing, and so cordial to the customers. She feared that if he were straight, his personality would be less accommodating about the habit. Savannah needed happy customers who ate and drank and got high for the entire night.

Elia was asleep when she entered. She put the food on the table, not waking him. The sooner he could get back to work the better. She left quietly. There would be no sales tonight, but she could tell the customers that Elia would be back in a day or two.

A Growl from the Salal

THE ISLAND'S ENERGY SHIFTED from that of a deep secret crime, hidden in the past, to an intensified agitation as Grace's visions threatened to reveal the killer. Scout could feel the transferal. Grace had started it and now Grace, Michael and Leo were looking for evidence that would expose the man who had taken a life and seriously injured others. The killer was near but not yet directly aware that there was a power beyond his control that would decide his fate. This man thought he was untouchable, but hubris has its weakness. It made him careless. His confidence would be broken and then the energy of his carefully kept secret would leak and eventually be out in the open.

Scout heard the ancestor's message clear and strong. Levis's actions threatened danger and Grace was right in the line of his intentions. As soon as he became aware of what she and her friends were doing, he would try to kill them. Levis had no intention of spending his remaining days in detention; his drug-running business was too lucrative.

Scout kept watch in the salal and growled as the winds of retribution gathered. He could see Grace, her friend Michael, and her father as they enjoyed the closeness of a family meal. There was much love between them, especially with Michael, who would not reveal his true intimate feeling for Grace. Soon, they would all face the wrath of a killer. The

Ancestors and Scout had vowed to protect them, but the man's force of evil was strong.

Grace's gift of sight would bring her up against danger. She needed to remain focused and strong. Goodness and justice had to prevail, but she would need help.

Levis Hardcastle

L EVIS WAS AT THE HELM of the Auriga. Sailing put him at ease. This West Coast place was like heaven, the mountains, the ocean, the vastness of the sky and the clouds that billowed. He breathed in the air. He was part of a network, one that was lucrative, and without the encumbrances of bosses and goals and targets set by management. Resentment still festered in his mind. Ridiculous, he thought. All management has illicit affairs with each other's wives. What he had done was no different from the rest. But she had complained and it got him fired. Yet, he had gotten a good deal out of it: a hefty severance package, anonymity, and the Auriga. This separation from society was not so bad. Here, he could do what he wanted and no one would judge or disparage his actions. Anyway, Levis Hardcastle was more a brand than an identity. Not even Annie knew. Poor bitch that she was—a devoted wife who would do whatever he said or wanted! Levis snickered at the thought of the power he had over her. She loved him. How she deceived herself.

Today was his weekly drop-off at Heriot Bay, his contact another stonehead of a runaway. He'd deliver his illicit drugs and then he'd sail back to Von Donop Inlet where he'd drop anchor in an obscure cove, leaving the boat there and returning home to a regular life as a regular island resident, a devoted husband, and the mayor of Galliano—

however unofficial that title was. He loved his life here among the secluded West Coast Islands. Here, he was someone important. In a few days, he'd pull anchor to go back to Campbell River Marina, right after his midnight run to Lewis Harbor. Elia would need another supply by then. He'd be healed and sufficiently motivated to up his quotient. Or else. As for the girl? Well. She was an added bonus and a bit of fun. Good thing she was stoned that night. She'd never recognize him. *No worries there.* He laughed out loud as the thought made him go hard. No one knew who Levis Hardcastle really was. It was the perfect situation.

Among his other weapons—his handgun and rifle—Levis kept an automatic weapon on the boat. There were other dealers who vied for his territory. He had been challenged before, but with the power of an AR-15 aimed at their boat, they quickly withdrew, not to bother him again. This territory was his. He would take no shit or intrusion from others. Levis ruled this territory!

It was also good to let his pushers know that if they stepped out of line, or dared give out information about the *Auriga*, or Levis, that their days were numbered. Levis had no qualms about it. He would kill them, bring them on board, and after a pleasant sail out somewhere in the Strait of Georgia, he'd turn them into fish food just as he had with that bitch, Tamara. She'd never be found; she would be just another missing aboriginal girl. He'd kept the glass beads with the cross at the center that she always wore, as a token. He hung it from a nail in the wall of the helm directly overhanging the steering wheel. It reminded him of his power.

Levis always took extra efforts to be discreet at Lewis Harbor. Although, Levis hated to admit, his midnight runs to that place always gave him the creeps. Between the phosphorescence and the dancing fireflies at the spot where he had first buried her on the beach, the place was spooky as hell. It was the spot where she'd come back from the dead. *Was I high or did I really hear voices coming from that starlit sky and then from below in the sands that lit up like sparks of fire that came from Hell?* He growled. God and Satan could fight with each other all they wanted. He, Levis Hardcastle, owned this land.

Levis shivered as he remembered a hand coming out of the sand. *How stupid could I be? I didn't hit her hard enough.* The blow would have killed anyone else, but she had a feistiness about her that kept her fighting back. He liked that she was tough and fought back. But it didn't matter. He'd finally put an end to her, or so he thought. It almost gave him a heart attack when her hand snaked up through the sand. This bitch just wouldn't give up—wouldn't die. As he unearthed her writhing body, she struggled with the strength of a supernatural monster. She clawed at his face, a scar he still carried, one that his friend Leo stitched up while he told the good doctor he'd injured himself while working on his car. *She fought like a banshee.* He'd had one hell of a struggle to restrain her with the ropes. *How could such a skinny bitch have so much strength?* He took her tied-up body onto the *Auriga* and out to the open waters of the Strait and then dumped her overboard. "Such a bitch. Such a bitch. But that's women for you."

Hugo's Suspicion

HUGO LOOKED AT HIS WATCH. The 3:50 ferry would have docked and Grace, Michael and Leo would be back at Abalone Hideaway. Maria had received a text from Leo and had told Hugo, if he still had questions, to come back.

Hugo liked Maria, such a gracious lady. He felt bad that more questions needed to be asked. But it wasn't Hugo who had the questions. Rubin seemed obsessed with drilling Grace about something that had happened in Toronto. What did that have to do with the assault case? Danton was in Ontario. Here on Galliano, neither Hugo—nor Rubin, for that matter—had any jurisdiction over a case in another province. Rubin had mentioned the Danton Case so just for his own information, Hugo made inquiries and learned that both Grace and Michael had witnessed a fatal accident at the Danton plant. The CEO, Evelyn Loudon, had fallen from a catwalk high above the factory floor while Grace and Michael were on site doing project work. The courts ruled it an unfortunate accident after the autopsy showed Evelyn was intoxicated, probably enough to make her careless. The case was closed, so why was Rubin badgering Grace? His persistence bothered Hugo. It was like an obsession to Rubin.

Hugo didn't want to feed into whatever Rubin was doing or trying to find out. Yet he had told Maria they would be back later, after the Walkers had finished the special evening meal Maria was preparing. He looked at the time again. It was nearly 7:00 PM. They would likely have finished.

Right now, Rubin was getting coffee from the Sunset while probably asking Savannah questions about Elia. Rubin was a cop through and through. He couldn't make conversation per se. He only knew how to ask questions. He seemed suspicious of everything.

Hugo drew in a deep breath and shook his head as he exhaled. *What an awful way to go through life.*

Rubin came in with two large coffees in takeout cups. "Thought you could use a caffeine fix." He handed one to Hugo. "We should go back to the Walker residence. I have more questions. There's something they aren't being upfront about. Do you feel it, too?"

"No," Hugo said. "I think you're way off the mark. They had nothing to do with the assault."

"But they went back to the scene where Elia and Holly were attacked. Why would they do that?"

What the hell? "Rubin." Hugo let out a loud sigh. "Leo has a boat that he moors at Lewis Harbor. If I had a boat at the scene of a crime, I'd want to check it out, too. In case it was vandalized, or damaged in the skirmish. That makes perfect sense."

"They found something. I know it. I can always tell when a person holds back." His voice dropped. "Besides, there's something eerie out there at the Walker property."

"It's the ocean wind as it whips through the trees. My Island Nation Band say it's the voices of our ancestors." Hugo laughed at Rubin. "If you're scared, I could go alone."

"You're Island Nation Band?" He stared at Hugo.

"One hundred percent, born and raised. You got a problem with that?"

"No, but that explains why the weirdness doesn't bother you."

"Let's go. I'll protect you if we run into the boogeyman."

Strange Discovery

R EBECCA SAT AT THE OUTDOOR KITCHEN enjoying her special blend iced tea. She turned to see who was coming up the driveway. It was Grace, right on time, to pick up Maria's weekly order of eggs. She liked it when Grace came. She liked Grace's mysterious side. She had felt it from the first time they met at Lewis Beach. Such a strange day that was. There was a brief connection—seconds—where their minds joined, like Grace had reached into Rebecca's mind to read her thoughts. Then the appearance of a wolf, Rebecca's attempt at shooting what she assumed was a dangerous animal, and Grace's defending it, saving its life. No ordinary person does that. There was a quality about Grace that showed she took in not only her surroundings, but the emotions of people she came in contact with. Grace most certainly had a special gift and such a person was privy to visions. She wanted to talk to Grace about it, but was concerned that such talk would drive her away.

"Maria has some baking for you." Grace said as she placed a pan of butter cinnamon cake on the table in front of Rebecca.

"Your mother is so kind."

"It's a thank you for the fish and prawns. And as you probably know, Maria loves to bake."

Their laugh was interrupted by a breathless Joseph who had come to the outdoor room with rifle in hand. Frowning and breathing hard, he laid it against the wall.

"Joseph! Has something happened?"

"I was hunting for duck at Hathayim when I saw something strange." He sat down with the women. "You know that the inlet is not well-traveled by boats, especially the unknown coves."

"We took the *Serenity* into the inlet the day before Elia and Holly were attacked," Grace offered. "We saw two boats there. One belonged to Savannah, but Leo didn't know the other boat." She frowned. "You're saying that boats don't usually go there?"

"That inlet is very shallow in places. It's not for inexperienced sailors." Joseph had caught his breath. "But this boat was anchored in one of the coves. You wouldn't see it from open water. But I was hunting. And there it was. I called out but no one was on board. Then I saw a rubber dinghy tied to a tree."

"Did you see anyone?" asked Rebecca.

"No. And you don't pull into the coves without a special reason. I would guess it's the drug dealer who supplies Elia with his cannabis."

"Did you see a name on the vessel?" Grace asked, her voice quivering as she looked off into the trees.

She's trying not to look obvious, thought Rebecca. *And not doing a very good job of it. She knows something.*

"The name started with an A."

Rebecca felt Grace react. "Do you think Leo might know of this boat, Grace?"

"I'll ask him."

She knows.

"Why would anyone go ashore there?" Grace said. "Isn't that a forested area? Hiking maybe. Yes?"

"I don't think so," said Joseph. "Galliano has very specific trails that are much easier to navigate. Whoever it is doesn't want to be seen or found."

"We need to let Hugo know about this." Rebecca's mind was reeling. "I'll get your mom's eggs. Iced tea? Would you like some of my special iced tea?"

Rebecca wasn't surprised that Grace declined.

As Grace reached her car, bobbling the egg cartons as she opened its door, Rebecca said to Joseph, "She knows something. She knows something."

✳ ✳ ✳

Back at Abalone Hideaway, Grace updated everyone on the conversation and the location of the Auriga. They wished they'd asked for more information at the marina. Porky had said that the Auriga was in and out of its moorings all the time. And they believed that they had seen it leave the marina that morning. Did that mean it would come into Lewis during the night? Surely Elia was in no condition to get his regular supply so soon. But then, there was no way of knowing how long it would hide out in Von Donop's secret cove. If only they could get on board; see what clues they might find. But it would be a dangerous bit of sleuthing, not to mention, most likely illegal.

"Rebecca and Joseph suspect that something isn't right about that boat," Grace told them. "And, I get this really weird feeling when I'm around Rebecca that she connects with me. I wonder what she'd say if I told her about the vision. Not about Tamara. The vision of the assault on Holly. What do you guys think?"

"I think it's a bad idea," Michael said. "They'll assume you're having some kind of psychotic event. Or worse still, it will implicate you in the crime. You'd have to explain how you know this."

"But Joseph has seen the boat and says no one is on it. Elia has barely recovered so he isn't going to meet with the dealer yet. The timing might be perfect. I really think we'll find answers on the boat." Grace was determined. "And the only way we can do that is with Joseph's help. He says the boat is well-hidden in a cove off the main inlet. He's the only one who knows how to find it."

Michael's cell rang. It was Heatherton with more information about Rubin. He put it on speaker for all to hear.

"Guess who owned the *Auriga* before Levis Hardcastle did?" Heatherton paused for dramatic effect. "It was purchased by a snow-mobile company about five years ago. Levis bought it for a steal from a security officer at Danton—none other than Rubin Machowitz, who had owned it for only a short time."

Michael's jaw actually dropped. "Rubin is involved in drug sales?"

"Not necessarily. I said he owned it and sold it. It was registered as a Danton asset for a while. Evelyn would have had to approve any ownership change. If it was bought as a perk for company executives, I certainly didn't know anything about it. Evelyn may have used it to entertain her boyfriends. Strange that a Danton company asset had Rubin Machowitz's name as owner."

Maria cut in. "So why was Rubin at the marina asking about it?"

"Probably because he's investigating Elia's attack and somehow found out about a boat that occasionally shows up here on Galliano. One that he once owned! He wouldn't want anyone to know that he once owned it." Michael snorted a "gotcha."

"But from whom would Rubin learn that?" asked Leo. "No one is aware of the *Auriga* except for us."

As a police officer, it might be easy for Rubin to find out about a boat, thought Grace. Hugo knew they went to Lewis and would spend the night there. Elia probably told Hugo that Holly and he had stayed on a friend's boat. Maybe he'd even told him the name of it. Hugo may have mentioned that to Rubin and that's why Rubin was in Campbell River? Not on "police business," but to find the boat and who owned it now.

They had to hurry to stop Joseph from reporting it to Hugo. Grace wanted to check out the *Auriga* in the secret cove where Joseph had spotted it, and before the police found it. Her powers drew her toward it. That vessel held information that was linked to her visions. Perhaps there was enough information to help them find the killer. Even if it held no physical proof, the residual energy of struggle and terror would still be there.

Michael and Leo agreed that Grace was probably right, that they needed to get on board the *Auriga* even it meant causing Grace to have another terrifying vision.

✳ ✳ ✳

As the four visitors approached Rebecca and Joseph on the summer porch, a wind stirred the trees with a rhythm that sounded like frenzied chanting. It was a sign, a sign she'd learned about from her mother. The white man's residential school had not succeeded in erasing the ways of Rebecca's people from her spirit. When she returned from their school, her mother, a healer, had reacquainted Rebecca with Island Nation Band spiritual ways. Rebecca knew that the Ancestors watched and guided those who sought the truth. Today, the truth was being brought to them by an outsider: Grace. Grace's gift was subtle because she didn't want others to know, but the Ancestors knew, and they sang of her strength through the voices of Nature.

As Joseph walked out to greet them, pointing to the porch, Rebecca arranged the chairs in a circle. She called out as Grace, Leo, and a man she did not know approached. "The Ancestors are here with us, Grace. Do you hear their voices in the leaves? Do you hear them, Grace?"

✳ ✳ ✳

Grace heard the leaves but had yet to understand what the signs meant. Did it have to do with what Joseph had discovered in the secret cove at Von Donop Inlet? Were the ancestral forces trying to guide her? Were they bringing allies to help her solve the mystery of the murder on the night beach?

"I don't know what the feeling is," Grace said. "Only how to describe it." She felt both the agitation of a vision pulling her and the need to keep it hushed. Somehow, she knew she could tell Rebecca. "I have something I need to tell you but you have to be open-minded. It will sound strange. You might even think I'm crazy."

Rebecca's kind smile told Grace she need not worry.

"I have an ability to see things that have happened. And I know something about what happened to Elia and Holly."

"You are a seer. I could feel your power the first time we met on Lewis Beach." Rebecca shrugged her shoulders at Leo. "Sorry. I didn't see her there when I tried to scare off the wolf."

Leo's nod was one of forgiveness.

To Grace she said, "That was a spirit wolf, wasn't it? I didn't know at first, but when I put the signs together…"

"After Elia and Holly were attacked, we went to Lewis Harbor to see if I could pick up any violent energy that would have been left behind. In my vision, there was a boat at the very end of the dock. I believe it's the boat Joseph saw at the inlet. It had a name on the bow. I saw the name as it pulled away."

"And you want me to take you guys there," said Joseph. "It's a very long hike through rough trails."

"Could we access the cove by boat?" Leo asked. "We could take my *Serenity*."

Joseph ran his hand through his hair as he turned to look at the trees at the back of the property. As he did, the wind grew stronger. "The cove is well hidden by the surrounding forest, but…" He turned back to Rebecca.

She nodded, yes.

"I don't know if I could find the way in from the water. But we should try. Tomorrow. Not enough daylight left today. The Inlet is not easy to navigate in the first place. Too many shallow areas for a boat to run aground on. It would be best to go in the morning."

"But if it's running drugs," said Michael, glancing at the others, "which we think it is, what if it makes a delivery tonight at Lewis and is gone by tomorrow?"

Grace could feel the trees' frenzied voices urging her to act. It unnerved her. She wanted to shut out the urgency, but her inner knowledge was taking over. Was it just her or did the others notice the agitation around them: a storm that wasn't due to weather? *Yes,* she thought, *we can wait until morning. Or, can we?* The Ancestors were guiding her, trying to give her a message. "Maybe we should stay on the *Serenity* tonight… in case?" She looked at her father.

Leo shook his head, no. "It would be dangerous if the *Auriga* came back. The man has a gun. You saw that in your vision."

Grace couldn't deny the truth of what she had seen.

"Well, we have rifles, too," said Rebecca. "Perhaps we should talk to Hugo. He's Island Nation Band. He'll stand with us."

"No," said Michael. "He'd bring that detective, Machowitz. The man who once owned the *Auriga*."

Joseph's mouth dropped open. "Not a good idea then."

"There has to be evidence on the boat," said Grace. "Why else would I see it in the vision? We have to try. It may be our only opportunity. Rubin may or may not have anything to do with what happened, but we can't take that chance. Don't tell Hugo."

"Leo," said Michael. "I think Grace's idea is a good one. How about we stay on the *Serenity* tonight and leave early in the morning? If the *Auriga* does show up, we can identify the guy and determine who kill—" Michael stopped short. "Uh. Find out who hurt Elia and Holly."

"If Rebecca and I wait in our car," said Joseph, "take turns sleeping, we'd be at a good vantage point. The parking lot is on high ground, well above the bridge. The bay will be right in front of us. From there we can see the approach of a boat for some distance. It'll give us time to get out of range."

Joseph grabbed his hunting rifle, cradling it in his arms. He was ready.

The decision was made. They would meet at Lewis Harbor at dusk.

Moonlight and Mystery

W HILE MICHAEL AND HER PARENTS stowed the supplies on the Serenity, and under the watchful eyes of Rebecca and Joseph at the high ground, Grace walked along the beach. Grace needed her sensory power more than ever today. She needed to soak in the energy that would warn her of what they might encounter. Also, she needed distance from the others to gather as much of the violent residual energy into her being, so when she encountered it again, it would welcome her intrusion and reveal what was hidden from the previous vision.

Grace was gathering whatever was lurking in this setting. She was a mixture of emotions. There was no one on the beach, but somehow, the area seemed occupied. She looked around again just to reassure herself. No one. She was sure she was alone but she sensed them—a presence—not one, but many. Uneasiness stole up her spine. She shivered and goosebumps rippled down her back. They washed over the familiar itch that accompanied a near vision. Was there a cold wind blowing off the bay? Or was that the chill of the energy that wanted to connect with her, something beyond an earthly link? Grace tried to push the message away. It had to be a cold breeze. At least that's what she tried to convince herself it was. Perhaps she should have worn a hoodie. Could she no longer tell the difference between the tingle that signaled a vision and the cold? She looked over at the *Serenity* and was relieved to know that she was in the sight of Michael and her parents. They watched. Just in case. Rebecca and Joseph were still watching, too. She could feel it.

The wind blew sharp across the water, making her clutch her arms around her. Tonight, she was on guard. Dusk was a magical time, the time when the sun had just slipped below the horizon, sending its last glow across the water while the moon was rising. The beach had a transcendent feel and a sound like music in the juxtaposition of it, perhaps the voices of some spiritual force. They seemed always present now. She had to trust it and give in. She had already accepted the mission to find Tamara's killer. She tried hard not to fear where it was leading her but she had no choice, did she? It was part of who she was.

"Grace," Michael called out. "It's getting too dark for you to be wandering around out there. Come on board. Your dad has the heater warming the cabin. Real cozy in here." He waved his arm at the boat's cabin.

She knew she should heed Michael's advice, but she wanted to soak up the last of the magic that was playing with her fretful mind. She spread out her arms and turned in a circle, breathing in the spiritual presences, confident that tomorrow's venture would give them the evidence they needed to solve the awful crimes that had been committed here. That's all she needed to do. Pass on the responsibility. She looked over to the parking lot where Joseph leaned against the car as he smoked a cigarette. How would she ever be able to let them know they were helping Grace find their daughter's killer?

The Ancestors

T HE ANCESTORS WATCHED from the Sunset Land. They knew Grace's fear. They also knew her strength. They admired her gift, her vision, and the pureness of her character. They had sent the man to her, Michael, the one who loved her but wouldn't admit his love to her—or even to himself. Strange, these humans, how they denied who they were and what they could do. If only the evil ones had similar misgivings.

They would guide her, protect her as best they could, but the evil one was unpredictable. They would have to depend on Scout. Scout would have to distract the evil one even it meant his life. The evil one had a gun and Scout was not immune to bullets. But Scout was smart, his instincts sharp. His greatest calling was to protect Grace. The Ancestors had powers and endowed him with special senses to keep her safe, senses that connected animal to human, the purest form of communication. Even now, Scout knew where she would face danger and he was already on his way to the place where the killer had hidden his boat.

Von Donop Inlet

T HE MORNING SUN had a different song. Like an alarm, it woke
Grace before the others. She was sore and stiff from the cramped quar-
ters. She'd had a restless night of unpleasant dreams. She turned on
the mattress that made a bed in a raised area of the bow. She was pinned
against the starboard wall of the Serenity. A breathy snore came from
Michael who lay beside her. She smiled. It comforted her knowing he
was so near. Her parents lay quietly in the bunk on the opposite side.
Sleeping with your boyfriend, though she couldn't call him that because
their relationship wasn't exactly defined, with your parents in a bed just
feet away, was weird, very weird.

She smiled, knowing that if she climbed over Michael, she'd probably wake him. She looked at the Fitbit on her arm. It was almost 6:30.
She rolled over close to him. He was warm and smelled of the herbal
body lotion Maria had left in the bathroom for guests. Grace breathed in
his essence then put her right leg over his body, supporting her weight
with her right arm on his left side. As if in automatic response, eyes still
closed, still seeming to be asleep, his arm reached around her waist and
he murmured something incomprehensible. She paused, looking down
on him. For a few seconds, she was on top of him and imagined being
intimate with him. It made her breath quicken. She heard Maria move

in the bed across from theirs, so she swung her left leg off the bed and found the floor, leaving Michael asleep with empty arms, and still murmuring incomprehensibles. Grace wanted to kiss him but instead, she pulled the blanket up over his shoulders.

"Good morning, darling," said Maria, climbing over Leo. "I'll make coffee. Toast and muffins?"

Maria made her way to the tiny kitchen area where she rattled the coffee pot and lifted the toaster from the small overhead cupboard to an equally small shelf at the side of the two-element burner. They managed to exchange hugs in the cramped cabin space.

Grace opened the hatch and climbed the two steps onto the aft deck. The *Serenity* swayed with the waves. The cool air was scented with the crisp brininess of early morning and the water mirrored the glare of the sun rising against the eastern skyline, silhouetting trees and mountains. Grace shielded her eyes as she scanned Lewis Harbor. *Did we miss a stealthy midnight visit from the* Auriga? Her intuition told her no. All was well. She looked over to the area where Rebecca and Joseph had parked their car. Rebecca was on the bridge leaning on the wooden rail, watching the sunrise. She waved to Grace as Grace jumped from the *Serenity* to the dock. Grace climbed the gangplank and then the steps to the bridge to greet Rebecca.

As Grace got closer, she spotted a tent a short distance from the car on the soft grassy area. Grace tipped her head toward the structure.

"It was better than trying to sleep in the cramped car seats. We were quite comfortable on the air mattresses and sleeping bags."

From the aft deck, Maria called to them. "Come join us for breakfast."

The sound of a heavy-duty zipper announced the presence of Joseph, looking tousled, as he crept out of the tent. "Did someone say breakfast?"

"The way to a man's heart?" Rebecca waved him over. "Maria has made breakfast."

Joseph disappeared into the trees.

By the time Rebecca and Grace had returned to the *Serenity*, Leo and Michael were awake. They, too, seemed sleepy and crumpled. What a sight everyone was.

With the toaster popping out slice after slice, the butter dish and the jar of Maria's blackberry jam were soon empty. The basket of muffins was next to go. Maria made a second pot of coffee. With stomachs full and caffeine jolting them to life, they were ready to head out after a quick trip to the water's edge to wash up.

Leo climbed to the helm, started the engine, and within minutes they had sailed out of the bay into the Strait. As they headed north, the water got choppier in the morning wind.

Grace sat on the vinyl-covered benches in the aft deck, soaking in the West Coast scenery, the wind playing with her hair, the fishy aroma of the ocean dancing in her nostrils. There was nothing as soothing as the sway of a boat on the open water. Joseph and Leo were at the helm. Maria and Rebecca clanked dishes in the cabin below. Grace heard the powerful swoosh of water from the boat's toilet and seconds later, Michael emerged from the lower cabin still fastening the belt to his jeans. He leaned on the port side rail looking like he might hurl his breakfast. Grace laughed. She usually felt the nausea of the waves but today she was fine. Michael was not so lucky.

"I have Gravol if you need it."

"How long before we reach the inlet?"

Maria emerged from the cabin with a glass of water and a tiny pill. Sometimes Grace wondered if Maria had sensory powers as well.

"Take this," said Maria. "You'll feel better long before we reach Von Donop."

Michael popped the pill and took a long slug of the water. He sunk down onto the padded bench and put his head on his knees.

Rebecca emerged from the cabin with her mug of coffee and sat beside Grace. "Beautiful, isn't it? There's nothing like being on the water. We should enjoy the peace. I have an uncomfortable feeling about what we'll find when we get there."

Rebecca's uneasiness radiated toward Grace. Grace's shoulders tensed. Would they find something that would prove that Tamara had been on board the *Auriga*? She hoped yes. And no.

✳ ✳ ✳

Leo pulled into Von Donop Inlet, the cliffs on either side screeching with seabirds, the Galliano petroglyphs visible high above on the stone face, making everyone wonder how they had ever been placed there. Was the water level higher centuries ago? So many mysteries. Mysteries? They were headed toward a mystery of their own.

With darting eyes, Leo and Joseph watched the trees on either side of the inlet. Since Joseph didn't know the exact location of the cove, they had to assess the approximate distance Joseph had traveled in from the land side. Hoping for the best was still guessing.

The *Serenity* slowed to a near stop, then maneuvered slowly into a grove of trees. With barely enough water on each side, branches were so close, they had to duck when the leaves brushed the sides of the *Serenity*. Grace wondered if they might run aground as Joseph had said was possible here. At one point, all she could see was trees. Then without warning, the trees opened up and there it was: the *Auriga*. She was anchored several hundred yards ahead in the center of the small cove, a cove so small, even a poor swimmer could swim ashore if they'd wanted to.

Joseph pointed to a pile of deadwood where, barely visible, lay a gray rubber dingy tied to a rotting downed tree. Whoever had exited the *Auriga* had rowed to shore and walked back into the bush to somewhere unknown, leaving the *Auriga* behind where they believed it to be concealed.

"Brace yourself," Leo said. "I'm going to try to pull aside the vessel so we can board it."

Grace held her breath.

Joseph came down from the helm to the aft deck, grabbed the boat hook and line, securing the rope to the *Auriga*'s port-side cleat. Leo cut the engine and Joseph pulled the boats together.

Not realizing that Michael wouldn't be of much help because of the rocking boat that was already bringing on another bout of motion sickness, Joseph called out. "Hold the rope taunt, Michael."

The *Serenity* swayed and rocked as they moved around the stern. Michael wobbled as he stood to follow Joseph's direction.

But Leo noticed his distress and took the rope. "You should probably stay seated."

Relieved, Michael sat.

The boats came together. and Joseph jumped onto the *Auriga*.

Grace knew that she, too, had to board the vessel, that the negative energy would bombard her the moment her foot touched the deck. She reached for Joseph's hand to steady herself and the *Serenity* swayed from her weight on the gunwale where she paused before hopping over the side.

Her feet thudded against the *Auriga*'s deck. The tingling was immediate and intense. Grace crouched, the truth grabbing and pulling at her. She knew what was coming. The message that lingered there was swift and urgent. It seized her hard, heaving her back in time to Tamara's final moments.

Darkness wrapped itself around her as the vision rushed in. First, she heard voices. The blackness lifted as she entered the mirage. A specter. Invisible. A body struggled on the floor of the deck, hands tied behind its back—behind *her* back. It was female. Blood from the woman's head splattered onto the deck.

A bulky figure stood over the woman. Grace both heard and felt the thud as the man kicked the woman's torso. The man's shirt was covered with dark red splotches.

The woman went limp, motionless.

The man growled. "Bitch. Bitch. I'll teach you some respect."

He tied a weight to her legs. Then, as though she were a piece of unwanted cargo, he picked her up and pitched her overboard, the splash swooshing onto the deck.

Grace could feel the woman's body sink into the cold sea with the bubbles bursting against her skin as Tamara displaced the water. Grace looked to the blackness of the water and saw the fireflies rise above the spot where Tamara's body had been. They flitted and hovered for a few seconds, scurrying in circles as though pleading for help before they followed her into the darkness.

Grace looked away from the water and there on the deck lay a necklace. It must have detached itself from Tamara's neck as the dark figure had flung her overboard. The colorful beads with a cross at their center had caught a ray of light. The necklace twinkled on the wet surface. Grace knew the necklace. It was the same one that had glinted in the moonlight vision on Lewis Beach. It was Tamara's. A bulky hand reached down and picked it up, held it out in front of himself for a moment, examining the cross and its meaning. The form chortled, turned toward the steering cabin and disappeared.

The vision continued to pull Grace along. The man, unaware of the visionary intruder, hung the necklace on a nail above the steering wheel, leaned back admiring his prize before his face contorted into a devilish sneer. He snorted and spat at it, the sputum flying and making a splat as it hit the wall.

The spell was broken and the vision faded back into the darkness.

Struggling to breathe, Grace felt herself fall onto the deck.

Leo handed the rope holding the boats together to Rebecca and jumped to the *Auriga*. Michael followed.

"Grace, are you OK?"

She was. It was over. She merely had to recover from it now.

Leo lifted her into his arms as Michael knelt beside them.

"I'm fine," she said. "I'm fine."

Leo and Michael helped her up to her feet.

She glanced over at Joseph who looked on, bewildered, a necklace dangling from his hand, his lower lip quivering, and his eyes black and wild.

A scream came from the *Serenity*. Rebecca had recognized the piece he held. Their eyes met in horror.

"We have to leave it here," Grace told Joseph. "Or he'll know someone was here."

Joseph stared at it. It was part of his daughter, all he had left of her.

Grace said it again, her voice stern. "We have to leave it here."

Joseph nodded agreement as he again caught Rebecca's gaze, her eyes fixed on what Joseph held. Her knuckles were white as she strangled the rope that was keeping the two boats side by side.

Michael steadied Grace as they climbed over the rails onto the *Serenity*. Maria was there to take hold of her daughter, seating her to prevent another fall.

Joseph and Leo remained on the *Auriga* for several more minutes. Leo had several plastic bags with swabs. He took samples from the floor and the steering wheel; and he took tweezers to lift something from the rope. He placed each of these carefully into separate, clear plastic bags. After a final scan around the craft, they jumped back to the *Serenity*.

Joseph embraced Rebecca. They were both sobbing, Rebecca shaking, too. They knew what the necklace meant. Tamara had been on the *Auriga*. She'd been there with a man they suspected was a brutal criminal.

"One thing's certain," said Leo. "A crime has been committed on the *Auriga*. But how can we let the authorities know? What we just did is illegal. We could all end up in prison and the murderer go free because of the way the evidence was found."

"Hugo needs to know what we found here today," Joseph said. "Tamara and Hugo… had a relationship." Joseph's voice was strained as if the words were stuck in his throat.

Leo nodded his head. "Very well. I agree." He raised his eyebrows at Grace.

Grace shrugged. She wasn't so sure about that. "But… How would we do that? We'd have to say that we came across an abandoned boat. That we called out. There was no answer so we boarded only to check if everyone was all right." She glanced at the others, hoping they would agree with her plan. "You can say you found the necklace, Joseph, but we left it because…" Grace didn't want to say that it proved Tamara had been aboard. To say more would be cruel. Rebecca and Joseph were already in grief.

"The forensic samples…" Michael met the eyes of everyone before continuing. "Without exposing Grace's extrasensory ability, we don't have any proof that they mean anything. Hugo and Rubin will want to know *why* we gathered them. Why Leo just happened to have Q-tips and plastic baggies in his pocket. No." He shook his head. "They can't know about Grace's vision."

"I agree," said Maria, slipping her arm over Grace's shoulders.

"At least," said Michael, "not until we can verify that any evidence we have leads to Tamara's disappearance. Right? How about I send the samples to Heatherton for forensic analysis? Rebecca, do you have anything belonging to your daughter that would help?"

Grace could tell that Rebecca was struggling to comprehend his request. Her breath came hard. She looked at Joseph for support. After a pause of several moments, she nodded. "Her hairbrush and toothbrush." Rebecca's questioning eyes searched Maria's and Leo's for support. "And Tamara's white shirt. The one with the blood on the sleeve. Her hand got impaled by a fishhook that time. You remember, don't you, Leo? You had to remove it."

"That's exactly what we need," said Michael. "That will help us."

"Anything to help." Rebecca wiped her eyes. "Anything to help find out what happened to Tamara."

Scout

S COUT WAS WATCHING from the shoreline, his fur blending into the landscape, making him invisible. He sniffed the air and caught the stench. Scout could smell the killer's scent, the malicious odor of evil. He stepped further back into the underbrush and went still as the ground beneath his paws.

Scout watched the man creeping toward a vantage point where he could better see the intruders on his boat. The watcher approached. He was near, very near the edge of the cove. In the stillness, he could hear everything they were saying.

The putrid essence of the killer's pheromones was unmistakable. Scout knew he presented a terrible danger to Grace, maybe to all those who were trying to help her. The man had already proven that he would harm or kill anyone who got in his way.

Now, more than ever, Grace needed Scout's protection.

Scout sensed the Ancestors' presence, too. They couldn't warn her directly, but they could call on the natural forces to bring the right people together to help keep her safe.

And Scout's telepathy had alerted his pack. If the watching man came near her, they would try to distract him. Hopefully, that would be enough.

Rubin, Like a Chameleon

RUBIN WASN'T EXACTLY PANICKING yet. He was worried. How and why had the Auriga shown up in Campbell River? It was like some external force was trying to implicate him in the current missing person case. Had he not been careful enough? The Danton case had been an undercover job. Someone had reported that people were acting strange, drugged perhaps, while working. Rubin's romantic involvement with Evelyn, staged as it was, and necessary to the case, could be construed as a conflict of interest. Whose side had he really been on? He had to admit that he'd asked himself that question more than once. Evelyn was shrewd, bad news, but giving into her flirtations was the only way to get privileged information from her. Wasn't it? Undercover work had risks, but the risks were supposed to be for Evelyn. He should have known better.

But Evelyn was too smart for that. Nothing was going to distract her from her fanatical ambition of making her workforce the most productive in the world. As far as Evelyn was concerned, ethics and the law could be damned. How had she not seen this coming? The implanted chips could not have gone unreported forever. The nano particles, programmed to control the actions and minds of Danton's employees, would eventually be detected by superior technology—or by an observant and caring eye, like Grace's. Rubin suspected all along that Grace had had something to do with it. What he hadn't expected was that he would have been so attracted to Evelyn. How had he fallen for her treacheries? How had he been seduced into overstepping the bounds of ethics. Even an undercover agent had rules. Deflecting the blame to Grace, falsely identifying her as an inside informer, would do the trick. But Evelyn was as beguiling as she was shrewd. Her lust for men was an obsession. He knew that but he was seduced by her anyway. He snorted at himself in disgust. In his own defense, though, her lifestyle, her promises, her flattery were so seductive to his male ego, it was like she was a sorceress and her spell had ripped the sense of reason out of him. She had lavished him with gifts. He had become her sex puppet. She had bought him the *Auriga*, refurbished it to a pleasure craft, and they had spent weekends on the Great Lakes, sailing to remote vacation resorts or to her private and lavish cottages in Northern Ontario. *Oh, the lifestyle I could have had.* After her death, he'd quickly put the *Auriga* on the market without ever reporting that perk. Now, here it was, implicating him not only in the drug scene Levis Hardcastle was probably involved in, but possibly in other crimes that Hardcastle might have committed. Rubin himself could become a person of interest in the missing aboriginal girl's case and in the assault on Holly Anderson, one that nearly killed her. He should have been up front with Hugo.

Rubin had used a sales agent to sell the *Auriga*. He didn't know or care who it was sold to, only that it no longer had Rubin's name on the registration. But it didn't take him long to find out who owned the boat now. It also didn't take long to find out about the new owner's background.

Levis Hardcastle was under investigation for assault, embezzlement, and who knows what else. The guy was bad news and here he was on Galliano, in the same place that Rubin had been assigned to, and the new owner of a boat Rubin had once owned. What kind of mess was this? This could ruin Rubin's career.

It wasn't just Grace's gentle and vulnerable personality that appealed to Rubin. He was sure that her long hair, fair skin, gray eyes and full lips would be attractive to any man. How could he resist helping her when he met her on the plane? She was in obvious distress. Wouldn't anyone have come to her aid? Yet, she was strong, persevering on her own after an obvious panic attack. Rubin couldn't resist. He wanted to help her. He wanted to sleep with her. She couldn't know that he'd taken this investigative assignment into missing women on the West Coast because of her. She knew more about the tragic end to Evelyn than she'd disclosed in her trial testimony. He was sure of it. Though, he had to admit, she seemed more of a victim than a suspect. His detective curiosity told him that Grace was somehow involved though; that she was an innocent recipient of Evelyn's plot. The two women were polar opposites. As sinister as Evelyn was, Grace was that innocent. He needed to find out more about Grace before his superiors found out about the *Auriga*. She was an enigma.

He vowed he'd find out what was missing from Grace's testimony, though he hated that he had to badger her to find out. He was sure that Grace would cave with his "bad cop" tactics. Maybe she would if it weren't for her support team. Why was Michael here? Was he a business associate? Or was there more to their relationship? Michael didn't appear to be her boyfriend. He did, however, appear to be very protective of her, as did her parents, though that was to be expected. Parents were protective of their children, but Leo and Maria seemed to be exceptionally so. Then also, Rubin got this eerie feeling whenever he was around their home, that there were ghosts hiding in the trees, even in the full light of day. Rubin felt watched whenever he was around Grace and her support team. Maybe it was his guilty conscience weighing on him? Yes. That had to be it. Because, for a case closed weeks ago, there were still too many loose ends, too many questions that had neither been asked nor answered at the trial.

Holly Vows Revenge

HOLLY SAT BY THE WINDOW of her hospital room, staring out at the Victoria cityscape, the water of the Salish Sea barely visible in the far distance. Her head and body still hurt. She felt violated, ruined. Her mind was tormented, full of anger. The person she was, the free-spirited flower child, no longer existed. The assault had beaten the feistiness out of her, knocked out her confidence and left her abandoned in a way she had never experienced. Despite how vulnerable she felt, a rage was building inside her. As her body healed, anger brewed. She didn't tell her therapist. That would keep her in hospital longer. Her therapist wouldn't send her back to an environment that threatened her mental health while in her fragile and vulnerable state. Holly had to keep it to herself. Already, she was planning to make her attacker pay. How could she hurt him? She would need a weapon. How do you go about getting a gun? She could still see the wooden butt of the one he'd used on her as it came toward her head. Why had she been so careless? She admonished herself for getting high and allowing this to happen. It was her fault. One thing she did know was that she would not let that happen again. She would recover, and get strong, and then above all, she'd find out who he was and make him pay. She gritted her teeth and let the plans ruminate. That piece of scum will regret laying his hands on me. He's going to pay with his life and I'll do it slowly, painfully. With the grizzly thoughts giving her comfort, Holly didn't notice Dr. Simpson, her therapist, walk into the room.

"Good morning, Holly. How are you feeling today?"

Holly liked Dr. Simpson. She was young, her straight blond hair always twisted into a knotted bun at the nap of her neck. She always wore stylish high heels with her white lab coat flopping open over a colorful figure-hugging dress. Red lipstick brightened her milky-smooth complexion. She reminded Holly more of a model than of a doctor.

Holly strained a return smile. "I'm good. When can I go home?"

"What's the rush?"

The words had no sooner left her lips when Holly realized that she should have complained about something. That would have made the doctor think that she was, in fact, getting better, coming to grips with the horrible attack that had almost taken her life. No one is "good" after that kind of trauma.

Dr. Simpson's smile waited for what else Holly might say, her eyes peering into Holly's.

"I was thinking about the flower garden at Hollyhock. It probably needs attention. It's my job to keep the beds neat and tended." Holly swung her feet off the bed. "It'll be great to get back. Put this ordeal behind me."

Dr. Simpson leaned forward, her head in a single nod. "I'll talk to your other attending doctor and see when that's possible. Don't rush it, Holly. You've been through a lot. It takes time to recover from these things." She patted Holly's hand.

The kind gesture made Holly tear up and this didn't escape the Dr. Simpson's notice.

"It might be good to spend time in the atrium. There's a garden there and it's sunny and warm outside. I'll let the nursing station know that it's okay."

Holly felt a tear slide down her cheek. She nodded agreement. The hospital was so clinical and being in a room here reminded her of the reason she was here in the first place. She would never be able to deal out retribution here at the Victoria trauma center. She had to get home to Galliano. She would call Maria. That's what she would do. Maria would get her out of here. "I'd like that," she said.

Calling on Hugo
for Understanding

R EBECCA RUMMAGED THROUGH Tamara's room to retrieve her bloodied shirt, fetched her hairbrush and toothbrush, and put everything into a clean, plastic Ziploc bag. After giving Michael the items that might verify that Tamara had been on the boat, Joseph and Rebecca decided it was best to report their findings—though not that Grace had had a vision. They would keep Grace's secret, but Joseph pulled some thing from his pocket. It was the necklace that Grace had asked him to put back. He hadn't.

If they hurried, Michael and Grace could catch the last ferry to Campbell River with what they hoped was evidence. They could just make the deadline to the courier center. The sooner they got the evidence to Heatherton, the sooner they could verify their suspicions. Heatherton had connections and would get results as quickly as possible. Grace already knew what the evidence would prove. Hopefully, that would end Grace's responsibility and her visions would stop.

✳ ✳ ✳

The last ferry usually wasn't full but it always sailed on schedule. They had just enough time for Grace and Michael to get back to Abalone Hideaway, get her car, and drive to the ferry landing.

Because they wouldn't make the last ferry back to Galliano, Michael and Grace would have to spend the night at a hotel in Campbell River.

When Grace hugged Rebecca, she could feel the dread in each beat of Rebecca's heart. Grace wished she hadn't been the person who'd exposed the truth to Rebecca and Joseph.

Grace wished that Joseph wouldn't go to Hugo to report what they'd discovered that morning. The forensic evidence they'd collected would verify that Tamara had disappeared after being on the *Auriga*. That would be enough.

✳ ✳ ✳

"How did you find it, Joseph?" Hugo asked.

Joseph knew he had to choose his words carefully. He could not disclose Grace's special power. "We were enjoying a day of leisure with Maria and Leo. They invited us to sail with them on the *Serenity*. Nice boat." Joseph paused. "Grace and her friend Michael were with us."

Hugo's forehead wrinkled. "And you just happened to sail into a hidden cove?"

"I came across it from the land side when I was hunting there yesterday. It's a good spot for quail and pheasant."

"I know."

"I thought it was strange. I told Leo and we decided to check it out. In case… In case somebody needed help or something."

"And did anyone need help?" Hugo's eyes narrowed.

"Leo and I boarded, but no one was there." Joseph decided to tell Hugo, straight on, what they had seen. "There were stains on the deck. It looked like dried blood. And this…" Joseph held out the beaded necklace with the cross. "… was hanging on a nail."

Hugo went pale.

"Did I just walk in on a personal conversation?" Rubin asked from the doorway. He set two takeout coffee cups on Hugo's desk, his eyes moving from Joseph to Hugo then back again. "What's going on?"

"Joseph found an abandoned boat and thought he'd report it."

Now it was Rubin's turn to go quiet. He grinned at Joseph but turned away from the men. "Guess I should have bought three coffees."

"I was just leaving," Joseph said and started for the door.

"I'll have the Coast Guard check it out and get back to you," Hugo told him. "Thanks for letting me know. It's probably nothing."

✻ ✻ ✻

The words "abandoned boat," rang in Rubin's ears. His heart thumped.

He didn't dare say anything further. If it came out that he knew about the *Auriga*, it would rouse Hugo's suspicions about him. And he knew Hugo was already suspicious. Rubin wondered if he should ask questions about what Joseph had found.

Hugo was looking at him. Waiting? It wasn't like Rubin to not be curious. "So where is this boat?"

"Von Donop Inlet. In a cove where no one would see it."

"So how did—What's his name?—find it?"

"Joseph. Hunts in the area. Spotted it from land."

Brief, vague responses. Interesting.

"Is there something bothering you?" Hugo asked.

Rubin grabbed his coffee and peeled back the drinking spout on the lid but set it down without taking a sip. He sat on the corner of Hugo's desk and looked up at him. He had to come clean.

"I have something to tell you." Rubin took a long slug of coffee and began. "I went to Campbell River yesterday to check something out. I once owned a boat. I sold it several months back but I recently found it at a marina in Campbell River." He sipped more coffee.

"And what does that have to do with anything?"

"The name of the boat is *Auriga*."

Hugo's mouth popped open, then he recovered. "So, do you know who owns it now?"

"A fellow by the name of Levis Hardcastle. He is suspected of drug trafficking, and I think he may be involved with the attack on Holly Anderson and Elia."

"You know him?" Hugo's eyes flashed with anger. "Why didn't you say something sooner?"

Rubin got to his feet and paced the room. He needed to tell Hugo everything, even if it would implicate him in the crimes. He had to tell the rest of his story.

"I had an undercover assignment in Toronto. It was at the same company that Grace Walker works for. There was a fatal accident at the Danton plant and Grace and Michael were on the scene when it happened."

"What does it have to do with the boat?"

"I was... involved with the woman who died. She bought me the boat."

"You were undercover and she bought you a boat? You don't think that was unusual?"

"It's complicated. You had to have known her. Evelyn is... was..." Rubin sat on the edge of Hugo's desk again, feeling ashamed that he'd made such a self-serving decision. "I didn't disclose the perk. I just sold the boat so no one would know. I'm fully aware of the conflict of interest. I regret it. I thought if I sold it, the transgression would disappear. And now here it is. It's like someone is trying to make it look like I have something to do with the assault and maybe with the missing Indigenous woman. The case I was assigned to investigate."

"Indigenous woman. You mean Tamara," said Hugo, his voice fading to a whisper as he turned his back to Rubin. "You were awfully hard on Grace Walker. What's that all about?"

"The court ruled the death an accident, but I think Grace knows more about what happened. Much more. I wanted to see if I could get her to tell me what else she knows about the accident. There's more to that incident than she gave in her testimony. I'm sure of it."

"The Walkers are good people," said Hugo. "If you wanted information, why didn't you just come straight out and ask?"

"I bent the rules. I let it get personal. It's messing with my head." Would it ever go away?

"Never mind that. Things are pointing to…"

"Murder? We can't prove anything yet, but the missing Indigenous girl is probably dead. And you had a relationship with her, didn't you?"

"Yeah. I did."

Holly

H OLLY WOULD STAY with the Walkers for a few days until she could move into the Hardings' house where she would house-sit for the fall and winter months. It would be much better than the bunkie she occupied for the summer. Hollyhock Resort would keep her on with limited duties and that would give her enough income to sustain herself until the next tourist season. The Hardings wouldn't be leaving until the following week, though. Maria was kind to let her stay with them, but Maria would watch her with a suffocating mother's care. Maria wouldn't let Holly out of her sight. And that would make it difficult for Holly to purchase a gun. She needed to see Elia. He'd help her.

Holly joined Maria the following afternoon to drop Leo off at the clinic. They were to go grocery shopping at the General Store afterwards but Holly had an agenda of her own. She told Maria she wanted to visit Elia at Savannah's place beside the Sunset Restaurant. Maria reluctantly agreed. She would meet her for coffee later at the Sunset Restaurant. Holly breathed a sigh of relief as Maria headed for the store.

In the front yard, outside of Savannah's clapboard framed house, Elia was working on repairing his bicycle. His hands were shaking, Holly knew, from withdrawal. She didn't mean to, but she startled him when she came up behind him.

"What happened to your bike?"

He jumped up, edgy. The wrench fell out of Elia's hand and his bike tipped over onto the ground with a clatter. It had only been a little over a week since the attack. Holly knew he would feel responsible for inviting her to be with him that night. But a wide smile lit up his face. "You're back."

His enthusiastic smile and the sound of his familiar voice touched her. She desperately needed a friend and Elia was always there for whatever she needed. She didn't even try to stop the tear from sliding down her cheek. She wiped it away with the back of her hand. Elia understood her.

He took her hand and pulled her close in a quick embrace. "Don't worry. I'm going to make him pay for what he did to us."

"I'm so happy to see you. And I'm going to help you." Through her sobs, she said, "But I want a gun and I don't know how to get one."

"I'll look after that. And we will find him. I promise."

Holly swiped the back of her hand across her nose. She took a deep breath. "I'm staying with the Walkers until the Harding cottage becomes available next week. I'm house-sitting again. After they're gone, you can stay with me. If you like."

"That would be great. I need to get away from here. Savannah's after me to get back to servicing her customers." Elia hung his head. "I'm not doing that shit anymore, Holly. It nearly killed us. Because we were so stoned, we didn't notice him coming at us. *I* didn't notice. I'm so sorry, Holly. I'm so sorry."

"Don't blame yourself. It's all on him and he's going to regret hurting us. Now. Can you get me a gun?"

Elia grabbed Holly by the shoulders and looked her in the eye. "Leave that to me. The bigger problem will be to find him. He hasn't shown up at the harbor since then. Or in town." Elia released her shoulders. "I've been watching for him, but it's like he's disappeared or something."

"Then you know who he is?" Holly had only seen a dark, bulky shadow that night, one she interpreted, because she'd been so high, as being an evil phantom. The memory sent a shiver up her spine.

Elia didn't answer. He walked back to his bike and resumed the repair.

"You know him, don't you?" she asked again, pressing for the identity of her assailant.

"I'll get you the gun and then we'll get even with that bastard. Trust me. It's best you don't know what I know."

If there was one thing Holly knew about Elia, it was that he was not a snitch. Not even if he was as high as a kite, stoned out of reality, it would never loosen his tongue. It was something she kind of liked about him. He was predictable, loyal and completely reliable.

"Holly," Maria called from the Sunset's patio. "Let's get a coffee."

So that was that, then. Would Maria pick anything up? Would she sense that Holly was upset that Elia seemed to be more interested in his bike? That he wasn't responding to her? Had Maria heard anything? *I need space.*

"I'll join you in a minute," she told Maria, then turned to Elia. "Elia?" But he kept working on his bike, with no response. "Let me know when… you have it. The gun. I have the money. I'll pay you for it."

This time, Elia turned to her, his forehead wrinkled, his voice tense. "It not about the money."

Painters Lodge

T HEY HAD ONLY MINUTES before the courier office would close.

The clerk, who was processing what appeared to be the last package of the day, looked angrily at Grace and Michael as they rushed into the office with only minutes to spare. He huffed his annoyance, then looked up at the clock. It said 5:58 PM.

"You guys are really cutting it short."

"It's an urgent package." Michael shrugged his shoulders, an apologetic smile on his face.

The clerk processed the package and threw it onto the waiting truck whose engine was already running. Its driver had revved it. Twice.

"Sorry," said the clerk. "He gets impatient."

They had no sooner stepped outside the Courier office door when the lock clicked behind them.

Grace breathed a sigh of relief to see the truck move out into the highway traffic. Soon, she would have what she needed: hard evidence they could give to the police without mentioning anything about her vision. It was just a matter of time before the evidence confirmed what Grace already knew. Her part in it would be complete. The police would take it from there and she would finally have some peace. Her visions would stop.

Michael texted Heatherton to let him know the package would be in Toronto the following day. Minutes later, Heatherton, always on the job, texted back.

> I have the lab on notice. They will give it priority treatment. You should have the results in a few days.

✳ ✳ ✳

Michael's sigh was loud enough for Grace to hear. "Mission accomplished." He laid his hand on Grace's shoulder. "So, I guess we're stuck here." He looked around the darkening scene, at the city and harbor lights that twinkled over the water. "No more ferry runs today. Right? Any idea where we should stay?"

"Maria made reservations for us at Painters Lodge. It's a couple of miles out of town." She pointed. "That way, I think. Maria said we can't miss it. But I'll use the nav-system so I don't get lost." She giggled. It was usually Michael who arranged things.

She made it a point to walk ahead of him to the car and she exaggerated the sway of her hips, wondering if it might finally cause a reaction from the usually staid Michael.

✳ ✳ ✳

The trees and bushes around Painters Lodge were lit with twinkling lights, giving the place a tranquil atmosphere. Everything sparkled against the darkness of the water. It made the hotel seem very elegant. Grace had to admit that the place looked rather romantic. From the corner of her eye, she watched Michael, wondering if he had the same thought. Not that they were here for that purpose, she reminded herself. No, they just needed a clean, comfortable place to spend the night. Maria would have made sure about that.

Michael grabbed their overnight bags from the trunk and followed Grace to the reception area.

"We have a reservation under the name of Walker," Grace told the young male receptionist. "Two rooms."

She thought the receptionist gave her a funny look. He looked at Michael, back at her, then checked his computer before giving Grace a confused stare. "The reservation is for one room only. Is that… OK? I hope so. It's all we have available. We're fully booked."

Grace wanted to ask the clerk to check again, but deep inside, she was fine with that. She shot Michael a look to see what his reaction was.

Non-reactive. Neutral. As usual. He shrugged.

An uncomfortable moment passed.

"Its fine," Michael picked up Grace's bag as the young man gave Grace the key card. "Come on. We're adults. We can handle this." He motioned with his head toward the elevator.

Grace followed him to their second-floor room, number 2016. She unlocked the door to find two queen-size beds, a flat screen TV, the typical desk and single chair, and windows overlooking the water. *Nice view. Everything one might expect for a romantic retreat. Maria, what are you up to? But yes. It's perfect.*

Michael put her overnight bag on the queen by the window, his on the other by the door. *OK,* she thought, his words "'We're both adults'" echoing in her ears. *What did that mean?* Was Michael hoping for the same thing she was thinking? Neither of them commented.

"Let's see if we can get dinner reservations?" He stared at her and waited for an answer. "The dining room looked… fancy. At least from what I could see of it on the way by."

"Maria said the food is world class. Gourmet."

Michael held the door for her.

This was getting awkward. Michael, Heatherton and Grace had often gone to "grab a bite," but this was just the two of them. They were going to dinner together, like a date.

❋ ❋ ❋

The tables in the diffused light of the dining room were covered with white linen tablecloths, with a lit candle in a cut crystal holder at the center. The maître d' led them to a table for two by a window with a clear view of a boat dock across the stretch. Currently, passengers were debarking there, no doubt guests for Oak Bay Resort, their hotel's sister. They watched as a hotel employee led them up the boardwalk to stairs that would take them inside the hotel. Across the other side of the strait, glittering lights outlined the Quadra resort. Grace couldn't help being enchanted by how lovely everything was. It was all so pretty. Romantic was the word that popped into her head. It was all so romantic. She smiled at Michael.

He shook his head and whistled softly. "Yes, very fancy." He grinned back at her, but turned away as soon as their eyes met.

They ordered the fish: halibut in a creamy wine sauce and bottle of local white wine. Maria was right. The food was world class. They chatted about the room, the hotel, and how nice it would be to take a stroll outside, just to see the place, in case either of them might want to come back.

After they had finished their meal, they did exactly that. They took a stroll around the grounds, ending up where the boat had unloaded the sister resort's guests. Their silhouettes stretched out toward the end of the dock, spreading up against the wooden railing of the lookout area. The hotel's sound system had speakers that piped music outside to the boardwalk. The late summer breeze was cool so Grace wrapped her arms around her shoulders for warmth.

Michael took off his jacket and put it over her shoulders.

Grace held her breath. He was so near.

He leaned in, hesitating for a second, and then pulled her close to kiss her softly.

She heard his breath, in harmony with hers.

They kissed again, this time with a frenzy that should have been in private.

"Should we go back to our room?" Michael asked.

"Yes." Grace was ready. Michael did have feelings for her. She hadn't imagined it. She laughed as he took her hand.

They sprinted back inside.

The elevator was taking too long so they dashed across the lobby to the stairs, the patrons in the lobby looking over to see what the ruckus was about. The orientation of the second floor's stairway exit was different from that of the elevator's so they were momentarily confused. Jaunting along the carpeted hall, they counted off room numbers.

"We're at the far end," Michael said.

They reached their door and as Grace placed the key card in the reader, she noticed something lying on the floor. A business card. She bent to pick it up. She turned it over and gasped.

"What is it?"

All passionate inclinations gone, Grace handed the card to Michael. Handwritten on the card was one word: *Auriga*.

Michael reacted immediately. He looked up and down the hall, grabbed the key card from Grace's hand, opened the door and pushed Grace inside.

"Stay there. Don't move."

Cautiously, he checked the closet, the bathroom, and out the window. At the window, he motioned for Grace to come stand beside him.

"Do you see something?"

"Look." He pointed to a man running along the boardwalk and waving at a boat that looked like it was about to head out. "Was he there all along?"

"I was too busy looking at you," said Grace. "He knows. He knows where we are, doesn't he? He knows where we are." Her panic was increasing. "He knows where we are."

Michael threw the key card onto the side table, then snatched the two overnight bags from the bed and placing them under one arm, he took Grace's arm in the other and pulled her toward the open door. "We have to get out of here."

Fear swelled in Grace's chest as they raced to the stairs. Once on the first floor, she took one bag from Michael and they ran outside to where her car was parked.

Too rattled to drive, she tossed the key fob to Michael. They threw their bags into the back seat and drove off into the night, back toward Campbell River where they'd hole up in a two-star near the ferry station until morning.

The whole way, they watched to make sure that no one followed them.

Morning

T HE SCREECH OF A SEAGULL woke them. They lay beside each other in a double bed, still in their clothes, sunlight coming in through the sliders from a balcony that overlooked the waters of the strait, already busy with honking boats. Noisy bird. The gull was persistent, pesky, looking for its morning meal. Falling asleep again would be futile.

"What time does the first ferry leave?" Michael asked.

Grace fell out of her stretch to look at her Fitbit. It was 6:45 AM. She reached over to the bedside table where she'd placed the motel's information pamphlet with the ferry schedule.

"Good news or bad news?"

"We've missed the first sailing out of Campbell River. But we can catch the 7:30. The first one out of Heriot Bay is at 9:00." She stretched again before throwing her legs off the bed. "We'll make it without any problem. It's only a couple of blocks away."

✳ ✳ ✳

Michael eased the car forward as directed, to the left outer bay, and stopped a hair's width from the car ahead of them. He turned off the engine. "And now, I guess, we wait?"

The ferry horn blasted as the gate was being secured. Grace couldn't shake off the feeling of being watched. She looked around at the other vehicles on the ferry. Even on this early morning run, the Quadra ferry was packed, packed tight. There was nowhere to move to, to get out of the way. *If he's here, it will be easy for him to take a shot. How would he do it?* Grace knew that somehow, Levis Hardcastle had seen them on the *Auriga* and now he was out to get them before Grace could put suspicion on him. Right now, they were easy targets. Michael and Grace remained watchful, but they had no idea whom they had to watch out for. They didn't know what Levis looked like. Did Levis know that? Would he also be on the Valdez Point ferry? It could be anybody, and only twenty-six vehicles would board the Valdez Point ferry, easier yet to spot her and Michael. She caught Michael's expression. She read the worry on his face.

He reached over and took her hand. "We'll let Hugo and the Toronto detective know what happened. I think it's time. We can't keep this to ourselves anymore."

Grace shrugged, uncomfortable with the idea, but let the suggestion marinate, hoping she'd warm up to the idea of exposing her special abilities.

They kept watch but it was like watching out for a lightning bolt in a sunny sky.

* * *

It was 10:15 by the time the BC ferry docked at the Valdez Point landing. Greeted by a familiar setting, Grace felt a measure of security. This was her territory, one that held a mysterious web of protection. As they drove off the ferry and up the incline of the road, Scout ran out from the protection of the trees and stopped in front of the car.

Startled, Michael jammed on the brakes. "Why is that thing? It's just standing there."

Scout's eyes met Grace's, that now-familiar mind connection reassuring her. She felt the net of his protection. Somehow, Scout let her know that she was not alone but also that she had to be careful. Their telepathy had grown stronger, a language unique to only them. This was no time to let down her guard. Grace could feel Scout's warning. She'd let Michael know that Scout was warning them to be careful, even if it caused him to think she'd gone off her rocker.

"The wolf's name is Scout. He's warning us. He's here. Levis is here."

"Then we go to Lewis Landing first. We tell our story. Hugo has to believe us. As for Machowitz? Well, who cares?"

Grace could almost hear her heart thumping. Yes, of course that's what they had to do now. She could feel the danger closing in on her and Michael. Did Levis know where she lived? That thought added panic to the fear that pulsed through her body. That would put Maria and Leo in danger as well. Where was this deranged creep? Was he stalking the grounds at Abalone Hideaway? They had to hurry.

Elia

E LIA HAD WASTED NO TIME. He had acquired the gun and needed to get it to Holly. His feelings for her had grown even stronger. He couldn't wait to see her again. Damn that Hugo. He was always getting in the way. Elia knew that Holly still loved Hugo, but Hugo had knocked up Tamara. Tamara had told Elia about that just before she disappeared. If Holly knew about that, she wouldn't be so happy with her old flame, would she? Holly deserved better than Hugo. Not that I'm any better but at least I have feelings for her. Honest feelings.

He pedaled his bike faster as he headed to Abalone Hideaway where Holly was staying.

❊ ❊ ❊

"Elia, it's nice to see you," Maria said. "Are you going to come in? Annie and I are having tea and biscuits. Care to join us?"

"Holly said she was staying here for a while. Can I see her?"

"I think she's out in the garden," Maria said. "Let yourself in through the side gate." She pointed.

The latched gate was just off the driveway. He thanked Maria and walked over to the gate, unhooked the latch. Holly was on the lower porch, curled up in a lounger.

Maria went back inside to the upper deck and resumed her conversation with Annie.

✳ ✳ ✳

"Michael is a lovely young man. I think Grace is fond of him and it's clear that Michael likes her," Maria said. "I don't know what's holding them back."

"Young people can make things complicated these days," Annie said. She winced as she took a sip of her tea, her swollen lip still tender and sensitive to the heat.

"Where did you say Guy was?" Maria asked, hoping to get Annie to start talking about the injury to her lip.

"Campbell River, getting parts for his car. That old beast is an obsession with him." Her strained voice faded to a whisper and her gaze focused off into the distance. "I hardly ever see him. These days, it seems he's always away getting something or other for his hobbies."

Maria had always sensed that things did not go well in their marriage. The bruises verified that. She wanted to ask her friend why she didn't leave him, but any therapist knows that only drives a patient further into denial.

"Grace has gone to Campbell River," Maria said, not even trying to hide what she knew would be a glint in her eye, and a subtle smile on her lips. "Michael is with her. They won't make the last ferry back to Galliano, I'm afraid, so I booked them a room at Painters."

"A room? One room?"

Maria nodded and looked off to the sea in the direction of the city.

✳ ✳ ✳

Holly looked up when she heard the gate latch click followed by the creak of the rusted hinges as it swung open. She jumped up when she saw it was Elia approaching her. She stepped off the lower porch to meet him, grabbing his upper arm and pulling him to walk with her further into Maria's garden.

Holly looked toward the upper balcony where Maria and Annie were chatting. "Let's take a walk to the back part of the garden." She kept her voice low, whispered, so Maria and Annie wouldn't hear. It was OK if Maria and Annie could still see them, but Holly would make sure she and Elia kept their backs to them. Holly knew why Elia was here and she was more than happy about that. The exchange would be discreet.

Elia followed her to the pond where they sat on the soft grass and watched the goldfish flit around in the gurgling water from the fountain she'd helped Maria rig up.

"Have you got it?" she asked.

Elia took his knapsack off his shoulder and laid it on the grass in front of them. He sneaked a peek over his shoulder at the balcony as he carefully bent forward, reaching inside. He pulled out a pistol, just right for Holly's small hand.

She snatched it up, fondling it for several moments before putting it deep into the pocket of her oversized jacket.

"Do you even know how to use it?"

"Yeah. You pull the trigger. Duh. How hard could it be?"

Elia huffed. "There's a bit more to it. Can you get away? I'll give you a lesson."

They walked back to the house and Holly called up to Maria who came to the rail and leaned over it, smiling down at them. "Would you like to join us for tea and biscuits?"

"We're going for a walk. Down the hill. To the beach."

"It might be too much for you. That hill is quite a workout. You're still healing. And that damn hill must be at a forty-five-degree slope."

"Don't worry, I'll look after her," Elia called up. "We'll take it slow."

They quickly left through the gate before Maria could say any more.

✳ ✳ ✳

Elia had lined up chunks of driftwood along a two-foot-diameter downed log, washed smooth by weather and waves.

Holly handed him the pistol and Elia demonstrated how to load the cartridge and release the safety. Then, holding the pistol with both hands, he aimed at the targets that lined the log like driftwood soldiers. His aim was true. His first shot knocked a warrior off the log.

The loud pop startled Holly and she brought her hands to her head to cover her ears. She looked around, wondering if anyone had heard the blast. She was shaking. She hadn't anticipated that she might not have the nerve to carry out her inner need for revenge.

Elia handed the pistol back to her. "Your turn."

Her hand quivered as she reached for it.

"It's OK," he said. "You can do this."

Holly aimed. Pulled the trigger. The kickback made her hand veer off toward the water. She tried again, this time visualizing her assailant as the target. The boom pierced her ears, but she knew she'd been closer. She planted her feet, took a firm grip with both hands, and aimed.

Bingo! The driftwood jumped into the air and like an acrobat, was propelled backward off the log, crashing into the stones on the rocky beach.

Laughing out loud, Elia whooped in excitement, his arms in the air like someone had just scored a goal at a major league game. "Wow, I wouldn't want to meet you in some dark alley. You've got this. Make sure you put the safety back on."

He picked her up and spun her around in celebration. They both hooted, but as their faces met each other in mid-spin, close enough to feel each other's breath, the elation disappeared.

Elia set her down.

Holly pulled back from him, confused.

"Sorry, I didn't mean…" Elia walked away toward the demanding angle of road that led back to Abalone Hideaway.

Holly said nothing. She followed him.

Maria was right. The uphill grade was more than Holly could handle. She had to stop again and again to catch her breath. Her head was pounding from the exertion of the climb. The uphill grade of the road was too steep. They were almost at the top of the hill when Holly thought to ask, "Do you think Maria heard the shots?"

"Yeah, probably. You should make sure to keep that thing out of sight. I'm thinking now that this was probably a bad idea. We should've gone somewhere further away."

Holly stopped, barely able to take another step. "I… can't…"

Elia was ready to carry her, piggy-back style, when they heard a car approach. It was a black SUV.

As it came closer, they realized it was Maria. She had come after them. She stopped and got out of the car, the concern in her voice evident as her question scolded before she'd even reached them.

"I heard gun shots. Are you kids OK?" She looked freaked as she approached them. "Did you see anyone out there shooting?"

"Yeah," said Elia. "We heard them so thought we'd head back."

Holly was still trying to catch her breath.

"Are you OK, Holly? Look at you. I knew the hill would be too much. Let's get you into the car. You need to rest. Elia, help her."

Holly was exhausted and welcomed Maria's concern. She could hardly make it to the back seat of the car. As Maria turned the car back up the road, Holly elbowed Elia and reached into her pocket. Elia responded, moving his knapsack closer, opening the pocket flap to allow Holly to slip her gun inside the knapsack, beside Elia's larger revolver.

What? she mouthed at him when she saw it.

He shrugged.

They drove back to the house where Maria tucked Holly into bed before offering to drive Elia back to Savannah's place. Elia accepted the offer, leaned over the bed to hug Holly, putting her gun under her pillow as he did so.

Coming Clean
with Hugo

I T WAS A SLOW MORNING in Lewis Landing. The Community Center, where the police station was located, seemed deserted. Not a single car sat in the small potholed parking area.

To Grace, it felt eerie, like an alien had teleported all human life off the planet. Michael said he'd noticed that, too.

They hadn't slept well the night prior, keeping their eyes and ears open, alert to whoever had left the telltale card at their hotel door. They were both jumpy.

They got out of the car, scrutinizing the road, the parking lot, and the building they were about to walk into. Levis could be anywhere, but it didn't appear that anyone was around. Had Hugo and his buddy, Rubin, gone out on a call?

There was no one in the office.

"Now what?" asked Michael.

"We're here now. We should wait for them to come back." Grace had finally mustered up the courage to report what had happened, so she could surely wait a few minutes for their return.

She scanned the empty room then spotted a stack of reports on Hugo's desk. She picked up the one on top to read it.

"Joseph reported finding the *Auriga*." She snorted. "This says that

375

evidence was surrendered. A necklace." She felt like she'd been stabbed with a knife. "I told him to put it back so Levis wouldn't suspect we were there."

"That still doesn't explain how Levis found us."

"He could have been watching us. Maybe from shore? I bet that's it. He was watching as we searched the *Auriga*." She was trying to restrain her anger and was not doing a very good job of it.

She put the report back on the desk just as the door opened hitting the wall with a resounding bang. The noise scared her and she jumped, knocking the pile of papers to the floor.

It was Hugo, with Rubin right behind him, each balancing a soft drink in one hand and a bag of some takeout food in the other. From the Sunset. Grace recognized the logo on the bag.

Like a thief, she crouched to the floor, shuffling the papers together in a frenzied haste before standing up, the reports still in her hands like a kid caught in the act of snooping.

"What the hell are you guys doing here?" Hugo demanded. "Why are you going through my police reports? That is confidential information. I could lay charges."

"I suppose you could," said Michael. "But then why did you leave them out in plain sight? Kind of careless of you, I'd say."

Hugo glared at Michael then his face softened. "You're right. I should have put them away." To Grace, he said, feigning anger, "Under lock and key, yes?"

Unmoved by Hugo's reactions, Grace said, "I see that Joseph reported what we found on the *Auriga*." She set the reports back down on the table, not bothering to stack them neatly again. "Actually, we're here to provide more information. And evidence."

Hugo put his food on top of the file cabinet. Rubin did the same.

"Have a seat," said Rubin. "We were actually going to pay you a visit later."

It seemed to Grace that the word "*Auriga*" had erased the smug "gotcha" smile from Rubin's face. His body posture stiffened, but of particular note to her, were his eyes. They were wide with fear. And there was more. The air in the room had changed. It was sharp with the electricity of tension, and the source of that tension emanated from around Rubin's body. Grace could feel the trickle of Rubin's anxiety move toward her.

"We were in Campbell River," Michael said. "To courier a package to Toronto." He paused, waiting for a reaction from either Hugo or Rubin. Their facial expressions didn't change. "It was late and we'd missed the last ferry back to Galliano so we stayed at a hotel. Painters Lodge. After we had an evening meal, we went back to our room. And this had been dropped at the door."

Michael handed Rubin the blank business card, plain side up.

Rubin shrugged as if to say, *Blank. So what?* Then he flipped it over where the handwritten word, *Auriga*, was. "*Auriga*? What's this all about?" It appeared to startle him more than Grace had expected it to.

Hugo took the card from Rubin. "What do you think this means?"

Michael said, "I think someone saw us on the *Auriga* and they didn't like us snooping around. That person, whoever it was, followed us and is trying to scare us off. Maybe kill us. And he left a calling card to make his point."

Grace faced Hugo straight on, her hands on her hips, letting Hugo and Rubin know she wasn't intimidated by their questions. "Or are you thinking we're just being paranoid?" She let her hands drop to her sides but still kept her eyes on Hugo's. "Rebecca told me that you and Tamara had a relationship. The necklace Joseph gave you? That was Tamara's necklace."

Grace turned to Rubin. "And you looked surprised when you saw the card. Is there something about the *Auriga* you're not telling us?"

Hugo and Rubin stared at each other.

"You can't lie to me," said Grace. "I'll know if you do. I can read the wind."

"That she can," said Michael.

"I was in Campbell River the other day," said Rubin. "I was following up a lead." He paused. "This is hard to explain. I don't even understand it myself. I sold the *Auriga* several months ago. It was my boat."

Grace already knew this. It hadn't taken Heatherton long to get this information back to them. She would play Rubin, as would Michael. "You owned the *Auriga*?"

Michael made it look like he was processing that information. "You sold it." Another pause. "Then you know who owns it now."

"Only a name," Rubin said. "I can't figure out how or why the *Auriga* is here and what that means for this case."

Grace still didn't understand how Rubin could have owned the boat. She needed an explanation. There was more of a connection than Rubin was admitting. The energy in the room was at sizzle level. Her fingers were tingling, her head was buzzing, and she felt like she was being pulled into a vision. She sat down, dazed, staring at the wall across the room.

"What's going on with her?" asked Rubin, moving closer to her. "Looks like she's having a seizure. She on drugs or something?"

Michael moved between them to protect Grace. "Leave her alone." He held his arms out, trying to shield her.

As Grace's vision cleared, she was back at the marina in Campbell River. It was earlier in the day than when they had been there. The marine manager was talking to a man whose back was turned away from her. She recognized his body form, the broad shoulders and the way he planted his feet. The two men chatted for a bit, then exchanged business cards. The man turned to leave, walking toward her. It was Rubin. He watched as a boat, the *Auriga*, left the bay, then scribbled notes—and the vision faded.

Grace came back to the reality of the room but carried Rubin's underlying motive with her. "You're here because of me. Aren't you? What *is* your connection to the *Auriga*? It's more than just having once owned it! What's really going on? It's like you have some kind of unfinished business that I have a part in. And I don't like it. Not one bit."

Then everything went blank and Grace collapsed into Michael's arms.

✳ ✳ ✳

Rubin was stunned. Grace had just unraveled his deep-seated secret through some kind of seizure. He lost his breath and sat down.

Grace was pale, perspiration dotting her forehead.

"Is your father at the clinic?" Hugo asked, phone in hand.

Grace waved her hand for Hugo to put his phone away. "This happens to me sometimes."

So this is why she's so antagonistic whenever I question her. Conflict. She wants to tell me the truth but doesn't dare because I'll think she's crazy. "Is this what happened to you on the plane? I thought it was a panic attack."

"Not exactly a panic attack," she said. "I have an acute sense of my surroundings. I know that Tamara... is dead. There are signs, clues, and definitely evidence. I think we can all agree that the person on the *Auriga* is the killer."

"You're a seer?" Hugo's face told Rubin that Hugo was both fascinated and frightened. *What's he afraid of? Was he more involved with Tamara than I've been led to believe? And how much does Grace know about it?*

"I think you're going to need more than Grace's 'acute senses' to convict him, won't you?" said Michael. "So if you don't mind, let's not make this central to the crime. We're trying to find a killer—you're trying to find a killer—so we need each other's help."

Rubin considered what this could mean for him. Were seers for real? Or was this something like those crazy mediums the police used on occasion to solve crimes? Had Grace foreseen the fall that killed Evelyn? If so, perhaps she also had the power to see unethical behavior. His. If she told anyone, he was done. His police career would be over. He wouldn't press further. Maybe she didn't have that power at all. Yet it would explain why she hadn't said anything about it at the trial. Why would anyone believe her? He wasn't even sure he believed it. Did Hugo's people believe in that sort of thing? He'd ask Hugo in private.

"The card proves that the killer followed us to Campbell River," said Michael. "That means he knows who she is and he probably knows she's staying with her parents. And I'm sure his intentions are more than just trying to scare us. Look what happened to Holly and Elia. Are you going to help us? Or do we have to take things into our own hands?"

"I'll make some calls," said Hugo, tapping his cell phone. "We'll secure the grounds at your parents' place." Hugo shook his head. "Do you really think this guy would target all of you?" Hugo didn't wait for an answer. Phone already to his ear, Hugo turned away, giving orders.

Michael's right, thought Rubin. *Grace is in danger and so are her friends and family.*

Abalone Hideaway

MICHAEL AND GRACE LEFT the station. Now they had to tell Maria and Leo. If the killer had seen Grace on the Auriga, he would have seen who was with her: Leo, Michael, Joseph, Rebecca... They were all in danger and all because of her.

Guilt washed over her.

Yes, Joseph was a skilled hunter, and Rebecca was probably a good shot as well, but would it have to come to that? Could they actually shoot someone to protect themselves? I couldn't, thought Grace.

When they pulled into the driveway of the Abalone Hideaway, they noticed that the SUV was away. Was Maria picking up Leo from the clinic?

"Maybe she left a note," Grace muttered, more to herself than to Michael.

Holly was at the door when Grace and Michael walked in.

"I heard your car drive in and it woke me up and—"

"Where's Maria? Where's my mother?"

"She said I could stay here till my housesitting job was available. Sorry."

"So where is she?" Grace was worried.

"It's nice to see you're all right," Michael said.

Grace felt his hand on her arm as he tried to calm her. She knew he was wanting to drill Holly with questions about the identity of her assailant now that they had an idea of who it could be. Grace wanted to know that, too, but Holly didn't look well at all.

"You scared me," Holly said. She was almost shaking. Her face was pale.

"We're sorry we scared you. Aren't we, Grace?"

Grace felt herself nod.

"Wake me up when Maria and Leo get home," said Holly. "I'm going to rest for a while longer." Slowly, she walked away down the hall to her room, shutting the door behind her.

"Hugo and Rubin should be here shortly," said Michael from the window near the driveway.

"I hope Maria and Leo get here first," said Grace. "I want to be the one who tells them what happened in Campbell River. About the card. That we're all in danger. Even them now. And it's all my fault." She began to pace.

"Think of something that will take your mind off it until then, OK?"

Grace looked around for something, anything, she could occupy herself with, a distraction that would replace the unsettling thoughts that raged in her mind.

"What about food?" Michael suggested.

Grace headed for the kitchen with Michael close behind her.

"Or maybe wine?" Michael said, opening and closing cupboard doors as Grace peered inside the fridge.

Maria had left a pasta dish, something with red sauce and shredded cheese on top. Grace took it out and placed it in the oven. Surely her parents would be home soon.

Two wine glasses in one hand, Michael reached over to turn on the oven with the other. He set it to 350.

"You've done this before," said Grace, already feeling better.

Michael reached into the fridge to retrieve a bottle of West Coast Riesling. He poured some into the glasses, put the bottle back, then bumped the fridge door with his hip as he handed one of the glasses to Grace.

"You're good," she said, happy to see the smile on Michael's face and feel the one on her own.

"Let's sit out on the upper deck," he said.

Grace could tell he was still holding back with his emotions. She wanted him to hold her in his arms. Instead, she walked to the door that Michael held open for her. They picked the patio chairs facing out to the rough area beyond the fence line and kept watch, taking note of any movement in the bushes or the grass, questioning every breeze that rustled or disturbed the vegetation. Was the movement due to the wind or was someone or something out there?

"How does someone figure out where you live?" Grace asked.

Michael shrugged. "Easy. Phone book. Ask someone. All your information is on the Internet." Michael set his glass on the railing. "What are you getting at? Where are your thoughts going right now?"

"You think that this Levis guy, a person no one knows, would just go up to someone on Galliano and ask where the Walkers live? Wouldn't that cause a Galliano resident to wonder why?"

"He'd have to know who to ask for," Michael said. "Let's ask Hugo if he knows if anyone's been asking about you. "

"Even if he Googled it, he'd still have to know a name. Just watching us search the *Auriga* wouldn't give him that information. Would—?"

The grass rustled and a shot of fear sped up Grace's back.

But it was only Scout patrolling the perimeter. He had put the thought into Grace's head: *You know the killer. The killer knows you and your parents.*

"It's the wolf. My wolf," Grace said, pointing. "Scout wouldn't show himself if Levis was lurking." She took a sip of her wine, allowing it to wash the tension away from her throat. "We're safe for now." She leaned back and closed her eyes. If only her muscles would relax. She felt like she was going to snap into pieces.

✻ ✻ ✻

Michael took her hand. He wanted to hold her in his arms, but she was not as fragile as she appeared sometimes. She was strong at the same time with so much psychic energy bombarding her. This was no time to confuse or distract her with romantic signals. Though he wanted it desperately. At least she could rest easy for a moment. Soon, when everyone was here, a new wave of tension would rise again. That strange power she had was calling to her. Her power was the strangest thing he'd ever encountered. It was both real and unreal. This mystic power had bequeathed her with the responsibility of unfolding crimes, this time, to bring a killer to justice. That was a heavy burden. Michael went to the railing and stared at Scout. The wolf stared back. Nope! Michael did not pick up any voices or messages. It was something only Grace could do.

A car pulled into the driveway. Maria and Leo were home.

✻ ✻ ✻

"Something smells good," Maria said as she hugged Grace. "You guys put supper on. I was hoping you'd do that."

Grace opened the oven. "Yes."

Maria frowned at Michael. "What's up?"

"We're going to have company shortly. Hugo and Rubin are on their way."

The door slammed, signaling that Leo had come in. "How's Holly?" Leo walked over to the counter and set down his black bag.

Grace and Michael exchanged glances prompting Leo to ask, "How was Campbell River?"

Maria shook her head, no. Not now.

"Hugo and the Toronto cop are on their way over," Grace said. "I'll set the table."

"What happened?"

"Grace and I picked up a business card on the hallway floor in front of our hotel room. It was blank on one side and the word *Auriga* was handwritten on the other side."

Leo froze.

"We went to the Galliano police station and brought Hugo up to date on everything. Everything."

Grace nodded.

"The guy knew we were there," said Michael. "I think we might be in danger. Extreme danger. All of us."

"How much does Hugo know?" Maria paused, waiting for Grace to say something but Grace wouldn't look up at her.

"Hugo and the cop weren't there when we arrived," Grace said. "There were reports on the desk and I looked at them. It said that Joseph reported what we found on the *Auriga*. That Joseph gave Hugo the necklace. That I'd had a short 'episode.'"

Maria took the remaining cutlery from Grace's hand and set them on the table. "And then?"

"We didn't explain," said Michael. "We just said that sometimes these episodes happen to her. She told them Tamara's dead and we have additional evidence that we sent to Toronto for analysis. But that Rubin guy… He's really freaked out about the boat. He admitted that he once owned it."

"That cop from Toronto owned the *Auriga*?" Holly had just walked into the room. "What does that have to do with anything?"

"Wait," said Grace. "Didn't Heatherton say that the cop once worked for Danton, the security team?"

"That's right," Michael pulled out his cell phone and started texting. "Heatherton needs this information about the ownership of the boat that just happens to be involved in an assault and murder here on Galliano."

"What murder?" asked Holly. "There was a murder?"

"Holly," Grace said. "There's evidence that suggests that Tamara is… gone. But don't say anything. Rebecca and Joseph only recently discovered certain information. But they kind of know."

Holly's knees gave out on her and Leo rushed to her side. Maria helped move her onto the couch. Leo grabbed his medical bag and came back to Holly's side, taking her pulse and blood pressure. She was clearly shaken.

Leo handed her a pill, insisted she take it, telling her it was something that would take the edge off the stress of the news. Maria helped her back to bed.

Rubin Speaks Up

A VEHICLE RUMBLED TO A STOP in the driveway. Grace, her parents, and Michael watched from the window as Hugo and Rubin got out of Hugo's car to wander around, checking the immediate perimeter around the house before coming to the door.

"Not a surprise to see you, Hugo," said Leo. "Grace and Michael told us you'd be dropping by."

"Did they also tell you it seems like we have a suspect in the Holly and Elia case?"

As Rubin entered, he pointed toward the back of the house. "There's a wolf hanging around the far end of your property." Rubin pushed his jacket aside to reveal the gun holstered there. He let his jacket slip back. "That doesn't seem to worry you."

Grace answered in slow deliberate words. "The wolf is harmless." She glanced over at Maria. "Sort of a pet, really."

Maria nodded.

"We're not worried about him." Standing straight and tall, Grace crossed her arms over her chest.

"Please," said Maria, indicating the dining room table. "Make your-selves comfortable. Tea? Coffee?"

Hugo shook his head and smiled a thank you as he pulled a plastic

391

bag containing the card from his pocket and set it on the table. "I can see how this might cause you concern. But as evidence, it poses no direct threat."

Grace spoke up, her voice insistent. "Really? Well let me tell you that there's something about the *Auriga* that Rubin is very uncomfortable with." Grace shot Rubin a look. "If Rubin is unsettled with the mere mention of the name, then why don't you think the card is a threatening message to us, too? I think someone has gone to a lot of effort to make sure we know we're being watched. And that somebody wants us to be scared. It's too much of a coincidence."

Rubin's eyes went from one person to the other around the table. He shrugged at Grace. "I was involved with Evelyn Loudon. We were... a thing. Look. I know I stepped over the line, but it happened. She bought the boat and put it in my name as part of an agreement for me to be her personal bodyguard because she said someone was trying to steal her technology. She was..." Rubin hung his head. "Very generous."

"Keep going," said Hugo, and not in a friendly, cop-buddies way.

"I don't have proof, but I think it was you, Grace, and Michael, who launched the complaint about Evelyn endangering the health of the Danton workers. I think that's why she fell from the catwalk."

Grace could feel Rubin trying to read her. She kept her face passive.

"She was after you that night. Wasn't she, Grace? But you didn't mention that in your testimony. Did you?"

"The court ruled it an accident," snapped Michael. "Evelyn was paranoid and was always after everyone. We were nowhere near her when she fell." His eyes glared into Rubin's, straight on.

Grace patted Michael's arm. Rubin didn't need to know what really happened. That Evelyn was after them. That she had a gun and would have killed Grace. Heatherton had removed it and disposed of it. It was never found. Heatherton, Michael and Grace had gone through the plant to cover their tracks. There could be nothing showing they'd been to the research center, that Heatherton had disabled the chip implantation program. That this had effectively put an end to Evelyn's devious plan.

Without the nano tech program, workers would be safe. There was no need for anyone to know anything. They had done nothing but protect those workers.

"You know who owned the boat," said Grace. "You need to tell us. That person is trying to kill us because of what we know."

Rubin's expression told Grace nothing. "You told us Tamara is dead, yet there's no body. And without a body, there's no proof of death. Does that make sense to you?"

Grace didn't like the apparent sarcasm emanating from Rubin.

"So it becomes a cold case."

"There was blood on the floor of the *Auriga*, Detective," Michael put in. "We've sent off samples of Tamara's hair and saliva to see if there's a match. That and the necklace—her necklace, identified by her parents—make for strong evidence. It would be difficult if not impossible to find a body dumped at sea."

"Her body was thrown overboard," said Grace. "I know this beyond doubt."

"How?" Rubin and Hugo asked at the same time.

"I read the residual energy on the *Auriga*. I'm empathic. I have visions." There, she'd said it. "It was so strong, I saw it. The whole thing. I saw her thrown overboard in my vision."

She turned to Rubin whose anger seemed to have subsided.

"You have a secret you want us to keep. Don't you, Rubin. We'll keep yours. I need you to keep mine. Visions are not evidence. No court would believe me. Tamara is dead. I saw it and we need you to help us find the killer. It should be easy because he's after us."

Hugo looked over at Rubin. "There are Island Nation Band legends that tell of such things. There are people who have special powers. People who can see what has, and sometimes what will happen. These people are connected to everything around them."

"Well," said Rubin. "Forgive my skepticism, but in my line of work, evidence—physical evidence—is all that counts. I'll keep her secret a secret if you agree to keep mine a secret, too."

"Good," said Leo. "That's settled. Now. What remains is that this person—the current owner of the *Auriga*—has given Grace, my daughter, and Michael, her friend, a warning. He needs their silence. One way or the other. My guess is that he is opting for 'the other' option. How do we keep them safe?"

"We'll set up surveillance around this area," said Hugo. "Rubin and I will take turns."

"We'll keep a close watch as well," said Michael.

✳ ✳ ✳

Holly was woozy from the effects of the sedative, but wobbled her way to the door of her room to listen. What were they talking about? What did they mean by "Grace's vision," the special power that Hugo was talking about. Then… My assailant is here? Close by? I have to tell Elia. If Levis is coming to us, we won't have to hunt him down. Groggy, she staggered back to her bed. I'll call him later. That bastard will regret what he did to us.

Protection

T HE AREA OUTSIDE THE FENCE around Abalone Hideaway was thick with brush and grasses. Further into the old growth, the forest floor would be carpeted with pine needles. If anyone was hiding out there, watching the house, there would be foot imprints and signs of trampled vegetation, perhaps tracks that would give away signs of a lurker. Hugo had hunting skills that would come in handy but so did people he knew. People who would keep watch for him while he and Rubin expanded their investigation. He'd ask them, but would check with Rubin first.

Back at the police station, Rubin considered what would happen to his reputation when they caught the suspect. He knew who the man was, Levis Hardcastle, but did Levis Hardcastle know who he was, as the previous owner of the Auriga? He did. Rubin's name was on the registration papers. What if the document were put into evidence? Rubin would have to explain why he had sold the Auriga. Why he'd owned it in the first place. It wouldn't take long before his conflict of interest in the Danton case would become apparent.

* * *

Hugo also ran his own consequences around in his mind. He considered the questions that would be asked. He and Tamara had been a thing. Everyone on Galliano knew it. Tamara had confided in Elia that she was several months pregnant. Now—according to Grace—she was dead. He had failed to protect her. Then Holly, the woman he really cared for, was attacked. These were things he didn't want known. He had noticed that Tamara was gaining weight, but Hugo didn't want to be—couldn't be— tied to Tamara in that way. He struggled to write the report.

✳ ✳ ✳

Rubin had sensed Hugo's anxiety. He knew that neither of them wanted to be open about their involvement in the case. Rubin wanted to cover up his relationship with Evelyn; Hugo was covering up his relationship with Tamara. Most certainly, the killer wanted to remain anonymous. Add that Grace had visions. How do you report this kind of stuff?

"This is the weirdest case I've ever worked on," Rubin said.

Hugo looked up from his computer. Rubin knew they both wanted to do the right thing, but also needed their personal entanglements to remain private.

"I have a really bad feeling about this," Hugo said. "We know this guy is out there. We know he murdered one of our own and assaulted two other people, resulting in serious injuries. And now he's after Grace. Maybe her friend, too. Maybe even her parents. If we don't stop him, we'll have more murders on our hands." Muttering to himself, Hugo typed a few more strokes. "Just the facts, ma'am. Just the facts." He looked up at Rubin. "My father used to say that all the time then laugh. But it's not even funny, is it?"

"No, it's not. Those facts, my friend, are going to get us in trouble."

"People are dead, hurt, and being threatened," Hugo said. "It's our job to bring the criminal to justice and protect the innocent. We can't let our personal interests stand in the way of doing our job."

They both nodded. They would do what was right.

Holly on the Hunt

H OLLY DRIFTED FROM THE NIGHTMARE of being attacked, to redemptive dreams of retaliation. She could feel herself teetering between fear and courage.

She wasn't going to be a helpless victim. Her anger had bolstered a strange kind of bravery. She dreamed of how she would do it.

She would stalk the guy; make him feel an increasing measure of fear. First, she'd shoot him in the leg, immobilize him so he couldn't run. Then she'd shoot him in the arm, disarming him. She laughed at her own pun. Shoot the arm to disarm. The impact of the bullet would make the rifle fly out of his hand and as he lay there on the ground, wounded, immobilized, she'd approach and hover over him, maybe make him beg for mercy. She'd make him say it over and over again, plead for his life. She'd enjoy his pleas, "Don't shoot me, please, don't shoot me." She'd reply, "Yeah, like you did when I begged you not to rape me." She'd laugh at him as she took aim, hearing the click of the trigger of the pistol. She'd shoot him in the gut and leave him to bleed to death. She would retreat, carefully covering her tracks back to the house. She and Elia would have already made arrangements to leave the Island never to be seen again.

When Holly woke from her medication-induced nightmare-dream, she felt refreshed and already vindicated. She sat up, realizing where she was and snorted a laugh. *Aren't I ambitious and evil? How can I ever forgive myself? Easily!* She laughed and forgave herself, knowing it was only a dream-plan, not a real plan. Or… Was she really capable of doing that?

She could smell coffee and bacon, heard a pan clanking on the stove in the kitchen. The sensual sounds, the sizzle that made her stomach rumble. Maria was probably making breakfast.

Holly rolled out of bed, pulled on the jeans she had left on the floor and the wrinkled T-shirt, ran her fingers through her hair to untangle the knots, and went to the kitchen.

Maria must have heard her approach, because she looked up from the stove to assess her, smiling before stacking pancakes and bacon on a plate for Holly.

"How are you feeling? Hungry? As you can see, I've made the heartiest bunch of pancakes possible. With bacon. Leo's and Grace's favorite. Help yourself to coffee."

Maria was so very motherly. Nothing like her own mother who never gave a damn if Holly ate or not. Then again, let's forgive her. Her mother worked the night shift. She was always in bed at breakfast time. Her mother worked hard just to keep a roof over their head. Nonetheless, this was everything she'd ever dreamed of how a family should be.

Holly poured herself a coffee and took a quick sip of the delicious brew before sitting down at the table. Maria laid the plate of pancakes in front of her. *Wow,* she thought. *Having someone so caring is nice.* She regretted that she would be leaving in a couple of days for the housesitting job at the Hardings. She'd be on her own again. Holly would have liked to stay under Maria's doting care.

"Smells delicious. Thank you." Holly turned her head toward the staircase where she'd heard footsteps. The rhythmic heavy steps sounded thunderous in Holly's aching head.

It was Leo, with Michael right behind him, both sniffing the air and muttering compliments.

Leo kissed and hugged Maria as Michael watched on, a timid smile lifting the corners of his mouth. "A guy could put on a lot of weight if he lived here." He smiled at Maria as he poured himself a coffee.

Maria scooped more pancakes onto plates for the men.

Leo took his plate and sat across from Holly.

"Eat up. There's lots," Maria said as she poured more batter onto the skillet.

Yes, I could get used to living here.

"You're up early. Maria's going to drive you to the clinic later. You're still healing from your injuries. We should keep an eye out."

"You mean to keep an eye on my mental state," Holly said, her agitation flaring up again. "What if I don't want to go?"

"Maria was a psychologist by profession. She'll help you with... with anything you'd like to sort out. We're here to help."

Holly squirmed. What she really wanted was revenge, but she couldn't tell that to Leo. Then Holly noticed that everyone had stopped eating. Had they noticed the edge in her voice? Or were they actually concerned about her? She forced a smile. The Walkers were kind. What was the matter with her?

"Yeah, I should make sure that I look after myself. Maria, would you mind driving past the Harding place. I should pay them a visit to familiarize myself with their house again. Especially their security system. You'll probably be glad to get me out of your hair." She allowed herself to emit a strained giggle, trying to make a joke of it.

Maria sat beside her. "You stay here until you're comfortable with what happened. OK? The Hardings aren't leaving for another week yet. Lots of time."

✳ ✳ ✳

Despite Holly's protests, Maria and Holly left for the clinic later that morning. Holly's physical state was improving, at least enough for Holly to move around without limping or groaning, but she still noticed the stiff and bruised tenderness of where she'd been brutalized. Holly would have to make it appear that her focus was on healing. She'd hide her need for getting even. Under normal circumstances, no one got away with insulting her. But physical and emotional injury were something she'd never forgive. There had to be payback. Holly had grown up on self-preservation. With each step, her sore pelvis reminded her of that and fortified her resolve to get back at the bastard who had done this to her.

Footprints in the Old Growth

W ANTING TO SEE IF LEVIS MIGHT HAVE been bold enough to come back to the scene of the crime, Michael had taken Grace's car to go to Lewis Landing Harbor. Hugo would join him just in case.

That left Grace alone and somewhat exposed at Abalone Hideaway. Uncertainty and unease tickled her stomach like a vision was about to ambush her, so she poured herself a coffee and took it to the upper deck balcony, hoping that the air and calmness of the morning sky and the sounds of nature would sooth her. But the sky boiled with darkening cumulus mounds. They billowed like monsters, blocked the sun, made the day seem ill-omened.

She listened for the usual reassuring voices in the wind. None. But they were guiding her. She knew that. Were they as anxious as she was? They could only warn her. The rest was up to her. Grace had accepted the task but that didn't give her the courage or physical strength to fight off the psychopath who was stalking her. He could be out there right now, waiting for an opportune moment. *That business card. Sick bastard.* Grace could almost feel his evil taunting. Was he watching her as she sat there on the upper deck? The thought made her skin feel like it was on fire.

She looked to the fence perimeter, searching for Scout. Grace didn't

407

know why, but these days, the wolf made Grace feel safe. He'd been there yesterday when Rubin and Hugo had come over. She didn't see him now, but she did see the bushes move. She also detected a flash of dark clothing, a jacket maybe, and a hat. As the grasses rustled and parted in predicable fashion, she was sure it was a human.

She froze. Had Levis found her? Was she able to conjure his thoughts? The tall grasses began to move in a line toward the lower fence area by the pond. The man's arms thrashed, parting the grasses. She knew Levis carried a gun. Could a rifle have that kind of range? If yes, then she was a sitting target.

Grace pulled back, hoping he hadn't seen her.

A man in a plaid shirt and with a Stetson hat perched on his head, emerged, crouching to examine the ground by the fence. It was Rubin. He was probably searching the area for signs that indicated that someone was out there watching the house, as promised.

Now that she knew it wasn't Levis, she could feel the color coming back to her face. She would go out to the garden and talk to Rubin, happy he was on the other side of the fence. She'd always felt uncomfortable around him. His changeable behavior couldn't be trusted, but he did seem to have had a change of heart.

※ ※ ※

Rubin saw Grace approach. He watched her long legs as she ran toward him. Her body was lean, nimble and strong like an athlete's. She had a profound effect on him. He wanted her. Under different circumstances, they might have been friends. Or more.

"Did you find anything?" she asked him. He moved right up against the chain link fence, then sensing her nervousness, he shook the lustful thoughts from his mind and stepped back from the fence.

He squatted down and pointed at the trampled areas in the grass. "Have any of you guys taken a walk in this area?"

"It's rough on that side of the fence. Burrs and bugs. We usually walk on the road down to the beach area. That way."

"This trampled area starts here and goes about a hundred feet toward the trees. Someone has been here. I don't think an animal would do that."

"You think Levis might we watching us from out here?" Grace came closer to the fence to see for herself. This might confirm her worst fears.

"I'll talk to Hugo. He'd know better if the depressions are animal or man-made."

"What should we do?"

Rubin studied her face. Her brow was wrinkled and her arms were folded tightly around her chest. Was her lip trembling? It reminded him of her distressed state when the plane had landed in Comox when they had first met.

"If it's OK with you, I'll come up to the house and stay until Hugo arrives. He should probably see this.

"That would make me feel... safer."

As she walked back to the house, Rubin wondered if she could read his thoughts. It appeared so. She was reacting to him as though he were coming on to her. But wasn't he at least hoping for the opportunity to do just that?

Elia Finds Levis

E LIA'S WITHDRAWAL SYMPTOMS were easing. He'd been straight for a couple of weeks. It had never occurred to him that his dealer might be closer than he thought. He always thought of him as "that guy" who sailed around the Discovery Islands, taking advantage of the remoteness of the area to evade the authorities while exploiting the locals and whatever tourist trade the Island attracted—a criminal who regarded himself as an entrepreneur earning a few extra dollars from the sale of drugs. But back then, Elia had always been too stoned to care; and critical thought was not his strong point in the first place. Galliano didn't have great job opportunities and he needed enough money to get by. All he cared about was earning some "dollars" the easy way. Selling cannabis and other recreational drugs at the Sunset was as easy as falling off a log. Now that he was seeing things with eyes unobscured by drugs— while not the full one hundred percent positive about it—Elia had realized who Levis was. Better still, he had a good idea where to find him, so now they could plan how they would ambush Levis. It seemed that revenge was contagious. They had the same resolve. Revenge.

Once Holly had moved herself to the Harding residence, they could perfect their shooting skills without anyone hearing the gunshots. Despite himself, he grinned at the thought of staying with her. Only a few days to go. He savored the thought.

Her appointment at the clinic wouldn't take that long. He hoped it wouldn't. The Hardings had given Holly permission to use their Island car, a beater, as they'd described it, one they didn't mind being roughed up by the potholes in the tarred-and-pebbled roads. With the use of "their own car," they could surprise-attack Levis anywhere on the Island without worrying about having to hitch rides to get to him, which would be laughable. This way, they'd find him and make their move when the opportunity presented itself.

Elia saw Holly walking down the hill from the clinic. She was alone. Maria must have stayed behind at the clinic or stopped at the general store. He waved to let her know he had seen her. Holly glanced around before waving back, then quickened her pace. Elia met her half way.

"Maria's driving me to the Hardings. They want to give me the keys now, and details of what to look after while they're away." Holly smiled. "A few more days to go and the place will be ours."

Elia was excited not only about being able to spend time with Holly but also about getting away from the pressures that Savannah was putting on him. Savannah expected him to resume his duties of supplying drugs to her customers. If Elia didn't comply with "serving her customers," she'd kick him out of her guest house. He would be homeless. He didn't care. He wasn't going in that direction anymore.

"It'll be great to get away from Savannah."

Holly nodded. Elia knew she understood the demands Savannah put on him. And right now, Elia was Holly's ticket to making her revenge happen.

An old car, moving slower than the speed limit, rumbled past them, its driver straining a look at Savannah's Sunset Restaurant before pulling off on the road to stop at the parking area further up the road. A man in a big hat that shielded his face got out, pausing to assess Elia and Holly before descending the steps into the sunken patio area in front of the Sunset Restaurant. He glanced over at them again before disappearing inside.

"I know who our assailant is," said Elia.

Giving him the nod, Holly took a deep breath. "Then we're agreed?"

"We are. I have the ferry schedule. We leave the island immediately after. Okay? Just remember. He deserves it."

Holly nodded, turned and went up the hill to the general store to meet Maria at the car.

At the Hardings

T HE HARDING PLACE WAS A CLASSIC West Coast house: large, timber framed, with a metal roof. The windows faced out toward the sea giving a splendid view. The interior was modern and well-appointed with high-end kitchen appliances and expensive furniture. No wonder they wanted a caretaker while they were away.

Holly was happy to take the job. She and Elia would certainly live in style—for a while, a short while.

Bruce and Lillian Harding greeted them in the driveway and invited them into the house. Holly noted their expensive clothing. They were sophisticated and rich, way out of her social class. But they greeted her warmly, and seemed kind and welcoming. They were friends of Maria and Leo and that made the meeting less awkward.

"How lovely to see you again, Maria." Lillian hugged Maria and wrapped her arm in hers. "And how are you, Holly?" she said, turning to Maria for any comment that might smooth the conversation forward.

News traveled fast on Galliano. The Hardings knew all the details of the terrible attack that had happened at Lewis Beach. It appeared that Lillian didn't want to say anything that would upset Holly.

"Holly is staying with us until the two of you are ready to head out for the Bahamas," said Maria. "She's back from the hospital in Victoria and doing well. I've told her that Leo and I will help her with any difficulties she might run into while she's here."

Lillian seemed relieved. She smiled. "Let me show you around and familiarize you with where things are and how they work."

The place was amazing, everything clean and well-maintained. Holly couldn't believe that she'd be staying in such an elegant place. She was beginning to believe that the attack had opened new opportunities for her. If only circumstances were different.

They toured the house and grounds for the next hour. The car the Hardings had described as an Island beater, was last year's model Mercedes. Beater, indeed! Lillian showed her where she kept the fob and gave her a credit card for gas. This was beginning to sound unbelievable.

❊ ❊ ❊

The following Friday, Maria announced that the Hardings had left on the first ferry to Campbell River. They would take the morning charter out of Campbell River to Vancouver Airport and then south to the Bahamas, to their other home, their vacation home.

Maria and Leo drove Holly to the Harding house after breakfast, stopping at the General Store for staples so Holly could get settled, not that Lillian hadn't already looked after that. Then after making sure Holly was OK, Maria would reluctantly leave her to her own devices.

Maria had misgivings about leaving Holly alone but that's what Holly wanted, what Holly had planned, and Holly was not Maria's child. She had to trust her, even though her gut told her things were not right with Holly.

❊ ❊ ❊

Holly felt it, too, a strange sort of disconnection with her surroundings. It was quite a change from her summer lodgings, the six-hundred-square-foot bunkie at Hollyhock. Transplanted into this luxurious place, she was conflicted with her plans. She struggled against her inner rage, with what she was resolved to do. She feared she was about to cave in. She could get used to this lifestyle.

A *click* and the door opened.

Elia walked in. Whistling loudly, he turned in circles to see the house. "Wow. We're staying here until…?"

Their eyes met and Holly could read Elia's hesitance about carrying out what they conspired to do.

"Yeah, rich people don't like leaving their stuff unattended." Holly's sarcasm echoed in her own ears even as the overtone of gratitude for such an opportunity resonated there, too. They would have been there the entire winter until March. Except that their plan included an exit from Galliano once they had given Levis what he deserved. They'd have to leave it all behind.

"I know where he is," Elia said. "We shouldn't get too comfortable here. I'll make arrangements for us to leave before we close in on him. Agreed?"

"Agreed." She couldn't look him in the eye again. Instead, she fiddled with the remote to turn on the large-screen television. She wasn't sure anymore how she felt about their plan. Then again, what if her assailant came after her? She and Elia were still alive. Maybe he'd want to change that.

But meanwhile, the Hardings had Netflix, and beer and wine in a beverage fridge so she could worry about that later. Holly pulled out two Labatts, and she and Elia settled in on the sectional, scrolling through the selection of movies on Netflix.

Hugo's Assessment

F ROM THE UPPER DECK, Grace watched Rubin fighting his way through the overgrown vegetation outside the fence line. He made his way back to the driveway just as Hugo and Michael returned. Grace had heard the cars' engines, so came out to greet them.

"Find anything out there?" Hugo asked Rubin who was brushing leaves off his pant legs and plucking burrs from his sleeve. He cast an alert eye toward Grace.

"There's some interesting stuff beyond the property line. On the other side of the fence." He motioned with his head for them to follow him back to where he'd been.

Hugo crouched to the ground, examining the flattened and broken vegetation. "This wasn't made by an animal." From that angle, he looked toward the Walker house. "A nice clear observation point. What do you say, Michael? Rubin?"

Michael crouched beside Hugo and confirmed the vantage point.

"Joseph's a hunter," said Hugo. "He'd know more than I do about how or who could make these imprints. He'll be able to follow it further. Maybe back to where it started."

"So. You're saying he's been here?"

Hugo nodded, yes.

Hugo knew they didn't need Joseph or his expert tracking skills to tell them that the house, Grace in particular, was being watched. He could see Grace, still standing on the driveway, and he knew she knew that the men didn't like what they saw or what it meant.

Scout

S COUT WAS NEAR and waiting. So was his pack. Things were falling into place. Grace had attracted all the right people. She had drawn the evil one close. The Ancestors commanded the elements to help guard the empath. It was not their intent that she be harmed. She would be the one to free Tamara's earth-bound spirit and that of her unborn son. Time was not a concept to spirits in transition, especially ones trapped between two worlds. The father of her child, the police officer, would help, but it would be Grace who would bring the evil one to justice. She had set the forces into motion, forces that could easily fall out of control. Evil was unyielding, destroying whatever stood in its way.

Their combined energy was strong. But as the Ancestors had observed, things were already in motion, another human would be caught in the wave. Evil held a great threat—often a lethal one. There would be another who would also be welcomed into the peace of the Sunset Land.

As evening descended, those who held righteousness in their hearts could hear the songs of redemption. Even the detective from Toronto, the one who had lost his way, could feel the pull of honesty. Somehow, Grace had attracted his help to the cause as well.

Grace's Assessment

A s THE MEN APPROACHED, Grace anticipated that they had information she wouldn't like. Surely the signs in the bushes indicated that the killer already knew their location. She just couldn't figure out how he had tracked her here. Perhaps he'd seen the name of Leo's boat, had investigated to learn who was the owner of the *Serenity*. Of course. That had to be it.

Michael approached her first. "Hugo's pretty sure the house is being watched." He pointed to the mound lookout.

In her heart she knew it all along. Grace had felt the ill-omened energy for days.

Hugo spoke up, trying to reassure her but without success. "Joseph will be able to tell us more about where the tracks started. Maybe where they originated. That would give us enough information for us to go get him before…"

Grace tensed and Hugo saw it.

"Before anything happens."

That didn't make Grace feel any better. She clenched her hands and buried them deep into the pockets of her jacket. "I'm scared."

"I'll call Joseph right now and try to get him here as soon as possible."

Hugo left immediately, leaving Rubin to guard Grace and Michael.

"He could be right there. Right now," said Grace. "He might try to kill me. All of us."

Joseph, the Tracker

CROUCHED ON ONE KNEE, Joseph examined the ground. He swished his hand over the trampled grass, reading the way the blades had been bent. He got up and moved to the bushes at the treeline, noting the direction the twigs now faced, then went back down on his knees to look for depressions by raking back the dead undergrowth. He went further into the trees where the ground vegetation grew sparse under the acidity of fallen pine needles. He bent down several times to touch the surface. He moved with stealth, as if he were hunting a dangerous wild animal: methodically, quietly, so as not to alert the predator. He followed the trail further and further until he came to Seavista Road. He crossed over, hoping to pick up the trail again.

He scratched his head. *Which way?* His finely honed tracking skills told him, *Down. Down toward the ocean.* He walked further along the road, stopping abruptly at a driveway. His eyes moved back and forth, putting together what he was learning. He knew this place but decided not to go further. If the footprints and disturbed vegetation came from someone who lived in this house, and if Joseph were noticed snooping around on this property, it could result in retaliatory action. He didn't like how close it was to the Walker residence.

The woods on the other side of Seavista Road started less than

437

twenty feet from the shoulder. It was the same woods that ended behind Abalone Hideaway. If the killer had a connection to this house, the person who was watching from the woods had easy access to the Walker property line.

He made his way back through the low scrub brush and into trees again, moving slowly, calculating how someone might approach, becoming a phantom so as not to disturb a twig or leaf.

Moments later, he was at the fence that enclosed Abalone Hideaway, where the others were waiting for his return.

"What can you tell us, Joseph?" Hugo asked.

"Tracks are freshly made. Could be a hunter but… somehow I doubt that. Just a feeling. Also, there are wolf tracks. And wolf scat."

"Think someone might be hunting wolves?"

"Not wolves."

Joseph and Hugo made eye contact.

"We have to tell them," said Hugo.

Joseph looked up to the roof-line of the house. "Do they have a security system?"

Hunting a Killer

E LIA DECIDED NOT TO TELL Holly where they were going; he would tell her to just follow his directions. Being in the Mercedes as it seemed to float over the rough Island roads made him feel stoned. He wasn't sure he liked that. When they got to where they were going, he instructed Holly to pull over to the roadside.

"Know where we are?" he asked.

"Yeah. The Walkers live right over there."

"I'm sorry for talking you into traipsing down that hill yesterday. And especially up it again."

"You're forgiven," groaned Holly as she pulled herself out of the Mercedes.

Elia wasn't sure anymore if he should take her through the bush. Could she handle it? They'd have to battle through the roadside brush, then across the cushions of slippery pine needles, protruding roots and rocks of the forest floor for what would feel like miles to her. And the thing Elia liked least about going through here was that even in the light of day, the woods would be dark. That always made him feel afraid.

He took her hand. "Let's do this."

❋ ❋ ❋

"Here we are," Elia whispered to her as he put his finger over his lips, pointing ahead through the trees.

In the back yard of a house, a woman was hanging wet clothes on a clothesline. A tall man, rather thick around the middle, approached the woman.

A surge of adrenaline made the blood run out of Holly's head. Fear saturated every cell in her body. She became dizzy, and terrified that her tired legs might give out. She crouched down as best she could, still able to see through the cover of the trees what was going on. She didn't recognize the face, but his body form was unmistakable.

"Where's the stuff I bought yesterday?" the man demanded.

Holly was trembling. Maybe she didn't want revenge after all. What she wanted right then was to run, get the hell out of there.

Elia placed his hand on her arm, his face asking if she was all right. She shook her head.

Elia motioned for Holly to stay there, to put her gun back into her pocket. His own gun in his hand, he rose and moved toward the forest edge.

The man roared again. "Where's the stuff I bought?"

The woman shrugged her shoulders, stepping away from him.

He struck her across the head and she fell to the ground. He walked away grumbling, leaving her crumpled form on the ground below the bedsheets blowing in the soft breeze.

Holly waved at Elia and mouthed, *Who is that?*

Elia's lips curled into a vicious snarl. He mouthed back, *He's the one who did that to us. To you.*

Holly went silent as her psyche retreated back into that horrible memory. *We need to help her.*

No. He'll see us.

Then the man returned to the woman, grabbed her by the front of her blouse, lifted her up and struck her, hard.

Holly gasped, putting her hand over her mouth.

The woman slid to the ground again.

Elia shushed Holly and pulled back into the old growth, his foot snapping a fallen twig.

The snap resonated against the muted sounds of the forest. It caught the attention of the man. His head went up, looking toward the forest as he backed up toward the house.

Within seconds, he emerged with a rifle propped against his shoulder, and moving with stealth toward the woods where Elia and Holly were hiding.

The woman on the ground stirred. She sat up, eyes wide as she saw the gun, that he appeared to be after something in the woods.

"What are you doing?"

"Shut up, woman." The man was getting closer to the treeline.

Elia crouched lower and motioned that Holly do the same.

The man entered the wooded area, his body silhouetted against the sunlit backdrop.

As he closed in on their position, Holly heard him snarl and she panicked, her muscles acting reflexively. She leaped up from their concealed hiding spot and ran.

The man started after her. As he passed Elia, Elia rose to full height.

Behind her, Holly heard Elia calling out, "No. I won't allow you to hurt her again." Then a bang.

Then the man's voice, "You? You bastard. Think you can outshoot me with that little toy pistol?" The man howled.

Holly heard two bangs but she kept running in spite of the fatigue in her legs. Her feet barely touched the ground as she sprinted through the forest back toward the car, adrenaline surging. She expected that any moment, the man would grab her from behind and take her down. She had no idea she could run so fast.

Ahead, through the trees and brush, there was sunlight. She could see the road. Her body blasted through the last of the underbrush as if propelled by magical force.

The Mercedes waited a short distance ahead. She didn't feel her feet on the hard surface of the road or the exhaustion in her chest. An elastic force pulled her forward landing her inside the car. The Mercedes roared to life as she turned the key then pounded her foot onto the gas pedal and drove away at lightning speed, leaving Elia behind.

❊ ❊ ❊

His aim had been true.

The hole in the kid's chest oozed blood. He could tell the kid was trying to talk, but without success. The kid dropped face forward into the pine needles and lay still, the needles going black beneath him as he bled out.

❊ ❊ ❊

Her first instinct was to save her own life. She floored the gas pedal of the Mercedes and drove, not knowing where she was or where she should go. But she also knew she had to get help for Elia. The gunshots had been distinct: one from Elia's pistol, another from a rifle. The blasts were different. Holly was familiar with the sound of a pistol. She and Elia, each with their own, had practiced. Did Elia get him? Or had Elia taken the man's bullet?

Holly's heart pounded with dread as the Hardings' so-called beater sped erratically along the undulating road, her mind and subconscious fighting with each other as if she were in some nightmare's wrestling match.

She drove until she could see another vehicle ahead. She was going so fast she hardly had time to apply the brakes. The sudden deceleration caused her to drive off the road into the ditch then up again onto scrub brush before coming to a stop so abruptly she hit the windshield with her head. The car's horn blared and the world went dark even as she heard a person opening the car door.

"Holly! Are you all right?" It was Hugo. "Talk to me."

As he pulled her off the steering wheel, her vision returned. She tried to talk, but only sobs would come out. "Elia…" She pointed in the direction she'd come from. "Elia…"

"What about Elia?"

"Gunshots…"

Hugo helped her out of the car and onto her feet. "I know. I heard them, too."

Closing In

M ICHAEL AND RUBIN HAD HEARD gunshots and were outside to patrol the perimeter of Abalone Hideaway, looking for an intruder, almost instantly. When they heard the sustained blast of a car horn, Michael jumped into Grace's rental car, Rubin almost falling to the ground as he got into the passenger seat to go along with him, and sped to the road behind Leo and Maria's property.

Michael pulled in behind Hugo's car and he and Rubin jumped out of the rental.

"Holly's been shot?" Michael asked.

"No," said Hugo. "Michael, you stay with her. Rubin, you come with me." They rushed to the cruiser and drove off.

In the rearview mirror, Hugo saw Holly jump into the Mercedes and take off in the direction from which she'd come, leaving Michael to stand there, hand on the back fender of Grace's rental, bewildered.

✳ ✳ ✳

The road dead-ended near the entry lane to the beach, but right now, a woman, appearing distraught and wandering aimlessly, stepped out of a driveway onto the road as the cruiser approached.

Hugo slowed, stopped, and he and Rubin got out of the cruiser and approached her. Other than the sound of the waves cresting on the rocky shoreline further down the hill, all they could hear were her frantic sobs. Hugo knew her, and speculated that she, too, had been part of the trauma Holly had just endured.

"Annie? What's happened?"

Annie was bleeding from the forehead, her left eye red and swollen. She appeared to be disoriented, in shock, perhaps.

Hugo wasn't sure if Annie even recognized him.

Rubin motioned, cocking his head toward the driveway. "I'll go search the area."

"No. Wait for me. You'll need backup."

Hugo settled Annie into the cruiser, then pulling his revolver, he joined Rubin who waited at the driveway entrance.

With their guns drawn and their eyes darting everywhere, their steps calculated, they moved along the driveway until they came to the clearing where the house stood. The door to the house was open but otherwise, everything seemed quiet.

They scanned the area around the house, and surmised that Annie had been hanging clothes when whatever it was happened, had happened. A basket of wet sheets lay on the grass and the clothesline lay on the ground. Rubin pointed to the trees where the salal had been trampled. Hugo and Rubin stared at each for a few seconds before moving with caution into the woods. Hypervigilant, they proceeded into the darkness of the trees.

Hugo knew that trees had a way of distracting you, each one standing as a barrier, pulling your eye in multiple directions. The ground was soft with pine needles so only the snap of slender twigs would acknowledge your presence. Was someone hiding among the forest's sentinels?

He and Rubin had walked several hundred feet into the woods where it seemed as though they'd been swallowed by another dimension. Hugo could feel the forest's silence screaming as it drew him toward what he feared most.

They stopped. Ahead of them lay a male. Face down. Not moving.

This was the most unfavorite part of Hugo's job. He bent down to turn the body over. He didn't have to feel for a pulse, the hole in the guy's chest said it all. It was Elia.

Against the Code of Nature

N*ATURE IS TOLERANT.* *The call of the wild is cruel but necessary for survival. Animals abide by a sacred code to take only what they need, defend if threatened. Break the code and Nature will seek justice. Scout watched, saw what the man had done, and called on the Ancestors to put matters right.*

❊ ❊ ❊

Damn it. Curse words tumbled from Guy's lips as he tripped and stumbled through the old growth. His mind raged as he realized how his life had so utterly been deviated from his ambitious corporate plans. He should have been running a company. But then, who needed the corporate world? The Montreal firm could kiss his ass. He could make it big without their rules and their protocol. And the boss's wife? That woman had started it by flirting with him. It wasn't his fault. She was the one egging him on. So what if it didn't fall within the limits of proper social acceptance? Who cares? She's the one who should have been disciplined. Not him.

And now, instead of meeting his corporate goals, here he was, in the boonies of Hell, running from a murder he'd committed. A second murder. Two. Ridiculous. He had no intention of going to jail. How had everything gotten so messy? So very messy. Those who could point to him would also have to die.

Guy, also known as Levis Hardcastle, hadn't built up his illicit business only to be captured because that Elia kid was weak. The kid wasn't cut out for the kind of work Guy was good at. The kid didn't have the ambition. Didn't he realize it was about money and staying ahead of the law and nothing else? Yes. It was a lucrative business but you had to be smart, too. And ruthless. Make your own laws. That's how it was done. Civil law was arbitrary, laws made up to suit its elite. And people were stupid enough to accept that without question. But if you were discreet, you could operate within its cracks.

Guy had relocated the *Auriga* to another cove near Lewis Landing Harbor, also discreet, almost imperceptible, but with some added effort, accessible enough. It wasn't very far from here. A few hours' walk through the forest and along a short stretch of remote shoreline and he'd be there. He'd sail away to another set of islands and be rid of this place once and for all. But first he had to clean up the loose ends.

The drug trade had no boundaries. His product was in demand everywhere. As for the *Auriga*, a few alterations and it would be unrecognizable, like a new boat, never be found or connected with Galliano. He'd make those arrangements as soon as he'd paid Grace a visit. It was her doing and she needed to suffer the consequences for her interference.

He didn't understand that certain spookiness about Grace. When she was around, his discomfort increased measurably. And his misfortune had started when she arrived at the island. If she'd never come to Galliano, Guy's life would still be perfect. But she started asking questions, sleuthing as though she were in some ladies' mystery novel or something, and she'd somehow put it all together. How had she done that? There was not a single physical trace of Tamara anywhere. Aboriginal girls went missing all the time and no one ever came looking for them. How could Grace possibly have known anything?

Guy slipped further through the forest trees, his thoughts in turmoil about Grace. Did she have some kind of power over him? And if so, what was it? He snorted. He'd never allow another woman to control his life like that Montreal bitch had. But right now, none of that mattered. Out here on the loose, he was incognito. He was Levis, king of the drug trade and he made his own laws. Grace would regret bringing attention to the *Auriga*. He'd slink through the cover of the woods and wait for the perfect opportunity. He'd make her disappear just like he'd made Tamara disappear.

He cursed himself as he caught his foot on a tree root. He tried to steady himself but could not stop himself from falling face down onto the pine needles and twigs of the forest floor. His mind went back to Elia's body, face down on the forest floor's carpet of pine needles in the woods beyond his house. A lucky miss or he would have been the one lying face down in the pine needles back there.

Guy was certain that Hugo and that city detective would have found the kid and would no doubt be trying to find him now. Guy had recognized the woman who ran. It was that Hippie girl from the Sunset, the one who got stoned all the time with the kid. She was the one who had come to the boat that night, the one who was asking for it but had gotten away, would bring the cops to the *Auriga*, would ruin his business.

Guy picked himself up off the ground, reached into his pocket for his whiskey and took a slug. Anyway, Elia could have been caught by a stray hunter's bullet. Yes. The wolves on Galliano were plentiful this year. The Island residents were all on alert in case one might cross their path. There was no law against shooting a predatory animal intent on foraging for food around the place you lived. It was for your own protection. In the end, Hugo would have to close the case as accidental. But then there was Annie. Perhaps the Hippie. And, of course, Grace. He snarled as he thought about how he could silence them. All of them. Bitches were always a problem.

The conditions on Galliano had turned against him. He slowed his angry thoughts as best he could. He wouldn't allow it to distract him from his plan. Guy Boisvert would be no more. His identity would have to dissolve into someone else. Soon, no one would remember him. He took another slug of his mickey. But Levis would carry on. He grinned as the thought comforted his mind. He'd be carefree and easy setting up new markets and pushers at different ports, making his midnight runs on nights of the full moon.

Guy crouched in the bushes at the fence line. He could see Grace on the upper balcony of Abalone Hideaway. She was too far away to take a shot that would land where he wanted it to. He had to come up with another plan, one that would distract her enough to get her away from there, to get her on the *Auriga* where he would make her disappear as he had with Tamara. The thought warmed him.

He pulled out his flask again, took a long slug, then another, grinning and thinking. If only he could make it look like her boyfriend had sent her a message to join him at Lewis Landing. Yes. That that would do it. He'd wait for her, have his way, then drag her on board and sail to the disposal spot. Neither Michael nor Leo would suspect anything until it was too late. He walked back his own house, carefully looked around to make sure no one was there, and got into his Cadillac. Why walk? He knew the perfect spot to hide it, and then go unnoticed to the clinic where they would all be gathered to investigate what had happened. He'd wait for an opportunity, disable Michael, steel his cell phone, send the message to Grace.

He's Out There

G RACE HAD FELT disturbing ripples all day. She wondered if it was because she knew Levis was watching her and that's what was putting her on edge. It was a different sensation from an imminent vision, but it was palpable, pulsating waves. Energy is timeless, she supposed. If past energy left a residual signal, perhaps it also reached forward as well. Grace didn't like this feeling. Could she push it away like she could sometimes do with an impending vision? She should have tried harder to change its trajectory. Could she have changed the energy path to save Elia? She already knew he was dead. It sickened her. She didn't have the visual of what had happened, though she felt it just the same. But the man… She knew him and he made the elements scream with signals of evil. It was Guy Boisvert, Annie's husband, and Leo's good friend. She shuddered at the thought of their friendship. He was out there in the old growth. Grace could feel his vibrations. They hovered near. The forest was almost hissing with his toxic presence. The wolves' low growls mixed with Guy's malevolent energy.

She was alone here in Abalone Hideaway. Leo and Maria had left for the clinic. Hugo had phoned him. Leo was needed to examine Elia's body and to attend to the trauma that both Annie and Holly had sustained. Michael and Rubin had left as soon as they'd heard the shots, thinking that leaving Grace behind would be the safest option. She wished she'd resisted them and had gone along. She didn't feel safe in the house. She was exposed.

Grace jumped at the sound. Her phone pinged. It was a text message from Michael.

Meet me at Lewis. Come as soon as you can.

She stared at the words on her cell phone. They were curt and felt foreign. Something didn't feel right about his message. It had an unfamiliar tone. But Michael wasn't someone who sent messages without good reason.

She grabbed her knapsack, the keys to Leo's car, went outside where she pulled the tarp off Leo's seldom-used car and drove off.

Holly Makes up Her Mind

H UGO HEARD A PANICKED CALL for help. He rushed outside the clinic to respond to Holly.

She had felt the need for some air, she'd told him. She needed relief from the vigorous questioning that was taking place, she'd said.

He wasn't sure he'd believed her but after what she'd been through in the last several days, he allowed it.

"Hugo. Over here." Holly was crouched down on the pavement.

Michael lay there, unconscious, a trickle of blood dripping from a gash on his head. His hand was still in a gripped position as if he'd been holding something.

Hugo bent down to see if Michael was breathing. He was, and was starting to come back to consciousness.

"What the hell? Where's my phone." Michael rubbed at the gash on his head. "Someone hit me from behind."

Hugo helped Michael into a sitting position.

The clinic door opened and Leo rushed out. "Help me get him inside."

But Michael was already on his feet and walking around, his hand fumbling through his pockets. "They took my cell phone. I had it out. I was about to text Grace. See if she's OK."

Eyes wide, Holly cried out, "He's after Grace!" She ran to the Mercedes and drove off.

Hugo followed in the cruiser, Michael and Leo in the SUV behind him.

Rebecca's Meditation

R EBECCA FELT AN INCREASING SENSE of restlessness, a strange unease, a quivering that was imitated by the surrounding trees. Was she
picking it up from them? Or were they picking it up from her? What was
going on—this apprehension that was gripping her? She paced the
porch, back and forth. Nothing seemed amiss, but something was calling to her, pulling her to a task, but she couldn't read it. Grace came into
her thoughts and then a feeling of dread, the same fear she'd felt when
Tamara had gone missing. Deep down, she knew what had happened to
her daughter, but wouldn't allow it to come to the surface. Denial can't
always be contained so the truth rose to her awareness. The feeling
should have left her distraught, paralyzed with grief, but instead, she
was sensing agitation, a need to go somewhere. Her mind brought up
the encounter on Lewis Beach where she'd shot near the wolf to make
it go away and then realized that Grace was in the basin. She remembered the horror on Leo's face when he heard the gunshot. Rebecca now
felt his horror again. She knew she must go to Lewis Harbor.

She grabbed her clam bucket and went to her car. She lifted the
trunk lid and her eyes landed on the rifle she'd used that day at Lewis.
Breathing hard, she checked to make sure it was loaded. A voice in her
head told her she'd need it, that she'd need it to be loaded today. She

could feel a surge of urgency. She slammed down the trunk lid and hopping in behind the wheel, she started the engine, the wheels spinning as she put the gas pedal to the floor. Dirt and stones flew from the tires as she raced out of the driveway to the road.

Rebecca didn't understand what was driving this feeling, only that she had to go. Twenty minutes later, she was at Lewis Landing. She turned off the engine, got out of the car and looked around, certain she'd discover the source of what was troubling her. There was no one here. Was she having a panic attack? No.

Lewis was sunny and warm, peaceful, a place she loved yet a feeling of something off was overpowering her self-talk. She needed to calm herself so she started for the beach area in front of the harbor. When she reached the bridge, she stopped. Another wave of anxiety, an anxious flutter in her core, compelled her to return to the car to retrieve the rifle. She looked around, feeling ridiculous. What was it that nudged this feeling? No one was around so it wouldn't matter if she was walking around, armed with a loaded rifle and ready to use it. If it brought her a sense of security, why not? Maybe she was sensing wolves. After all, she'd seen a wolf here before. Yes, it might be prudent. She got the rifle, walked back to the bridge and then down to the sand and rocks of the beach, the waves retreating further and further with the ebbing tide. It seemed right to be there, but she didn't know why.

With her eyes bouncing from the water to the treeline and her rifle cradled across her arm, she patrolled the beach, while losing track of time. It seemed like hours. Finally, she felt tired and decided to rest. She had walked the length of the beach both ways, not knowing what the compulsion was.

She stopped walking at a shaded spot beneath the glossy leaves of the lone arbutus and sat down there, knowing she would seem to disappear among its low-hanging branches. She laid her rifle gently on the mulch under the tree and folded her arms around her chest then began to rock, trying to calm the agitation that resided in her being. She would wait for whatever it was.

✳ ✳ ✳

Grace pulled into a parking spot on the high ground at Lewis Harbor. She expected to see her rental car parked there, with Michael waiting inside it, but she saw no signs of activity.

The cramp in her gut cautioned her not to get out of Leo's car, but she thought she caught a glimpse of fur down on the beach. Was Scout out there? Why didn't she see Michael? She looked at the text message again. That was it. The message wasn't from Michael.

Something moved in the bushes up ahead. It was indeed Scout. He had been sent to protect her.

The scent of danger hung in the air. Grace sensed that he was there. She had been manipulated. How had he gotten hold of Michael's cell phone?

She got out of the car and proceeded to the bridge. Where was he? She could feel his eyes on her. Again, Grace looked up and down the beach but saw no one so proceeded down the steps to the sand where she scanned the harbor where the boats were moored. They were unmanned. She lingered, gazing out to sea, taking a moment to consider what to do next. Two harbor seals swam close. They looked at her, snorted, then disappeared into the water.

She heard the crunch of sand behind her and turned slightly, catching the sensation of a movement, and a presence. From the corner of her eye she saw him, but it was too late. He had grabbed her forcibly from behind.

A gruff voice, slurred with alcohol, whispered, "Didn't you know that curiosity killed the kitty cat, Grace?"

He maneuvered her away from the water's edge. She could feel the rifle that was hanging from the strap on his shoulder. It butted hard against her leg. He held her tight against his body as they moved in awkward unison away from the boats anchored in the harbor.

"Why are you doing this, Guy?" Grace tried to make herself sound strong, but she knew her voice sounded strained. It quivered.

"Guy is no more. And you are responsible for that. How did you know about the girl? No one knew. Are you some kind of sorceress? An evil one? Bitch?"

He kneed her in the back, the pain making her fall to her knees on the stones. He pulled her upright again, rough, slapped her across the face, then turned her, holding her firmly across the shoulders from behind. The barrel of the gun dug into her painfully.

Once on the sand, it became harder for him to control her movement. She sensed his difficulty. She felt his footsteps slip, his grip loosen, but he adjusted and regained his stance.

They moved along under the bridge to the beach on the other side. The tide had washed beach sand into a deep mound where he slipped again.

This was her opportunity.

As he lost his footing, Grace back-kicked him hard on his shin. This made the grip he had on her loosen even more. Then she thrust her elbow into his ribs but it wasn't hard enough to disable him, only enough to make the rifle strap slide off his shoulder. As he grabbed to secure it, she freed herself and ran with all her might down the beach, just as Tamara had done in that fateful vision, that fateful night.

"You can't outrun my rifle, you bitch," he called after her.

Grace pictured him lifting the weapon to shoot her in the back. The clouds, the waves, the wind, all seemed to scream, but most of all, Grace heard a mighty growl followed by Levis's scream.

She stopped running. She turned.

From out of the underbrush, Scout had sprung, burying his fangs into Guy's rifle arm. Guy threw him off. Grace heard a yelp as Scout landed on the ground, and then the shotgun blast that forced Scout to flee back into the brush for cover.

A narrow trail of blood led to the undergrowth.

"No, no, no," she yelled.

Guy had wounded him.

Grace stood her ground, facing Guy full on. "What makes you think you can keep killing and hurting everyone?" She was filled with courage, determined to call him out. If he was going to kill her, she was going to have her say first. He was going to hear the words from her own voice, how despicable he was. A complete piece of shit. Evil. She didn't care if he laughed or delighted in his position of power at this moment. If it was meant to be, she would go down strong, brave in her final moments.

Guy's mouth curled into a sneer. He fumbled for something in his pocket. Grace heard his pocket rip as he pulled out his mickey. Only a little of the golden liquid was left in the bottle. He slugged the last of it, burped, hurled the empty into the ocean. He whooped wildly, thrusting his rifle up over his head in triumph. He waved it out in front of him to make sure she could see it, know what was going to happen to her.

"This makes me think that I can do whatever I need to do to survive." He drew the rifle back to his shoulder, aiming at her.

She clenched her fists. Strangely, she was no longer afraid.

"You killed Tamara, but not here on the beach. You buried her, thinking she was dead. But when she rose from the grave, you freaked out. You took her out to sea and threw her overboard to drown. Maybe she'll come back to life again. This time from the depths of the sea. Get her revenge on you."

She'd made her point. Guy shuddered and looked over to where he had first buried Tamara.

"Her spirit lives on and has called on the Island Nation Band Ancestors and animal spirit guides to avenge her. Do you really think you got away with this? The police already know. They're looking for your boat as we speak."

"I taught her a lesson so she has no power over me anymore. And when I dispose of you, you won't either." He fumbled at his pocket for his whiskey. He switched his rifle into the other hand and dug into the pocket on the free side.

Straight and tall, Grace took a step toward him, then another.

He switched the rifle back and held it up to his shoulder, his gaze unsteady along it. "One more step and I'll pull the trigger."

Grace heard a click.

"Go ahead. And I'll pull the trigger as well." A woman's voice came from the bushes.

Rebecca moved forward to stand behind Grace. "I heard everything," she said. "Go ahead. Give me an excuse, any excuse, to shoot you where you stand. Please. You owe me that, at least."

"And so will I," another voice shouted from the bridge. A voice so feral it sounded like an angry feline. It was Holly. "I've literally been dreaming of this moment."

Guy moved his rifle tightly against his shoulder and a shot rang out.

Guy howled like he'd been processed by the devil. Blood exploded from his knee as he fell to the beach.

Then Hugo's voice: "Holly! No more. Stop! Holly. Rebecca. Guns down. Guns down. Grace, kick it away from him."

Grace did as told.

"Now step away," continued Hugo, approaching at a run. "We'll take it from here."

Rubin was heading for Holly.

Holly was crying and shaking, her gun still aimed at the whimpering scoundrel on the beach. "He has to pay for what he did to me."

Rubin approached Holly carefully. He spoke gently to her. "We'll take it from here, Holly. Give me the gun."

She handed the gun to Rubin then fell to the decking of the bridge where she curled up, sobbing loudly.

Rubin called out to Hugo who was in the process of handcuffing Guy. "Everything under control over there?"

Hugo raised a thumb as he spoke into his cell phone. "I need an ambulance. Lewis Harbor." He smiled down at the moaning Guy. "Take your time."

Grace couldn't help herself. She laughed.

On the Night Beach

T HE NARROWEST BAND OF SUNLIGHT hovered stubbornly across the horizon between sky and water. It was a new-moon night, so everything would be cloaked in darkness, time suspended.

Grace murmured incomprehensible words that could have been from another language. Michael noticed her breathing change as he lay there beside her, stroking her hair, and knowing she was witnessing something that might be troubling her. He thought of waking her up, but sensed that somehow, this was different, that she was OK, so he let her sleep. Even as she lay there, edgy as she was, she was beautiful.

✳ ✳ ✳

From far back on the ocean waters, the twinkling lights lit a path. The fireflies moved toward the harbor with great speed to a predetermined spot on the beach. The nearer the swarm came, the greater it was, until it stopped at the water's edge where the culminating light exploded into Tamara's spiritual form where the waves kissed the sand. She stepped from the sparkling glow, methodically looking for something. Then she threw out her arms and her unborn son of several years ran to play along the water's edge. He, too, was looking for something and called to the trees from which Scout emerged to join him in play. Joyful, they

477

skipped and danced in the glow of the fireflies that sang along with the laughter of the young soul, and delighted the wolf, two translucent forms enjoying all that the earth and water offered.

Tamara sang to the steady, rhythmic, hypnotic beat of the drums as she danced in ceremonial finality.

Then another form materialized on the beach. It was that of a young man. He had come from the trees, the old growth forest. He, too, had heard the call of the Ancestors. He'd heard the drums. He understood and obeyed. His part in the ceremony of retribution was just as important as anyone else's. His sacrifice had put into motion the last of the actions that had finally brought the man known as Guy, the same man known as Levis, to justice even though the price he'd paid was his own life. Now, with justice served, he, too, would be invited to the Sunset Land, a reward for his sacrifice, his contribution. He waved to Tamara to come and started toward the narrowest sliver of remaining light on the watery horizon. At first, he floated over the sand, then over the water, his ghostly form becoming more and more translucent, until it merged with the golden glow of the setting sun. Elia was at peace.

Tamara lingered, allowing her unborn to revel a bit longer among earthly pleasures that he had been denied because of Guy's evil. Her son had been cheated. He deserved this time. As the light grew dim, she called to him and he absorbed into her body as she melded with the last glimmer of the water.

Scout looked toward the horizon, sad. When he heard the call of the child, pulling him like a magnet into the one last strand of light, he joined them, disappearing with the other spirits. The singing and the drumbeats stopped, leaving behind only the swish of waves on the black and lonely beach.

✳ ✳ ✳

Michael watched Grace's face as a calm seemed to come over her. A smile touched her lips and a tear slid down her cheek.

He pulled her close.

Back at Danton

Aт Pearson International in Toronto, Heatherton waved to Grace and Michael as they exited the ARRIVALS doors. He hugged Grace warmly and then slapped Michael on the shoulder. "Welcome home, old boy."

"It's great to be back," said Grace. "I'm exhausted from the flight. Can't wait to get some sleep."

"I'll have you home at your condo in short order," said Heatherton as Michael put his arm around Grace's waist and gave him a cheeky grin.

"Actually, we're staying at my place," said Michael. "She gets into way too much trouble when she's alone."

Grace nodded agreement and smiled at Heatherton. It was amazing to hear Michael say it out loud.

"Well played, old boy," Heatherton said. "Took you long enough to let her know." He grabbed the luggage trolley and led the way to the parking garage.

✳ ✳ ✳

It seemed like Grace had been away for months instead of only a few weeks. It was rest and reprieve that Grace had sought in going to

Galliano. She had not found it. Not at all. When the energy calls, it has to be answered, no choices allowed. She'd been called there for a purpose. And no matter how much she tried to resist it, it was a part of her and demanded her attention. But now, back here at Danton, she knew she need not ever be afraid of her own power again. She knew her gift wasn't the curse she'd once perceived it to be. The routine and daily tasks—now that Evelyn's sinister plot to enslave innocent workers had been foiled—provided peaceful comfort to the people who worked there. Grace felt the new energy that permeated Danton now, no longer agitated and challenging, but welcoming and secure. Should the energy be disturbed again, her senses would be alerted and she would do what it called out for her to do to set the balance right.

She hoped that it wouldn't call on her too soon. But if it did, she had her backup team. Michael would always have her back, and Heatherton would be there, too. Next time—and she knew there would be a next time, sooner or later—she would be better prepared.

Acknowledgments

WRITING A NOVEL is a long and grueling task. Smart writers enlist the help of experts in the writing field. Alone, a writer can't bring their goals to fruition without the assistance of beta readers, editors/mentors, and publishers who do the technical work to put it out both to the online and physical world for readers to access and enjoy. I want to thank my daughter, Tiffany Eby Ferrie, for beta reading my work. Most definitely, I would never have realized my writing goals and dreams without my editor Jenna Kalinsky from One Lit Place. She's the one who constantly encouraged and made sure that the project went forward. She never once scolded or criticized. She always knew exactly what I needed emotionally to dispel the daemons that creep up on authors, giving them writer's block. Jenna's professional help was invaluable. I am equally grateful for the kind and supportive help of Sherrill Wark for casting another critical eye on my manuscript. The more eyes, the better. It is through her efforts that this novel came to market. Sherrill, herself a writer, is the owner of Crowe Creations. She is a designer of print and digital books slated for self-publication.

Writing has always been my dream. Thank you all from the bottom of my heart.

About the Author

I N ALL THE YEARS Marianne Scott worked in business, she never knew she had a flair for storytelling. Being tangled in the day-to-day challenges of meeting deadlines, dollar targets, and ever-tighter delivery expectations, left little time or energy for creativity. Yet at her core, she always felt something there. She didn't know how to name it, this yearning that grew inside her with every passing year.

At work, Marianne would jokingly threaten to write a "tell-all" about her colleagues, exposing the difficult personalities and the stressful foibles of the fast-paced manufacturing industry, but in fact, she found herself more interested in letting her imagination run with stories of conspiracy, forbidden affairs, corporate espionage and other sundry misdoings.

Once she left the corporate world, instead of penning non-fiction tales, she gave herself over to her imagined worlds. Her truest pleasure, amusement, and release soon came from turning the ordinary into the extraordinary. From this, *Finding Ruby Draker* was born. Then *Reinhardt*.